Praise for
Leslie O'Kane's Molly Masters mystery
The Cold Hard Fax

"Endearing characters, touching family and friend relationships, and a feisty heroine."
—Diane Mott Davidson

"O'Kane is certainly on her way to making her Molly Masters series the *I Love Lucy* of amateur sleuths."
—*Ft. Lauderdale Sun-Sentinel*

"O'Kane delivers a satisfying whodunit."
—*San Francisco Chronicle*

By Leslie O'Kane:

DEATH AND FAXES
JUST THE FAX, MA'AM
THE COLD HARD FAX*
THE FAX OF LIFE*

PLAY DEAD*

*Published by Fawcett Books

THE FAX OF LIFE

Leslie O'Kane

FAWCETT GOLD MEDAL • NEW YORK

A Fawcett Gold Medal Book
Published by The Ballantine Publishing Group
Copyright © 1999 by Leslie O'Kane

All rights reserved under International and Pan-American Copyright Conventions. Published in the United States by The Ballantine Publishing Group, a division of Random House, Inc., New York, and simultaneously in Canada by Random House of Canada Limited, Toronto.

Fawcett Gold Medal and colophon are trademarks of Random House, Inc.

www.randomhouse.com/BB/

Library of Congress Catalog Card Number: 99-60900

ISBN 0-449-00160-1

Manufactured in the United States of America

First Edition: May 1999

10 9 8 7 6 5 4 3 2 1

To Elisa Wares,
with gratitude and affection

Chapter 1

Nevermore

One look at this place and the women will kill me, I thought as I viewed my surroundings. In front of me, the cabin, composed of unpainted clapboard precariously balanced atop cinder blocks, looked like the combined efforts of the two less enterprising little pigs. Then again, that was an insult to the pigs.

I straightened the shoulder strap of my duffel bag and glanced behind me down the pine-needle-laden path. Currently on a starvation diet and unaccustomed to the altitude in the Colorado Rockies, my best friend Lauren Wilkins was already winded. Our eyes met. She gave me one of her winning smiles as she pushed her brown hair back from her round, flushed cheeks. "The kids are busy arguing over who . . ." Her smile faded as she stared past my shoulder at our cabin. She stopped beside me. "Are you sure this is the place, Molly?"

"This is it. Unit three of the Red Fox Resort. Interesting interpretation of the word 'resort,' isn't it?"

She tilted her head. "Maybe it's nice on the inside."

"I'll believe that when I see filet mignon sold in rusty, dented cans."

While we waited for our children to catch up, my disappointment turned into anger. Half a dozen women had already paid Celia Wentworth, my so-called business partner, to have me conduct a greeting card workshop here this weekend. Celia supposedly ran conferences for a living. This "resort" in Evansville

1

was only an hour's drive from Boulder. She should have checked out the place before she made our reservations. And *I* should have checked Celia's credentials before handing her ten percent of the proceeds. I'd merely taken a mutual friend's word on Celia's qualifications. Allison Kenyon, the mutual friend in question, was one of the women coming up today.

Behind us, the children's voices grew louder. ". . . *my* turn to carry our suitcase!" my son, Nathan, was saying as they rounded the bend with Lauren's daughter, Rachel, calmly leading the way.

"You didn't have to yank it away from me," my daughter, Karen, snarled. "So, fine! You can carry everything by yourself!" On that note, she tossed an armload of jackets and sweaters on top of him.

With his typical priorities, Nathan first smoothed his hair back into place—he used mousse to plaster down his curls—then growled and lunged at Karen.

"Hey!" I called. "Remember what I said about fighting?"

They froze. "We're not fighting," they cried simultaneously, then retrieved their belongings—though Nathan managed to step on Karen's jacket in the process.

That had been their standard response ever since I told them that each minute of fighting delayed our upcoming trip to an amusement park by one hour. My parental bribe/threat was inspired by the fact that Lauren was sacrificing her weekend to watch them as well as her own daughter while I conducted the workshop.

Karen and Rachel darted past us, Karen's fine sandy brown hair bobbing in time with Rachel's white-blond curls. "Is this cabin ours?" Rachel asked her mom in passing.

Eight-year-old Nathan, his tall, wiry frame built for speed, dropped everything on the ground and took off at a dead run. The three reached the cinder-block step at the same time. Rachel flung open the plywood flap that served as a door and rushed in after Nathan, a step ahead of Lauren and me.

"Yuck!" Nathan cried. "It smells like your socks!"

"It does not!" Karen said. "It smells like *your* underpants!"

A whiff of stale, moldy air reached me, and I silently agreed with both of my children—which said more about my laundry habits than I cared to assess. At a quick glance, the interior was even uglier than the exterior.

"What am I going to do, Lauren? These women have each paid two hundred dollars for a writer's retreat. I doubt any of them thought that included retreating from all physical comforts."

"Mo-om!" Karen called. "I thought you said we'd be staying someplace *nice.*"

"Well, that's what I was led to believe, but apparently the woman making the arrangements didn't check it out first."

"I guess not. This place stinks. Literally."

I glared at my daughter, annoyed at how much she sounded like me. If she was searching for role models, I would much rather have her choose Eleanor Roosevelt.

With a giggle, Rachel joined Karen in the doorway and whispered something in her ear. Though they were both ten years old, Rachel was half a foot taller than my petite daughter.

We took ourselves on a tour. The living room furnishings were rejects from a flea market, complete, no doubt, with fleas. To the left of the entrance, the kitchen area—as defined by the orange carpeting giving way to warped and stained yellow linoleum—housed a mini-refrigerator, small range, and a gray Formica tabletop built into the wall. Past the living room, the main bedroom was in decent shape with two newly made queen-sized beds, but the second bedroom, just off the kitchen, had obviously once been the bathroom. Bunk beds were located where a bathtub had once been, with the sleepers' view of the commode blocked by a partition.

"Eew. Sick," Karen said as she studied this bedroom. "Come

on, guys. Let's put our stuff in the other bedroom before Mom sticks us with this one." The three of them rushed off.

"Ah, well." I dropped my bag on the bottom mattress. The bedsprings squeaked in protest. "Tonight while I'm unable to sleep, sickened by the thought of how I've ripped off people trusting enough to hire me, I'll be able to vomit in the toilet without having to get out of bed."

"Maybe the other cabin is nicer," Lauren said, ever the optimist.

With the sleeve of my navy blue cardigan, I rubbed at a filmy pane on the window of our bathroom-cum-bedroom and pointed with my chin. "Unit four. That's it there. Looks identical to ours." I wanted to stomp my foot in frustration but was afraid I'd crash through the floor. "I can't do this. It's one thing for me to ask my family and friends to put up with this place, but I can't mistreat strangers like this. If all else fails, I'll refund everyone's lodging costs and move the retreat to my house in Boulder."

"But meals at the lodge are included, right?"

I winced. "I forgot about that. The only food at home is a tray of ice cubes and a can of Cheez Whiz. That won't hold off eight adults and three kids for long. Still, it beats staying here. I'm going to go see if I can find the manager."

Nathan had returned with the suitcase and now stood in the doorway, listening. His eyes were mirror images of Karen's, but his newly acquired adult teeth were uneven, which gave him a bit of a cocksure grin—the snails and puppy-dog tails to Karen's sugar and spice. "Karen," he called, "want to come watch Mommy get mad?"

Lauren put her hand on Nathan's shoulder and escorted him to the living room. "I'm sure we can find something more entertaining to do than that, if we all put our heads together."

"How can we have any fun with our heads stuck together?"

Forcing myself to allow Lauren to handle Nathan, I left.

Strange how sensible this trip had sounded in theory and how convoluted it all seemed now. My husband, Jim, was in Dallas on business for three weeks. School had just ended back in our present home, Carlton, New York, which meant Karen and Nathan would each in turn be trying to become an only child. Our former house in Boulder was between renters and temporarily unoccupied. Lauren's fiancé, Tommy Newton, was out of town at a weeklong police training course. They were getting married soon, and Lauren was nervous and in need of a distraction. My idea of two weeks in Colorado, partially funded by a workshop, had seemed to be a perfect solution to all of our problems.

I took a deep breath of the brisk, pine scented air. Birds chirped merrily. Deep blue, white-crested mountains in the distance met with the brilliant blue sky dotted with fluffy white clouds. It was hard to be in a foul mood, surrounded by the sensations I'd so missed in the last three years. I made my way down the mountainside of craggy rocks, sparse grass clumps, and lodgepole pines.

A black Suburban kicked up a dust cloud as it rounded the dirt road below and headed toward me. It looked like Celia Wentworth's van. That was odd. She wasn't supposed to be here. Yesterday she'd told me that my friend Allison would be driving up with the five other attendees. I strained to look through the tinted windows and grinned with relief at the realization that Celia must have learned our accommodations were atrocious and come to get this mess straightened out.

I waved and trotted down the path toward the road. Celia, easy to spot with her teased, frosted hairdo and heavy makeup, stuck her head out the window and called, "There's been a slight change in your roster, but I'm on top of it."

"Oh, okay," I murmured, distracted by an image of Celia standing on top of a roster. For some reason, that led me to the even sillier thought of her sitting on a rooster. This was an evil side effect of writing greeting cards for a living: wordplay sometimes sidetracked me at the worst possible moments.

"I'm taking your participants to the other cabin." She gestured back into the recesses of her large vehicle, where a number of women were seated. "We'll meet you at yours in ten minutes."

"Wait. There's a major problem. I'm going down to speak with the manager."

"You needn't do that. I'll handle any problems. That's my job, after all."

"Yes, but you see, I'm not willing to—"

"Hi, Molly," interrupted a woman who'd emerged from the passenger seat.

I stared at her as she rounded the car. "Allison! You're here!"

Her voice was the same, but my friend had changed radically in the last three years. Perhaps inspired by her recent divorce, she'd dyed her light brown hair blond, and she'd lost quite a bit of weight. This should have been the stuff of magazine makeovers, but even at a glance, her facial features looked almost haggard.

We greeted each other with a hug, then Allison called over her shoulder to Celia, "I'll walk back up with Molly."

I hesitated but decided my talk with the manager could wait; Celia had gotten us into this so she really should be the one to get us out. "How've you been?" I asked Allison, trying to keep the concern from my voice.

"Great. Splitting with Richard was the best thing I ever did for myself." Her voice was unconvincing. Her face was pallid and her eyes bloodshot.

How to inquire tactfully about her health? "That was some flu bug that went around this past spring, huh?"

After a glance at Celia's car, now rounding the bend above us, Allison grabbed my arm. "Listen, Molly," she said, lowering her voice, "I misled you by recommending Celia. She's loused everything up. She got the dates wrong. She just discovered the mistake last week. I was the only one who'd registered who could make the switch. Everyone else backed out."

"What? You mean—"

"Celia scrambled around and got four last-minute replacements. Five, counting herself."

"But I just met with her yesterday. She didn't say anything about this."

"You have to know Celia. She'll rewrite the entire rulebook rather than admit to an infraction."

"How could she possibly find four women interested in writing greeting cards on such short notice?"

"She promised them a luxurious weekend in the mountains."

I froze, a knot forming in my stomach. "Oh dear Lord. Was that a direct quote?"

"Yes. Why?"

"You could call this place rustic. Austere, maybe. Shitty, for sure. But not 'luxurious.' "

We climbed the steep course to the cabins at a quick pace, my concern for Allison momentarily forgotten. Having opted for a weekend in the mountains, my new "students" weren't going to want to switch venues to my house in Boulder. I could wind up having to make full refunds to them, plus pay for unused cabins and meals.

A woman cried, "This place is a dump!"

"Someone noticed," I muttered to myself. There went my last hope: that Celia's four last-minute replacements were all blind.

"That's Lois Tucker," Allison whispered as we got within sight of an irate woman emerging from cabin four. "Lives in that tan house between my house and Celia's. Did you ever meet her?"

I shook my head as I eyed the sturdy-looking black-haired woman. Her thick, dark eyebrows were drawn into a fiery glare.

My first impression was this was not someone I wanted to cross. And right now, she looked ready to kill.

"She always has to have her own way. She was a manager at IBM till she quit to home-school her son. Claimed once he reached middle school, his classmates were all thugs and junkies."

As a mother, such a radical statement about school conditions always gets my attention, but at the moment there was a mob of indignant women to deal with. Not surprisingly, they were throwing the phrase "luxurious weekend" back at Celia and me. In the meantime, Allison wandered into the cabin to see for herself.

Celia, who by all appearances had not yet seen the cabin, held up her palms and barked, "Ladies! Please!" She made a parting-of-the-seas motion to Lois and the three other women I hadn't met standing in the doorway. Wordlessly they stepped aside. She marched inside, came out moments later, and said, "Not bad."

This touched off another round of complaints. A strawberry blonde with a ponytail said, "Actually, I think the place is kind of cute." She looked some ten years younger than the rest of us—which is to say she was in her late twenties or early thirties. Though her makeup was tasteful, she wore black stretch pants and a bare midriff T-shirt. Under the weight of everyone's stares, she shrugged and said, "Who cares what the cabin's like? It's beautiful up here, so peaceful and pretty. Take a deep breath and smell God's air."

That certainly wasn't "God's air" *inside* the cabins, but I kept the comment to myself. Celia broke the silence to state, "I need to have a word with Mrs. Masters." The others joined Allison in the cabin to grouse about the conditions, and Celia took my arm and led me a short distance away.

"Molly, as Allison may have told you, there's been a slight

change in plans. Originally, you'd told me you wanted to do this next weekend, so I—"

"No, I didn't. I've told you it was *this* weekend since day one." Celia held up her palms, and I noticed that, though thin and attractive in all other respects, she had gelatinous upper arms. The woman could applaud with them by touching her elbows together. "As I've already explained, Celia, this is the first time I've tried to offer a class like this. It is extremely important to me. I'm flying back to New York next Friday, and I can't change that now, or it would foul up my friend Lauren's wedding plans."

As if she hadn't heard a word, Celia shook her head and said in a maddeningly calm voice, "Molly, you told me next weekend."

"I did not! I have the original faxes in my car, if you want to see them!"

"There's no sense in us arguing. We can't change—" She stopped as we saw that Lauren and the children were coming.

"Hi, Mom," Karen said. She rushed up to me and gave me a hug. "Is everybody here? Have they seen their cabin yet?"

"Hello, sweetie," Celia said in sugary tones, leaning to Karen's level. She cocked her head in Nathan's direction and, in a babyish voice, said, "I'll bet you're looking forward to a weekend in the mountains, aren't you?"

He held her gaze for a moment, then looked at me. "Mom, I want to go home. I'm gonna go wait in the car." He turned on his heel.

Lauren and Celia, who'd met briefly yesterday at my house in Boulder, exchanged nice-to-see-you-agains, then Lauren headed off with our daughters to catch up with Nathan. Over her shoulder, she called back at me not to worry—that she'd "get Nathan to come around." Sure. Nathan was so stubborn he could bring tears to a mule's eyes. In an hour or so I'd have to drag him out of the car and tell him either to obey Lauren or no amusement park.

"Let's continue this discussion in your cabin." Celia marched ahead of me without awaiting my response. Out of annoyance, I stayed put, but then the perky strawberry blonde leaned out of their cabin and called, "Molly? Just wanted you to know, we're voting on whether or not we stay. My name's Julie, by the way. It was nice meeting you."

Was? Uh-oh. I mustered a smile and a wave, then went inside my cabin. Celia, already seated on the brown-and-gold plaid couch, immediately began. "I've already collected the money from Allison plus your new participants. Unfortunately, that only covered the meals and lodging, and not your fee. Before you ask, I paid the resort in full and it's nonrefundable."

My mind raced through the arithmetic, and this was way out of whack. "But that—"

"You only have to give back four of the hundred-dollar deposits to the original registrants, since I already reimbursed one for my slot."

My heart was starting to race as I struggled to check my temper. "Refund the . . . what are you talking about? Wasn't their money already reimbursed by these friends of yours?"

"On such short notice, I couldn't very well expect them to pay full cost for the retreat, now could I?"

"In other words, you screwed up the dates of the retreat, and now you expect me to take the financial loss?"

She rose and wagged her finger and upper arm at me. "I resent your tone of voice! I've done my part. I got replacement attendees! If it weren't for me, you'd be out a lot more than four hundred dollars!" She reached into her pocket. "But here. Here's your check back for my services. I've decided not to accept payment because of our little misunderstanding. So we're even-steven. Neither of us is making any money on this venture of yours."

"You call that even?" I said, accepting what was indeed my original check. "I'm *paying* four hundred dollars to work this weekend!"

"And *I* paid for my food and lodging to attend a workshop in a subject I have no interest in! You and your friend get a cabin for free!"

"But it's *not* free! It's costing me—"

The door flew open and Karen rushed inside, closely followed by Rachel and Lauren. "Potty break," Lauren explained unnecessarily as Karen continued past us into our bathroom/bedroom. "Uh, you may have to talk to Nathan. He's sitting in the backseat and won't say a word to me."

There was a rhythmic rap on the plywood door flap, then perky Julie poked her head in. "Okey-dokey. We've taken a vote, and we decided to give you a chance, Molly. We're all ready to get those creative juices flowing." She accentuated her last sentence with a peppy little fist pump.

"Mom?" Karen called through the wall. "There's something swimming in the toilet."

Probably my career, I thought. Though if that were the case, it would be drowning.

"Come on, Molly," Celia said as she waltzed out the door. "Mustn't keep your students waiting."

Some ten minutes later, Nathan hated me but was with Lauren and the girls. My participants, who probably also hated me but were more discreet about it, were seated in a circle on the green shag carpet of their cabin. While dealing with Nathan, I had reminded myself that this retreat was an experiment for me and was not intended to turn a profit. I then vowed to resolve the financial ramifications with Celia later, ripped up her check, rapidly unpacked, and made the short walk to the other cabin to join the women's circle.

"Let's begin by introducing ourselves. I'd—"

"We've all known one another for years," Celia interrupted, her painted features smiling, but all the while giving me an evil eye.

"I'd especially like to know what you hope to gain from this workshop. I'm Molly Masters. I worked for a greeting card company in Boulder for five years before my husband's job brought us to New York three years ago. That's when I started Friendly Fax, my one-person company, which specializes in personalized faxable greetings."

To my left sat a woman of about my medium height with freckles, her straight auburn hair in an efficient bob. In a flat, emotionless voice, she said, "My name is Katherine Lindstrom. I'm an English lit professor at C.U. I have no interest in greeting cards per se. I don't send them. I don't receive them. However, I am doing a unit on popular literature next semester. Studying greeting cards allows me to start with the most banal form of the written word."

I studied her for a moment, but she seemed oblivious to the fact that she'd just insulted me. Making fun of my job, as if *she* were blazing new trails by being a literary snob in academia. Talk about "banal." Plus she dragged out the last syllable of that word in an annoying affectation. Nobody refers to the water-way in New York as the Erie Can-ahlllll, after allllll. Forcing myself to stay pleasant, I said, "Maybe once we get into this class, you won't find greeting cards quite so banal."

After a pause, the pretty, fortyish woman beside her said, "I just wanted to spend a weekend in the mountains." She had an olive complexion and white, shoulder-length hair. She wore a denim jumper and sandals. "My name is Nancy Thornton, and I'm a therapist."

"A physical therapist?" I asked.

She held my gaze an instant longer than I was comfortable with, then said, "No, I'm a psychologist. Greeting cards is one way people express emotions with low risk. It is so much easier and less revealing to purchase a prewritten card than to write your own letter."

"A thought just occurred to me, Nancy," Celia said out of turn. "Did you ever notice how the word 'therapist' spells 'the rapist' if you put a space between the 'e' and the 'r'?"

A conversation stopper if there ever was one. Nancy glared at Celia and said nothing. As I scanned the circle, it struck me that all of them sat clutching their knees to their chests, as far away from the others as possible in the small room. In fact, the tension in the room hinted at mutual disdain.

"Allison?" I prompted with a smile, glad to have one friend present. "What about you?"

She combed her fingers through her dyed hair. "I'm still an electrician, Moll." She frowned and made a slight gesture with one hand. "I used to know Molly when she lived in Boulder. I wanted to spend this weekend with *her*."

"My name is Julie, as you all know," our young happy person said next with no hesitation. "I'm an aerobics instructor, and I also breed dogs. Unlike Katherine, I absolutely *love* everything about greeting cards. Lois?"

"I'm Lois," she growled. Adding to her dark, sturdy appearance, she wore a plain black sweat suit. She sounded so grim and hostile, she had to have been a no vote for staying. "My son has graduated and moved on. I used to be at IBM but got out of the rat race."

While she spoke, I scanned the faces and reflected upon what a challenge this would be for me. Professor Katherine, therapist Nancy, and now grouchy mother Lois gave me the impression they'd desert my class in a New York minute if I allowed their interest to wane.

"Writing greeting cards sounded like a possible new career for me," Lois continued. "How much money do you make?"

"This really isn't something I'd recommend people get into

as a full-time career. It is fun, though, and you can make a little side income on it." Parking meter change was more like it, but no sense being too honest.

Lois's eyes widened in alarm anyway.

"We'll begin by brainstorming. It's June, so let's come up with some card ideas for graduates. Ninety percent of all cards are purchased by women, so you might want to start by—"

"I don't want to write graduation cards," Lois interrupted, folding her arms.

That surprised me, since she *did* have a son who just graduated from high school. "The topic was just a suggestion. Card companies actually buy six to nine months in advance. So you might want to think of ideas for Christmas cards. It's easier to brainstorm when you narrow your scope, though, such as . . . Christmas cards with cats. Then you think of sayings about cats. 'The cat's meow,' 'the cat's pajamas' . . ."

" 'Curiosity killed the cat,' " Allison interjected wryly. "Or vice versa. And then there's 'cat burglar.' "

"Um, that's getting pretty far away from the Christmas theme," I said, perplexed at Allison's attitude.

"I'm allergic to cats," Lois grumbled, "and I'm Jewish."

"Hanukkah with hamsters, then." I set a large salad bowl in the middle of our circle and handed out pens and stacks of small sheets of paper. "Toss captions for cards into the bowl as quickly as possible, without self-editing."

Still, no one moved. "This first exercise will be kept completely anonymous. I won't pay any attention to who wrote what, and until we're comfortable, I won't read anything out loud. There's no pressure. Just pick up your pens, write a sentence or two on the paper, and toss it into the salad bowl. Even if your sentence is 'I don't know what to write.' Eventually, your right brain will take over and you'll start coming up with concepts for cards."

Celia, I noticed, was writing away furiously. Eventually, the others started writing as well. To keep this anonymous, I doodled instead of watching them. With the concept of writer's block fresh in my mind, I sketched a dark, mustached man in old-fashioned clothes seated in front of a second man at a desk marked "Editor-in-Chief." The mustached man is eyeing a caged bird that's saying "Nevermore. Nevermore. Nevermore. Nevermore . . ." The other man says, "Mr. Poe, it's a shame about your writer's block. Maybe it . . . Let me get my blasted raven out of here so we can hear ourselves think."

Three slips of paper were in the bowl when I looked up. I snatched them and read:

Molly, how dare you hold me responsible for
what was obviously a simple matter of getting
our wires crossed? I'm just as disappointed
about our lodging as everyone else. It was
misrepresented to me over the phone. That
(over)
hardly makes this my fault. You could be a little
grateful for all my hard work! I would ask that
you stop and think of where you'd be right now
if I hadn't gotten my friends to fill in!

C. Wentworth

I'd be running a retreat for a group of people who wanted to be doing this, located in a place where the building wasn't about to collapse. I went on to the next one:

Birds give me fits
tho I kinda like ducks.
This retreat is the pits.
It really sucks.

Oh, well. Everybody's a critic. The handwriting, though, looked disturbingly like my friend Allison's. My spirits sagging, I looked at the last slip:

> Christmas. Graduation. No ideas. Nothing.
> I don't want to write cards. I'd rather be home.
> Scrubbing the toilet with my toothbrush.
> Better yet, with my husband's toothbrush.

I grinned, then scanned the room. The down-turned faces before me were tense, as if the women were struggling to write Shakespearean prose. "The key to writing greeting cards is empathy. You put yourself in the sender's place and sense what she thinks her receiver wants to hear. Just jot down anything, the faster the better. Let your subconscious do the work for you."

"Unconscious," Nancy corrected.

Dejectedly, I refined my sketch of Edgar Allan Poe. After a few more minutes, I snatched some papers out of the bowl. The first one contained a sketch of a mortarboard and read:

> Good luck, son.
> I promise not to turn your bedroom into that
> sewing room I always wanted.

I chuckled and nearly broke my vow not to read aloud. That had some commercial potential, though "slam" cards were often a tough sell. The next two slips had incongruous phrases:

> Deck the halls
> Christmas balls
> Niagara Falls
> Wish someone would wash them walls.

When's dinner?
Gad, this cabin stinks!
I've smelled nicer locker rooms!

This was encouraging. They were starting to get the idea of letting their thoughts flow. Maybe this weekend wasn't going to be a total fiasco after all.

I turned to the last piece of paper in my hand and read:

VIOLETS ARE BLUE.
ROSES ARE RED.
ONE OF YOU DITCHES
WILL SOON BE DEAD.

Chapter 2

Neither Sleet, nor Hail, nor Gloom of Night . . .

Shocked by the threat, I felt my cheeks flush and my palms grow sweaty. I scanned my students' faces for telltale clues that one of them was watching me—or deliberately not looking at me. They were all riveted to their task—writing cards—paying me no mind. If only I was still in Carlton, I could whisk the note off to Sergeant Tommy Newton for handwriting analysis. As it was, all I knew was that the block lettering looked nothing like any of the writing samples I'd seen so far.

Damn it all! One of these women hated the others so badly that she wanted to make them fear for their very lives. Whoever did this was using me as a pawn—expecting me to read the threat aloud.

Allison hadn't written it. I had yet to discover why she now looked so downtrodden, but we were friends. She would never do something like this. I studied Celia's lacquered face and hair. She could have set this whole retreat up just to anonymously threaten one of her "friends." But would she be so brazen as to do so when I had a signed sample of her handwriting?

Nancy absentmindedly twisted a lock of her prematurely white hair, a look of deep concentration on her pretty features. As a trained therapist, she should be in better control of herself than to write a death threat. Meanwhile, Professor Katherine had pulled her bulky tan sweater down over her knees and seemed to be trying to disappear into it, turtlelike. She was not as likable as I'd first hoped. Perhaps I'd been overly influenced by the friendly, girl-next-door appearance her freckles gave her. But as a self-avowed critic of the "banal," she wouldn't use that old roses-are-red saw. Likewise, Julie was so perky, she might never use the word "bitches."

Then there was Lois, who'd told Allison that middle-school children were "thugs and druggies." Purely from a note-writing standpoint, she was my prime suspect.

Nancy looked up at me, her eyes widening as she studied my expression. "Molly? Are you all right?"

If I went ahead and read this sick joke out loud, I would create the very state of pandemonium that the threat's writer had in mind. I needed to calmly call off the retreat and send everyone home, safe and sound. Not to be unduly self-centered, but if one of these women sincerely had murder on her mind, it was not going to happen on *my* shift, with my children right next door.

"This might be a good time for us to break for dinner," I said, palming the threat and inconspicuously stashing it in a back pocket of my jeans.

"Great," Lois said. "I'm famished."

"It's only six P.M." Celia shook her head at me while she spoke, as if we'd been asking for her permission. "This is a full hour ahead of when you scheduled the dinner break on your program."

"I realize that, but . . ." Desperate for a plausible excuse, I peered out the small, dirty window above the couch and found a good one. Thick gray clouds had blotted all trace of blue from the sky. Yikes! There was a storm brewing. I'd forgotten how drastically the weather could change in Colorado. "Look how dark it's getting outside. We might be in for some nasty weather."

"Nonsense," Celia said. "We need to stick to our schedule."

"I follow a schedule five days a week when the university is in session," Katherine said to Celia. "I refuse to do so during my *luxurious* weekend excursion."

I rose. "I'll meet you at the lodge, all right? I think I'll just check on my kids for a few minutes first." *Then I'll pack them and Lauren into the car, meet the others at the lodge, show them the note, and tell them I'm leaving and that they should, too.* I headed toward the door, willing myself to go slowly and not break into a full sprint.

"You're not planning on running out on us, are you, Molly?" Celia asked.

I whirled around, again catching sight of the forced smile with livid lips beneath her narrowed eyes and well-preserved hair. How had she known my intentions? Everyone was staring at me, wearing expressions of surprise mixed with hostility. An irrational but powerful vision of them as a coven of witches— with Julie as their token aerobics instructor—swept over me. Maybe I was about to be force-fed raw liver, or subjected to whatever witches did during induction ceremonies.

"Of course not," I lied, my voice sounding false to my own ears. "Don't be silly." I didn't want to reveal my cards too early, until my escape was firmly in place. Blast it! Why was I so frightened? This was just a sick joke!

"You do seem to be acting a little strange, Molly," Allison said slowly, peering at me from through her bleached-blond bangs.

"Do I?"

"Has something frightened you?" Nancy asked in thera-peutic tones.

I had a sudden desire to lay down on the couch and tell her my troubles. "Yes, actually. I had . . . a premonition that spooked me a little. I just need to check on the children and re-assure myself."

"Do you get premonitions often?" Nancy asked, still in therapist mode.

"See you at the lodge." I bolted out of there and trotted down the slope to our cabin. My Reeboks sometimes slid on the loose, gravelly soil, but I grabbed on to branches to maintain my pace and balance. One of the women back there knew precisely why I was behaving this way. But why had she done it? If she really wanted to kill one of us, why sacrifice the element of surprise? This had to be simply a nasty practical joke. Nothing else made sense.

I rounded the cabin. "Karen? Nathan?" I called as I threw open the door.

Silence. My heart raced. If Lauren had left, why hadn't she locked the door? Now I really *was* having a premonition that my children were in trouble, despite the fact that they were in Lauren's very capable care. Damn! "Where is everybody?" I cried, punching the doorframe with the heel of my hand.

Maybe they were already at the lodge having an early dinner. If so, I might be able to pack, drive down there, and grab them. As I sped through the kitchen in search of purse and keys, a piece of paper on the counter fluttered and caught my attention. I picked it up and read:

Molly, we found what looks like a great hiking trail. I took the kids out there. We'll meet you at the lodge for dinner at seven as planned. See you then. Hope the workshop is going well.

Lauren

Shoot! Now what? I took a couple of breaths to calm myself. Meanwhile, I was packing like a madwoman. I'd meet them at the dining hall, whenever they arrived, and take it from there. First, though, I needed my car keys. I'd linked my personal key chain onto the plastic key chain from the rental car company. This should have created a big lump of keys, too cumbersome to misplace. So where the heck were they?

Voices outside let me know the women were on the path to the lodge. Moments later, Allison knocked on the door and called, "Are you coming, Molly?"

"In a minute. Go on without me."

After several minutes of fruitless searching, I realized Lauren must have taken the keys with her. I had no recourse but to walk down to the lodge. I grabbed one of the door keys off a peg on the wall and realized why Lauren had left the place open. The plywood door was so warped, there was too big of a gap between the latch and the frame for the lock to work. Great. Someone had given me a death threat, and there was no way to lock my door.

Muttering a few choice curse words, I made my way down to the lodge. The sky was filled with gray clouds. A lightning bolt flashed in the distance. With this bad weather brewing, Lauren would cut the trip short and head to the lodge. Still scanning the sky, I sent up a quick prayer. I pulled my cardigan tighter around me and quickened my step.

From this angle, the lodge appeared to be your basic, albeit oversized, rectangular log cabin. It was built into the steep mountainside so that the front porch was just one step up, but the far side, where the dining room was situated, was supported by tall stilts of thick logs.

The entrance was through a small office, and I immediately went to the desk in search of a phone. Even if the police thought I was a kook, I'd feel better once I'd told them about the note in my pocket. I picked up the handset, then noticed that the base of the phone boasted a rotary dial that was locked in place. A small sign beside the phone read: INCOMING CALLS ONLY.

"Foiled again," I murmured to myself. This must be one of the last rotary phones in the United States. And *its* lock—unlike my cabin's—worked. Of all the paranoid, penny-pinching contraptions.

I wandered through the first doorway, which led to the dining hall. A mild fragrance of coffee beckoned. To my surprise, the room was glorious. An enormous moss rock fireplace took up much of the inner wall. The opposite wall was mostly glass, featuring a spectacular view of the tops of lodgepole pines and the Continental Divide, though its peaks were rapidly melding into cloud banks. The wide boards, finished to a high sheen, made for an elegant floor, and the two remaining walls were burnished and polished logs.

There was one major downside to the room, however. The furniture consisted of half a dozen white plastic tables, each with four white plastic seats—the kind you might buy if you needed spare lawn furniture and didn't mind chasing it across your neighbor's property with every little breeze. Furthermore, said furniture was occupied by the women in my workshop.

These folks had destroyed my rule of ten percent—that one out of any group of ten people is a jerk. I believe so strongly in the accuracy of that average that any time I'm in a room with nine truly delightful people, I try to keep my mouth shut. But here, five out of six women were bordering on jerkdom, with Allison being the exception. Okay, four, if you could tolerate Julie, the perennial cheerleader type. Possibly three, if you didn't mind Nancy's attitude that you were undergoing analysis with every statement that left your lips. Even so, at best we were at fifty percent.

Allison, Julie, and Celia were at one table; Nancy, Katherine, and Lois were at another. Julie immediately smiled at me and called, "There she is." While I was tempted to join them and get caught up with Allison, I sat at the other table where I knew no one. I wanted to keep an eye on them; this was a dining room, so they would soon be armed with sharp objects.

Lois greeted me with the statement, "Explain something to me, Molly. I can't understand why you would stick with the greeting card business when you can't make any real money at it."

While scanning the room for an employee who could give me a key to the phone, I answered distractedly, "I'm a full-time mom, part-time greeting card creator. Writing cards is something I enjoy, so anything I earn is a bonus. That's not hard to understand, is it?"

"Maybe not. But still. There must be lots of jobs you can do at home in your free time and earn better money at. Don't you think?"

"Molly is saying that making big bucks isn't a priority for her, Lois," Nancy said calmly. The overhead lighting cast an alluring sheen on her mostly white hair, a striking contrast with her olive complexion.

"Not everyone is as focused on money as . . ." Katherine paused as if thinking twice, then said, "other people are."

"You make it sound as if all I care about is making money, Katherine." Lois spoke semi-tauntingly, her heavy brow knitted, her strong features taut with anger. "*I'm* the one who quit my lucrative career to raise my child, remember?"

"How could I forget? You remind us all continually."

Both Katherine's and Lois's hands were fisted as if they intended to come to blows. "Aha," I cried, gesturing at a thin, bald man in a slightly soiled apron who'd entered through some double doors. "Here comes somebody who looks like an employee."

"About time," Lois said. "I was beginning to think no one was ever going to notice us."

As if *that* were possible.

The elderly man made his way toward us from the kitchen. "Evenin'," he said, a happy grin revealing his missing front tooth. "You from cabin three or four?"

"Both," I said. "Why?"

"It's gonna be a cozy gathering for dinner tonight. You folks are the only ones here this weekend. 'Course, it's been that way, ever since the board of health got all hot under the collar."

"Excuse me?"

He chuckled and waved his hands. "Don't take it the wrong way. It was just a minor plumbing problem. You'll be taking a shower and all a sudden the damn sewer backs up. Next thing you know, you're knee deep in—" He broke off and grinned sheepishly. "Just don't flush too often and you'll be okay. Plumbing in the kitchen works just fine. So don't mind me. I get to rattlin' on sometimes. I'll have a nice buffet set up for you soon."

Nauseated by this latest revelation, I asked, "Could I speak with the managers for just a minute?"

"Fred and Lucy? They're gone. Left me in charge. Anything I can help you with?"

The others were hanging on my every word, but they'd find out soon enough anyway. "I'm not overly pleased with . . . well, anything. I'd like to check out of my cabin, which is number three, and get my money back."

"What did you say, Molly?" Celia screeched from the other table.

"Ah," the man said to me, nodding. "That won't be possible. The managers. Fred and Lucy? You'd have to see them about that. 'Scuse me. I'll go set your dinner out."

"What's going on, Molly?" Allison called.

"We'd all be better off if we just chalk this up to experience and head home. Don't you agree?"

"That's the first sensible thing anyone has said since we arrived," Nancy said, brushing an errant strand of white hair behind her ear.

Lois let out a big sigh and said, "Thank goodness."

"You mean we get to leave?" Katherine asked, for the first time smiling and showing some of the energy she must possess in order to be a teacher. The faint lines on her freckled face crinkled appealingly with her smile.

At the other table, no one was smiling, not even Julie. Allison was the only participant I felt loyalty toward, and I planned on privately asking her if she'd consider spending the weekend at my house. I ignored Celia, who was snapping her fingers to get my attention, and followed the man into the kitchen through the swinging double doors.

"Um, sir? Sorry to bother you, but is there a number where I can call the owners?"

He looked at me, then at the doors, as if surprised a non-employee could pass through them. "No can do. They're on vacation. Won't be back for another couple weeks."

"They didn't leave you with an emergency contact number?"

"Yes, but the number's just for emergencies."

"This *is* an emergency."

He raised an eyebrow, which consisted only of three very long hairs, at me.

I continued, "Believe me. Things will be much better for everybody if I can just talk to the owners, get at least half of my money back, and get out of here."

"You may as well eat first. Can't call now. I got me a dinner for a dozen folks to put on."

"Dinner can wait. I really—"

He lifted a lid to a large pot on the stove. "Here. Smell that."

He hoisted the pot under my nose so that I had no choice but to oblige. A rich tomato-based spaghetti sauce, heavy on the oregano, made my mouth water despite my troubles. "Mmmm. Smells delicious."

"I wouldn't know." He drained spaghetti into a huge colander in the sink beside me. Fortunately, nothing came back up the drain toward the noodles. "My olfactory whatchamacallits are shot. Can't taste much, neither. Ironic, isn't it? A cook who can't taste from nothing? Course, it's kind of like Beethoven. Being deaf and all. That feller did all right for himself."

He dumped the pasta back into its huge pot, then poured the sauce on top and started swishing the ensemble around with a wooden spoon built for a titan. My finicky children weren't going to like this. Karen didn't even trust her own mother to dole out her sauce, so she always took it on the side. Nathan ate his spaghetti bald, except for a liberal dose of parmesan cheese.

The taste-impaired chef then poured his spaghetti into two shallow, square pans and proceeded into the dining hall. He gestured with his chin at two other pans on the counter. "Carry those in while you're at it."

Realizing there was no way to force him to call before he served dinner, I stacked the pans and followed him to the serving table. The others had already circled the table, no doubt attempting to eavesdrop on our conversation in the kitchen.

"What's the story, Molly?" Lois immediately asked. "Can we go home?"

I shrugged. "I don't know if we'll get any of our money back, but I think we should consider leaving anyway right after dinner."

"Sounds good to me," Nancy said.

"It doesn't to me," Celia said, pursing her bloodred lips.

The chef carried in a huge clear salad bowl. The oil-and-vinegar-based dressing had already been mixed and the croutons floated atop as miniature sponges.

"Dig in, everybody," he called, lifting the lids with such a flourish I half expected him to bang them together like cymbals.

"Excuse me," Julie said sweetly. "I'm a vegetarian. Is there any meat in the spaghetti sauce?"

"Not unless something crawled in there and died while my back was turned."

"You already put margarine on the bread!" Celia scolded. "I certainly hope you used polyunsaturated fat. Or at least unsalted."

"Is this low-calorie dressing on the salad?" Julie asked, still maintaining her positive demeanor.

"Yeah. Sure." He rolled his eyes as he neared me and muttered, "Boulderites. That town's graveyards are full of the healthiest corpses in the world."

"Can you make that phone call now?" I asked, doing my best not to whine.

He raised his three-hair eyebrow again but made no comment. For lack of a better idea, I grabbed a plate and got in line.

"What a dreadful man," Celia said to me under her breath. "I can't believe he didn't let us butter our own bread."

"That is a shocking disappointment. Did I happen to mention that Lauren's and my bedroom doubles as the bathroom?"

"Oh, don't worry about that. The couch in the living room pulls out into a double bed." She clicked her tongue half a dozen times and shoved the bread around with the tongs to make her selection. Anticipating that this could take a while, I slowly ladled my salad onto my plate.

"Where are Karen and Nathan?" Allison asked, pausing from dishing up spaghetti.

"Out for a hike. I hope. I'm not sure if Lauren knows how fast the weather can deteriorate here."

"Didn't you train your children in outdoor survival skills?" Lois asked.

I clenched my teeth. "They're only eight and ten years old. Outdoor survival hasn't seemed like a priority." A huge thunderclap rattled the windowpanes. "Till now." I stabbed myself a helping of spaghetti. "Is there some particular reason you chose to ask me that?"

"Why, no. I just meant—"

"Don't listen to Lois," Julie said. "Your children will be fine. There's no reason to worry."

"Thanks, but I like to decide for myself when to worry."

Julie frowned and headed toward her table. Now *I* was being nasty and bickering with everybody. Sheesh. This just was not a greeting card kind of gathering.

I reclaimed my seat. Battling visions of my children dodging lightning bolts, I pushed my food around, in between incessantly checking my watch. In the meantime, everyone else finished and moved on to dessert: pineapple upside-down cake. Celia explained to everyone, whether we wanted to listen or not, that the cake "should have been made with fresh pineapple rather than canned."

Torrents of rain began to pelt the windows. With this much force, it would soon be hail. Where were my children? What could be keeping them?

Professor Katherine rolled her eyes. "I told everyone we should have driven down here to the lodge. They all insisted they wanted to walk."

I checked my watch. Seven-thirteen. Maybe they were at the cabin, waiting out the rain. If only I knew which direction they'd gone, I could go look for them.

To my enormous relief, a clatter arose from the office, which could only mean my children were making one of their patented subtle entrances. I rose, and moments later, a giggling Karen and Rachel rushed in. They were wearing waterproof hooded jackets, but their pants were soaked. I crossed the room and gave Karen a hug and Rachel a pat on the shoulder.

"We got caught out in the rain," Rachel said. "Mom twisted her ankle a little."

"Where is she?" I asked, already making my way to the office entryway.

"Nathan's helping her get—"

Nathan opened the door and Lauren limped across the threshold. They were both sopping wet, but Lauren waved off my concern. "It's nothing a good soaking in hot water won't cure. We were walking down a hill and my foot slipped."

Nathan brushed past me and headed straight for the dinner buffet without a word. Moments later, his voice carried from the dining hall. "There's sauce on this spaghetti!"

I supported Lauren's weight as we entered the dining room.

Karen, standing on tiptoes beside her brother, said, "At least the bread's been buttered."

The cook emerged from the kitchen and stood, hands on hips, scouting us. He grinned at Lauren with his jack-o'-lantern smile. "Howdy. Is this the lot of you?"

Lauren looked questioningly at me, and I said, "This is everybody; they just need to wash up first. Where's the bathroom?"

As he pointed the way, which was back through the office, I called to the children, "Whatever you do, don't flush," and returned to my seat. With my children safe, my appetite had returned, and I fended off the women's questions and Celia's arm-jiggling attempts to usher me off to a private conference.

Lauren and the kids got their meals and took the remaining table by the window. For the next several minutes, we all watched a spectacular hailstorm cover the ground in a blanket of pea-sized ice. Though I knew I should be anxious under the accumulating circumstances, the childish part of me reveled in the pleasure of watching a summer storm while safe, warm, and dry. Well, two out of three anyway.

Rachel and Karen were having so much fun slurping their spaghetti that Karen forgot to worry about it being presauced. Even Nathan was getting into the act, once he'd finally broken down and taken his first bite. His exact response was: "This sauce is *way* better than yours, Mom."

Outside, the sky grew dark, but none of us wanted to venture out into the storm, which showed no signs of subsiding. I moved my chair beside Lauren and said quietly, "Let's go home tonight. I'll throw our stuff in the car then come down and pick you and the kids up."

"We're *leaving*?" Nathan hollered. "But I don't want to! I want to stay here and watch the lightning!"

"But, Nathan," Karen argued, "if we go back to Boulder tonight, we can go to Elitches a day early."

I winced at her mention of the amusement park in Denver, having no intention of going there on a weekend, but Nathan retorted, "I don't care. I like it here. Maybe we'll even get to see a tornado!"

"Now there's an appealing thought." Along the lines of a rotten cherry atop a melted sundae.

A hinge on the kitchen doors squeaked, and I held my breath as the cook entered and headed my way. With luck, he would tell me that we could get a refund after all.

Celia rose and stood in front of me, as if to block his path. "Molly, need I remind you that you have an obligation to—"

"Sorry to interrupt, ladies," he began, "but I jus' wanted to tell ya not to go making plans about leaving anytime soon. Heard on the radio that there's been a rockslide on Route Seven a mile or so down the road. It'll be early morning at best till they've had a chance to reopen."

Route Seven was the one and only road out of the mountains and back to Boulder. He turned on his heel, then left us sputtering our protestations at him, as if he were in charge of the news instead of merely its messenger.

"This must be a new rung of Dante's Inferno," Professor Katherine moaned, her doom-and-gloom tones in full force. "We're never getting out of here."

Celia, however, smiled, then clapped her hands once sharply. "This is for the best. We all committed to be here for the weekend. This is a sign that we need to fulfill our agreement to one another."

Thank you, General Custer. Me 'n' the troops feel much better now.

Julie and Allison rose, put on their jackets, and brushed past Celia. Allison said to me, "We're making a run for it, back to the cabin."

"Molly," Celia said, her hazel eyes glaring at me, "I hope you agree that, since we now have no choice but to stay, you must carry on with the workshop." She trotted toward the other two, calling, "Julie? Allison? If you would wait just a moment, I'll come with you."

"Karen, you look cold, sweetie," I said to my daughter, holding out my arms. While Katherine, Nancy, and Lois left, Karen got out of her chair, and I pulled her onto my lap to cuddle her. She hadn't really looked cold, but I needed to hug my child. I kissed her fine, light brown hair, and she leaned back against me. Even at age ten, she fit so wonderfully on my lap— a bonus of her diminutive size.

Nathan had gotten some cake and asked me what "the gooey stuff" on top was. When I told him it was pineapple, he made a face and shoved it onto his sister's plate, who objected vehemently, until Rachel told her it was "yummy." Karen then returned to her chair, took a bite out of each cake slice, and raved about the flavor while eyeing her brother as if he'd accidentally given her a winning lottery ticket.

"Why don't you go ahead," Lauren told me. "My ankle's not hurting much now, and I'd rather stay here as long as possible. To be honest, it's a lot nicer than the cabin."

I whispered, "There's something I need to show you." I pulled the note out of my pocket. "Just handle it by a corner. I plan to give this to the police for fingerprints."

Lauren carefully got the paper from me and read it solemnly. When she'd finished, I put it back in my pocket.

"What was that, Mom?" Karen asked.

"A bad greeting card idea."

"Can I read it?"

"No, sorry. It's for adults only."

Karen, bless her sweet, innocent soul, accepted my answer.

"How did you get that?" Lauren asked, her voice full of worry.

"I was having everyone slip greeting card captions into a bowl, and it was among them. Not exactly Hallmark material."

I longed to discuss the threat further but needed to wait until the children weren't near. Instead, I insisted that I would get the car and drive them as far as the parking lot. Lauren didn't have the car keys after all, but then, I lose my keys so often that my hunting for them qualifies as a hobby. They must be at the other cabin.

The rain was now a light but steady drizzle. In the darkness, I could barely make out the rivulets formed from melting hail that ran alongside the path as I made my way to the women's cabin.

"The roof leaks," Katherine said to me by way of greeting the moment I stepped through their door. They were all seated in the living room, looking wet and tired.

"Yes, but can you believe our good luck?" Julie said, gesturing. Even she, with her youthful complexion, looked bad, her mascara having run, which lifted my spirits. "The water dripped right into the salad bowl. Though that did ruin all of the card suggestions."

"My life's work was in that bowl," Professor Katherine deadpanned.

I glanced around. If something did happen to one of us, I would need handwriting samples. "Where are the slips I'd already collected?"

"Thrown out," Celia answered. Her makeup and hairspray had somehow survived the rain. "I spruced up a bit before we left for dinner. Are we ready to begin another writing session, ladies?"

"Maybe you can begin by rewriting whatever got soaked. In the meantime, I just need to find the keys to my car so I can go pick up my injured friend and my children."

"You stay here. I'll go get them," Celia offered, picking up her purse and rifling through it. "That way, you can start the class."

Lois groaned and smacked the floor with both hands. A

cloud of dust arose. "I've had it! I've been patient enough. I'm not going to sit here in a freezing room with a leaking roof, just to hear about some silly career no one can make a decent living at."

Celia looked up from her purse, wide-eyed. "Where are my keys?"

"Neither of you have your keys?" Lois asked. "What is this? Weekend with the half-wits?"

"Hey!" I glared at her. "That was uncalled for!"

Lois furrowed her heavy brow and said nothing. No wonder there was so much animosity in this group. I'd only been with them for a few hours, and I wanted to resort to violence. They, according to Celia, had "all known one another for years."

"Your cabin lights just went on, Molly," Nancy said, looking out the window. "Your friend and the children must have walked back up."

"Really?" I joined Nancy at the window. The lights were indeed on. "I think I'll see how Lauren's ankle is and be right back."

Celia stepped in front of the door, blocking me. "Nobody is leaving this cabin until the person who took my keys returns them."

"You must have misplaced them," Lois said.

Celia shook her head and turned up her already turned up nose. "I always put them in a special compartment in my purse. They aren't there. Somebody took them."

I gritted my teeth but then turned to the others and asked, "Did anybody borrow the keys to get something out of the trunk?"

A chorus of nos greeted me.

"My car is a Suburban, Molly. It doesn't even have a trunk." Celia's voice was so haughty, I fisted my hands.

"Think about what you're saying, Celia," Nancy said in

gentle, therapeutic tones. "Who would possibly want to take your keys? It's not as if anyone *wants* us to stay here."

Unless one of us intends to commit murder. Maybe I hadn't simply misplaced my keys after all. A chill ran up my spine.

"Besides," Katherine said, "the road is blocked."

Just then, an enormous flash illuminated the sky. Simultaneously, a tremendous crash resounded. We all gasped. An instant later, the lights went out. We were left in total blackness.

Chapter 3

She Mustard a Smile

I tried not to panic as I blinked, hoping my eyes would adjust. A death threat in my pocket, a room full of suspects, and the lights go out. During my far-too-short-to-end-now! lifetime, I had read more than enough mysteries to know exactly how this was going to end: One of us would be dead when the lights came back on.

Get a grip, I silently chastised myself. The note was just a sick joke. But just in case . . . "Can everybody please say their name? So we can get a feel for where we all are?"

"Celia Wentworth," Celia began without hesitation. She was still directly behind me, in front of the door. Her carefully plucked eyebrows would be drawn together in a stern mask. "Let's not lose sight of the fact that someone has taken my keys, and that I demand to have them back!"

"Lois Tucker speaking, and I'm so ticked off at you, Celia, if you weren't across the room from me, I'd wring your neck. I never should have listened to you! You lied to me about this weekend! You've lied to me more times than I can remember." She'd risen. I could just make out the silhouette of her sturdy frame in front of the window on the opposite wall. Her arms were akimbo, her hands no doubt fisted.

"Lois, Celia, please," Nancy said in her placating, therapeutic voice. "Let's all just take a couple of deep, cleansing breaths and count to ten. There's no sense in making this worse."

"*Cleansing* breaths?" Celia repeated in disdain. "Sounds like advice from a midwife."

"You sound angry," Nancy replied calmly.

"Brilliant deduction," Celia snapped. "That must be why you make the big bucks."

There was a dull noise from the center of the room.

"Ow! I just kicked the goddamned salad bowl!"

"Who said that?" I asked.

"That was me, Julie," came the small, embarrassed-sounding voice. "And please excuse my French."

"Julie?" Allison said. Her melodic voice was immediately recognizable. She was still seated on or near the couch. "That's the first time I've ever heard you swear."

"I know. I'm sorry. Truth be told," Julie explained, "I'm scared of the dark."

My mind raced through the layout of the room and my recollection of the voices. One had been missing. Our professor! "Katherine? Are you still with us?"

"Where would I go?" came her monotone answer. "We'll be here till the end of time. This greeting card workshop is our rock, which we, like Sisyphus, are condemned to push uphill for all eternity."

So long as there wasn't a ventriloquist in the room, everyone was still alive. "So, Katherine, are you saying you're not enjoying my workshop?"

I had hoped to lighten the mood with my remark, but nobody laughed. There was only the sound of a lot of shuffling and mumbled apologies as someone moved about.

"Allison, do something about this," Celia snapped.

"I'm trying to find my suitcase to get my flashlight," Allison answered, her voice coming from another room. "The lightning probably knocked out a main power line, in which case there's nothing I can do. But I'll go out and check the breakers."

Celia called out, "Allison? Once you find your flashlight, get mine, too. It's in the side pocket of my suitcase, located by the foot of my bed. Did everyone else bring theirs?"

"It isn't as though we had a lot of time to pack," Katherine snarled.

"Let me get this straight," Celia said. "We're on a weekend trip in the mountains, and only Allison and I thought to bring a flashlight. Is that correct?"

"Yes, that's correct. Want to make something of it?"

"Now, really, Katherine. I was simply making an observation. There's no cause to take it personally."

"That is so like you, Celia," Katherine retorted, her voice still so angry I could imagine how her students would cringe in their seats. "You refuse to be held accountable for whatever hurtful or vitriolic remark you make, yet you treat everyone else's verbal miscues as if they'd been etched onto your forehead."

This was deteriorating into a catfight. I opted for a convenient excuse to extricate myself before I, too, got clawed. "I've got to get to the other cabin and check on the kids. They must be scared stiff." Actually, they all had flashlights and were probably enjoying this.

I bumped directly into Celia and apologized as I tried in vain to get around her. "Wait just a minute, Molly," Celia said crossly. "Let's make sure Allison can find her flashlight before we go traipsing around on one another's feet. All right?"

"Well, fine. I'm sure worse things could happen than my stepping on your toes."

"Such as Lois stepping on them," someone muttered.

"Julie! How dare you!"

"I'm so sorry, Lois," Julie said in a near whimper. "We've just got to get some light in here. I'm starting to have an anxiety attack."

"Let's all relax and imagine ourselves floating down a river," Nancy said soothingly.

If I tried to follow her suggestion, I'd envision myself careening toward Niagara Falls without a paddle.

"I've got my flashlight," Allison called, "but your batteries are dead, Celia."

"That isn't possible. I checked the batteries before we left. You must not have pushed the button hard enough."

"I'm an electrician," Allison said. "I know how to operate a flashlight." The small, oblong light from Allison's flashlight played across the room. Everyone rose and followed Allison's light as if they were gypsy moths.

"Let me take that," Celia barked as soon as Allison reached us. "We'll escort Molly to her cabin."

"No," Allison said. "I need it to check the fuses." The glow of the light darted across the room in a frenzy as Celia and Allison played tug-of-war with the flashlight.

"But we need it to get to Molly's cabin," Lois said.

My temper finally snapped. "Nobody is going to my cabin but me! Let me out of here, Celia, before I have to hit you!"

"Just as soon as I get the flashlight, I'll move," Celia said, her officious tones setting my teeth on edge.

"This is just the way things turned out the last time we tried to go someplace together," someone whined.

The statement distracted Celia enough that she turned and said, "We all agreed we would never—"

She broke off as Allison seized the opportunity, shouldered her, and opened the door. I grabbed it before it could swing shut again and left. The damp, chill air was a welcome change.

Allison had already started up the hill to circle the building. The moonless sky cast little light. I made my way down toward my cabin, indistinct shapes all that were visible within the blackness. I crooked an arm in front of my face to protect it as I was thwapped by one soaking wet pine branch after another.

Each time I was rewarded by an extra shower of water coming off the needles. Occasionally the lightning bolts would illuminate my way. I wasn't worried about getting electrocuted; that would be too quick an end to this miserable weekend.

From our cabin window's dull glow, it was obvious the kids had turned on their flashlights. I felt around until I found the door, threw it open, and called, "Is everybody all right?"

"Yeah, sure Mom," Karen answered. "We're playing flashlight tag. Want to play?"

Several minutes later, Lauren and I convinced the children that it was bedtime, leaving them with two of the three flashlights between them. They would no doubt be wide-awake for a long time yet, but at least I finally had an opportunity to speak to Lauren alone.

"What are we going to do?" Lauren asked as soon as the bedroom door was shut behind us.

"All we can do is—" Just then, the lights came on. The sudden brightness painful, I blinked while the children giggled that we forgot to turn the lights out in their room. This led to another round of tucking children in and saying good night, but we managed to collect the flashlights—their greatest distraction from sleep.

Lauren was already seated on the couch when I closed the bedroom door behind me. "What on earth has been happening in the other cabin?" Lauren asked quietly. "I thought you said this was going to be a fun workshop."

"Well, I was wrong. This is about as much fun as a combination tax audit–root canal."

Just then, Lauren and I gasped as the door flew open. Allison stepped inside, held up an almost full bottle of red wine, and cried, "Success!"

"Is everybody all right over at your cabin?" I asked.

"Depends what you mean by 'all right.' I think you may have taken over my standing as Most Despised."

"Why would *you* have been Most Despised?"

Ignoring the question, she set the bottle on the counter. "I decided to break out some wine to celebrate having lights. Nobody over there wanted to join me, so I came over here." She started taking drinking glasses down from the cabinet.

"Count me in," Lauren said.

"Just a little for me." I paused, trying to decide what tack to take for gleaning information. "I've gathered that this wasn't the first time you women tried to take a trip together."

Allison nodded and handed an eight-ounce glass of wine to Lauren, who reclaimed her seat on the couch. "We took a trip two months ago, when Katherine won an award of a couple hundred dollars from the university. She claimed she wanted to treat her 'best friends' to a luxury weekend at the Broadmoor."

"Wow. That was nice of her." The Broadmoor was one of the ritziest hotels in the state of Colorado. I sat down beside Lauren.

"Except she changed her mind when she checked out the cost. Celia said she'd handle making comparable arrangements."

"You didn't end up here, did you?"

Allison laughed. "Not quite this bad, though the company stunk. If I'd had any idea I'd wind up having to spend another weekend with those bitches, I'd have refused to come here."

Lauren's face paled and she shot a nervous glance my way. My heart seemed to skip a beat. "Excuse me?"

"Oh, sorry. With these *unlikable people*. I forget how motherhood has tamed your language."

I stared at her, surprised and a little hurt by the snideness in her voice. Plus, her last remark made no sense. She hadn't even known me before I'd had children. "What's caused the bad blood among all of you?"

She held up a palm and let out a bitter chuckle. "I'm not

about to ruin a perfectly good glass of wine by opening that Pandora's box." She started to hand me a glass.

"That's way too much. If I drink more than half a glass, I suffer for the next twenty-four hours."

She pushed the glass into my hands nonetheless. "Aw, it's just a domestic. Pour out what you don't drink." She sank sideways into the upholstered chair and crossed her legs at the ankles across the armrest. In a nasty impersonation of Julie, Allison clasped her hands and asked, "So, Moll. Isn't this place just adorable? And aren't my friends just wonderful?"

The wine tasted sharp, almost sour, but that may have been a result of the current mood in the room. I asked again, "What caused the problems among you?"

Allison's features hardened and she raked her bleached-blond bangs out of her eyes. "I'd rather not get into it just now." She then gulped her wine without another comment.

Lauren, still seated beside me on the musty plaid couch, rubbed her sore ankle and also downed her enormous glass of wine at an impressive clip. Though I truly tried not to let my expression reveal my disapproval—Lauren occasionally drank too much and it worried me—I could tell by her sheepish smile that my concern hadn't been well masked.

I moved to a hardback chair next to Allison and insisted Lauren lie on the couch with her leg up. Once she looked more comfortable, I returned my attention to Allison, already on her second huge glass. "So, tell me what's gone on lately, Allison. Your last letter sounded as if things were starting to come together for you. But you seem, well, different."

She sat up a little from her sideways perch and peered at me. "Different?"

"Unhappy," I admitted honestly. "Weary."

Allison stared at her foot as she rotated it slowly in the air. Her thin hiking boots were covered with mud, which fit right in with the decor. "You have no idea what true unhappiness is.

That's called marriage to Richard Kenyon. Then to finally escape, only to find out—" She stopped abruptly. A look of such sorrow passed across her features that witnessing it almost moved me to tears.

"What?"

She drained her glass, rose, and emptied the bottle into her glass. "You know what they say about curiosity, Molly." She chuckled mirthlessly and said to herself, "Except this time, the cat killed curiosity."

"I don't follow. What do you mean?"

She said nothing, merely flopped back into her chair and gulped wine as if it were soda pop. I glanced at Lauren, who grimaced, but made no comment. Allison sighed and drained her glass. "I'm tired. I'm going to bed. Let's talk in the morning. I'll tell you the sordid tale then." With difficulty, she got to her feet.

"Allison?"

She met my eyes. I hesitated for a moment, then said, "A few hours ago, somebody slipped a death threat into the bowl instead of a card caption. It said one of us would soon be dead. Do you have any idea who could have written it, and why?"

Allison's face barely registered a reaction, yet looked as unnatural as Celia's hair. "No, I have no idea. Are you sure it wasn't just a practical joke?"

"Is that what you think it was?"

"Of course. It must have been." She opened the door, then stopped and looked at me. "You haven't told any of the others about the note, have you?"

"Only Lauren, and now you. But maybe I should go over there with you now and—"

"No! It will just rile everybody up and we can't leave till morning anyway." She grabbed the empty bottle off my counter. "Good night." She tripped on the threshold. She was so unsteady on her feet, I stepped outside to watch and felt a surge of relief when the muted light indicated she'd made it to her door.

"Is she always like that?" Lauren asked when I returned to the living room. "She sounded . . . hostile."

"No. She was always a private person—secretive even. But I've never known her to be so bitter." Had she been covering up her sadness all the time we'd been friends? Should I have tried harder to draw her out while we still lived in the same town?

Lauren let out a heavy sigh, her lids starting to close. "That wine sure packs a wallop. I'm going to bed."

While Lauren limped around the bathroom and readied herself for bed, I climbed into the top bunk and found catharsis in my usual way: my drawing pad. My head started to spin by the time Lauren got into bed. I tossed the pad onto the floor.

Lauren must have retrieved it, because a moment later she read out loud, "She mustard a smile?" in incredulous tones.

"It's intended as a freelance card. The actual cover will show a color photo of a hot dog and a hamburger. The burger's lips as she smiles at the hot dog will have been made out of mustard."

"So I gathered." Lauren said through her yawn, "You should change it so the guy is the hamburger and the girl is the hot dog."

"Too phallic for you?" I teased.

She said, "Mmm," sounding half asleep.

"I'm sure even Picasso had his off days."

"Yes, and I'm sure your fast-food drawings are every bit as good as his were. Good night, my dear. Sleep well."

I, too, felt exhausted. Must be the effects of the thin air. I flipped off the light and let myself drift off.

The next morning, my head hurt as I sat up and parted the curtains. The clouds were gone and the sun was shining once again. I usually get a headache from wine, but this time I'd only had a third of a glass.

Wanting to enjoy the scent of pine trees, I rose, then banged and jiggled the window, but it wouldn't open. I cheered myself with the thought that by now, the rockslide would be cleared, and we could leave. From their room next door, the children were chattering away, their joyful, infectious giggles wafting through the wall.

I headed through the kitchen. The bedroom door creaked open and my daughter craned her neck around the entrance.

"Morning, sweetpea."

"Morning," she said to me, then called over her shoulder, "Mom's awake. Now we can go get breakfast."

I shuffled into the living room and scanned my surroundings. Just as I was about to conclude that all was in order, something caught my attention. My purse was by the door. I could have sworn it was on the table last night. Someone must have moved it. To my surprise, there was a characteristic jingle when I moved it. Sure enough, there in the front partition were my keys.

Last night, I had searched this compartment and found no keys. "Weird," I muttered to myself, stashing the keys in the pocket of my jeans.

"What's weird, Mom?" Karen repeated, entering the living room. She was fully dressed.

"I found my keys."

"You're right. It's weird for you to actually *find* something. Rachel and I are going to go get breakfast by ourselves."

"No, you're not." My daughter's superior tones had rankled me—another precursor to the fast-approaching teen years. And she was my *easy* child; if she turned on me, I'd never survive. "Wait until I can get dressed and go with you."

I returned to my room, where Lauren was sound asleep. I soon noticed a second oddity: My Reeboks were missing. I searched the small cabin in vain. Lauren stirred a little as I searched our room for the fifth time.

"Lauren? Have you seen my shoes?"

She opened her eyes and blinked at me. "Huh?"

"My shoes are missing. Have you seen them?"

She yawned and rubbed at her eyes. "Shoes. You can't find . . ." She groaned. "I'm sleeping. Only husbands ask questions like that."

"I know. I'm sorry. But my shoes aren't here. This place is the size of a tollbooth, so I really mean it when I say that I've looked everywhere."

Lauren rolled over and mumbled, "Maybe you were sleep-walking last night."

"And did what? Went outside and buried my shoes? This is too bizarre. What am I going to do? I can't go around this place barefoot. I'm not up on my tetanus boosters."

She yawned and muttered that I could borrow her sandals while she wore her sneakers. Then she pulled the covers over her face.

"Lauren? I'm going to take the kids down to—"

There was a knock on the door.

"Hope that's a door-to-door shoe salesman." I went to answer it. Karen and Rachel had raced to the door, but waited for me, probably anticipating, as I was, that this was merely one of the women from the other cabin. I swung open the door and gaped in surprise.

"Tommy! What are you doing here?" I cried accusingly. "How did you get here? The road's washed out."

"Glad to see you, too, Moll. They cleared the road as of six A.M."

I studied him, still stunned. Tommy Newton, Lauren's fiancé and my longtime friend, was not wearing his police uniform, but rather workboots, jeans, and a green flannel shirt, his red hair a bright orange hue in contrast. "I didn't mean . . . Has there been an emergency?"

"Naw, I just—"

"Tommy!" came Lauren's delighted voice behind me. I stepped aside as Lauren vaulted into Tommy's arms and they kissed passionately in the doorway. There was no place for me to go, or even to look. Nathan opened his door, caught sight of Lauren and Tommy, said, "Yuck," then closed his door. I'd just decided to join the children, when Lauren and Tommy broke off the embrace.

"My class got cancelled at the last minute," Tommy explained. "The boys are at camp, so I figured, perfect time for me to go visit Colorado." He finally pulled his eyes away from Lauren and spotted Karen and Rachel.

"Hey, Karen. Hi, Rach."

Karen and Rachel said, "Hi," simultaneously. Rachel forced a smile. She still hadn't warmed to the idea of sharing her mother. That had been an ongoing battle for the last few months and had caused Lauren to delay the wedding on more than one occasion. That was merely my opinion though, as Lauren denied it and always claimed they were just waiting for the perfect time.

All of a sudden, Celia, Julie, Nancy, Katherine, and Lois were standing behind Tommy in the doorway. Tommy did a double take and looked a little unnerved at how outnumbered he suddenly was.

"Hello," Lois said to Tommy with a big smile. "Are you the owner?"

"Depends," Tommy replied. "The owner of what?"

"She means the resort," I explained.

"Resort?"

"These hole-in-the-wall cabins," Nancy answered.

"No, I'm not the owner. I'm just a friend."

"Do you have a car?" Katherine asked. "With keys?"

"Yes. Why?"

"Drive me to Boulder," she said, rummaging through her purse. "I'll give you my last dime." She truly must have been desperate, as she hadn't even waited to be introduced to Tommy. She had slept on her hair wrong, I noted. A sizable portion of

her short brown hair, which yesterday looked so neat and efficient, now stood on end.

"Speaking of dimes, the phones are out at the lodge," Julie
said, her strawberry blond hair, in contrast to Katherine's, every
bit as perky as her voice. "I stopped by there during my morning jog and spoke to the cook. He says the lines are down."

"Maybe we can get Allison to fix them, or something," Celia
suggested. She gave Tommy one of her patented plastic smiles.
"My name is Celia Wentworth. And you are?"

"Sergeant Newton. Tommy, rather. I'm on vacation."

"Where *is* Allison?" I asked.

Celia shrugged. "She must have gone down to breakfast."

"She took her suitcase," Nancy said.

"Yes, we know," Celia snapped, "but as I told you, the parking lot is partially visible from that crest over there"—she
pointed to a clearing above us as forcibly as if this were a disco
move—"and I could see both cars when I checked not fifteen
minutes ago. She must have simply brought her belongings
with her to the lodge. I'm sure she wanted to make a quick exit
after breakfast." She softened her tones and smiled at Tommy.
"I watched you walk up. Where's your car?"

"Down below. By the lodge. The cook showed me the path to
get to the cabins." Tommy looked at me. "Did you know that
the cook has no sense of smell?"

"Some people have all the luck," Katherine said.

"Did you see Allison while you were talking to him?" I
asked Tommy.

He shook his head. "Place was deserted."

"Then where—"

"She was probably just in the restroom," Celia interrupted.
"It was nice meeting you, Thomas. Ladies? Shall we?" Celia
signaled with a sweep of one hand for the troops to forward
march. She took a couple of steps, then looked back at me and
said, "By the way, whoever stole my keys has yet to return

them. We cannot leave until I have my keys." Celia marched down the path, head held high, seemingly oblivious to the fact that no one had followed.

"Mo-om," Karen cried. "We're hungry and everyone's blocking the door. Can we go out a window?"

"Wait for me," Lauren called from our bedroom. "I'm almost dressed. Tommy and I will take you."

"We're going to starve," Rachel whined.

"Let's go," I said, then called back to Lauren, "We'll save your seats."

We all started down the hill in a pack. Nancy tried to make polite conversation with me, but I couldn't shake the feeling she was analyzing me. Plus my concerns for Allison weighed heavily. Where was she? Her words last night describing herself as "Most Despised" nagged at me.

Something in the corner of my vision froze me just as we reached the turnoff to the dirt lot where my car was parked.

"Molly," Katherine asked, "are you all right?"

"I'm fine. Please go on ahead with the others."

"What's wrong?" Nancy asked.

I shook my head. "I'll join you in a minute. I want to make sure my rental car survived last night's hailstorm."

As soon as they grudgingly continued down the path, I doubled back and checked what I'd spotted in the foliage: an empty, dark green bottle. I picked it up and sniffed the lip. It was the wine bottle we'd drunk from last night, which Allison had taken to her cabin. I dashed to my car and tried to deny what I was seeing.

Allison, unmoving, was slumped against the steering wheel.

Chapter 4

Elementary, My Dear Watson

Allison's blond hair was fanned across her face, her head tilted away from me, toward the passenger side.

"Allison?" I thumped on the window. She didn't move. The door was locked. With shaking hands, I snatched my keys out of my pocket and opened the door. I put a hand on her shoulder to shake her but jerked back.

Allison felt stone cold.

"Tommy!" I hollered in desperation, hoping he was within earshot.

"Molly?" he called back. It sounded as if he was near the turnoff in the path.

"I'm at my car. Come quick."

I heard his footfalls as he ran toward me.

"Molly, is everything all right?" It was Lauren's voice.

"No, but just go ahead and catch up with the kids," I cried, my voice starting to break. It seemed to take forever until Tommy arrived. He dashed over to me, panting, his cheeks nearly as red as his hair.

"Please tell me it's my imagination, but she seems ice cold." I leaned over her and said, "Allison?"

Tommy gently guided me out of the way and leaned in through the car door to examine Allison. I turned my head, longing to escape, to block out the words I knew Tommy was about to say.

He straightened and faced me. "She's dead. Did you know this woman?" Tommy asked me, grimly.

I nodded. This couldn't be happening. "Allison. Allison Kenyon. She was my friend. This is all so . . ." My thoughts seemed at once to be swimming in slow motion and racing ahead of me. I wasn't sure what it was I wanted to say. "Something's all wrong. Allison couldn't be the target. What did she ever do to hurt anyone?"

"The *target*?" Tommy repeated.

"Why is she in my car?"

Tommy was staring at something on the dashboard. "Starter's been tampered with. Looks as though your friend here knew how to hot-wire it. Did you lock your vehicle last night?"

"Yes. Then I couldn't find my car keys. But this morning, they were in my purse, only they weren't there last night." I stared at Allison in dull shock. There were no visible wounds. On the passenger seat beside her was a gray canvas overnight bag.

Tommy had crouched down and was now staring at something on the floorboards. I craned my neck and spotted the object he was studying. An empty syringe.

Tommy raked his fingers through his red hair as he rose. He watched me, studying my features. "You gonna be all right?" he asked, his voice so quiet it barely registered.

I nodded. He probably wondered why I seemed so calm. I wondered the same thing. I wanted to cry but couldn't. Would Allison still be alive if I'd read that threat out loud? Had my decision to keep quiet cost her her life?

"Phone lines are prob'ly still down," he said, pulling a pair of keys from his pocket. He held them out to me. "I've got to stay here and secure—I have to keep anyone from touching anything. You have to go get the sheriff."

"But what about—"

"My rental car's the blue Escort down by the lodge. There's

got to be a fire station in town, and they'll radio it in. Don't talk to anybody else."

I nodded again, but all I could think about was my children. One of those women with Karen and Nathan right now was a killer. I had to get them out of here.

Tommy put an arm around my shoulders and led me to the entrance of the lot. Lauren was lingering on the path some twenty yards below us as if torn between tending to the children and making sure I was all right. Tommy waved at her to back up. "We got a situation here. You keep everyone down at the lodge while Molly goes for help."

She didn't move. Almost staggering, I wove my way down through the rocks and tufts of dead grass toward her.

"Did something happen to Allison?" she asked me.

"She's dead," I answered, feeling so numb it was all I could do to keep on my feet.

Lauren gasped. Her hand flew to her face.

"Molly!" Tommy hollered. He was standing above us, one foot braced on a large boulder at the entrance to the dirt lot, as if playing king of the mountain. "Can't you follow simple instructions? I told you to keep your mouth shut!"

"Well? I didn't know you meant Lauren, for heaven's sake!"

"You're gonna compromise the—" He stopped and took a deep breath. In calmer tones he said, "Both of you. Go straight to my car. Do not go into the lodge. Drive to the fire department. Do not speak to anybody else. Got that?"

We headed down the path without answering, but my thoughts were on Karen and Nathan. I was not going to desert them, even for a few minutes. Lauren, limping only slightly as she matched my pace, murmured, "Was Allison murdered?"

My mind slogged through a morass of thoughts. Allison could have been a drug user or committed suicide, but that wouldn't explain how she got into my car, especially since my keys had reappeared in my purse. "Probably. We've got to ignore Tommy's instructions and go into the lodge, you know. We're taking the children with us."

"Oh, absolutely."

We reached the lodge. Lauren started Tommy's car while I dashed inside to get the children. I tested the phone in the office. No dial tone.

I took a deep breath of coffee-scented air to collect myself as I entered the dining room. Celia was sitting with Nathan and the girls at the nearest table. The four other women sat at an adjacent table near the window. All of the women greeted me, their attempts at conversation a jumble of words about Allison and when we might leave. The children, focused on their meals and not on me, had heaped their plates with pastries and bacon, with tiny dots of scrambled eggs just for color.

Celia's painted features smiled up at me. "At last. I've been keeping the little ones company while you were gone."

"Thanks. I'm here now."

Celia didn't take the hint and stayed put. "Unlike last night's dinner, the breakfast is really quite good. Aren't you going to get anything to eat?"

"No."

At the other table, Nancy rose, patted her lips with the napkin, and came over to me. She said quietly, "Allison isn't here. The cook hasn't seen her since last night."

"Really? I hope she's all right."

She studied my face, my cheeks warming. How long could I keep up this act? For all I knew, Nancy could have killed my friend. One of these people had. I wanted to scream. One hateful, hideous person in this room had killed my friend!

"Is everything all right?" She'd slipped into her therapeutic tones. "You seem quite shaken."

"Lauren reinjured her ankle." I averted my eyes, afraid that with her professional expertise, she could read through my lie. "I'm taking her to a doctor."

"Oh, dear," Celia said, finally rising.

"What? What's happened?" Julie asked, leaping to her feet. "Is it Allison?"

"No," Celia said irritably, "Molly's friend went and hurt herself."

"Hey!" I snapped, in my raw state ready to pounce on Celia for anything. "She didn't do it on *purpose*!" Nancy and Lois, the only adults still seated, rotated in their chairs and stared at me. I turned my attention to the kids. They were watching me in total confusion. "Grab your plates. You can finish in the car." Rachel looked especially upset. I leaned down and said in a near whisper, "Don't worry. Your mom's fine."

Karen said, "I'm not hungry."

"Me neither," Rachel said, pushing her plate away.

Nathan, however, began shoveling food into his mouth as if this were bound to be his last meal. I grabbed his plate and his orange juice.

"Molly," Celia began, "I meant no offense. I merely—"

"Please excuse us." I waltzed out as fast as I could, Nathan's plate and cup in hand. My eyes were stinging and I realized dully that tears were running down my cheeks.

We reached the car, and I set the plate down on the roof and opened the back door. Rachel slid into the middle seat and immediately asked her mother about her ankle. While Lauren spoke to her quietly, Karen had stopped in front of the car door and was looking up at me, her expression full of worry.

"What's wrong, Mom?"

As I met my daughter's beautiful dark eyes, I felt a surge of both gratitude and fear for her very existence. Why were murderers living in the same world as my kindhearted, wonderful children? "My friend Allison Kenyon died in her sleep last night."

"You can die from *sleeping*?" Nathan asked, horrified. He stepped alongside his sister.

"No, not from—She . . . Nobody dies in their sleep at your age," I said, as the only reassuring thing I could think to say at the moment.

"But they do at your age?" Karen asked as she got into her seat at the opposite side of the car.

Nathan flopped down into his seat. "I'll bet this means we don't get to go to Elitches."

"Yes, it does." I thrust his plate and cup into his hands. "I'm making up a new rule. Whenever a friend of mine dies, we don't go rushing off to an amusement park. Okay?"

Both Karen and Nathan shrank back, and I instantly regretted my harshness.

"Sorry, Nathan. I'm upset about losing my friend."

I sat down, but rotated to peer between the seatbacks. "Nathan? Karen? Please understand that I'm going to be sad and maybe a little grouchy for a while. It doesn't mean that I don't love you or that you've done anything wrong."

"That's okay, Mom," Karen said. "We don't mind."

I winced, too emotionally drained to respond.

We headed into the town of Evansville and found a fire station almost immediately, as it was right on Main Street. The lone fireman in the office immediately radioed the information to the Boulder sheriff's department. He knew where the Red Fox Resort was and said he'd follow me up there.

Nathan had finished his breakfast by the time I got back to the car. We drove in silence, the fire truck right behind us. I shivered uncontrollably. When we reached the resort, Lauren drove us past the lodge and up the road toward the parking lot, until she spotted Tommy, who gestured for us to pull over. He jogged past us to speak to the fireman. Because the dirt road was too narrow to do anything else, the firefighter stopped his truck where it was, and we waited, engine idling. Tommy soon tapped on the window, which Lauren promptly rolled down.

"Nearest sheriff's units'll be here shortly. Why don't you all take the kids to—" He stopped and stared into the backseat, finally registering the children's presence. "How did the kids get—" He let out a sigh. "Never mind. Go on up to one of the cabins and stay there."

We hustled the children up to our cabin, and Lauren took them into the bedroom and got them involved in a board game she'd brought with her. I sat on one of the rickety chairs in the kitchen. I could hear sirens nearing but had no vantage point of the parking lot and its activities.

After shutting the bedroom door behind her, Lauren took the remaining chair beside me. She appraised my mood and said soothingly, "Tell me more about Allison. How did you meet her? Did she have children at the same school as Karen and Nathan?"

I shook my head. "She didn't have children. We met at a group golf lesson several years ago. She hit me with a three-wood. Wild backswing. She felt so bad about it, I finally agreed to let her buy me lunch, and we got to be friends. Golfed together several times every summer since then till we moved away."

"Were you close?"

"If you'd asked me that yesterday, I would have said yes. But that wouldn't have been true. It was strange. There was something about her I found so appealing. Maybe just the way she laughed at my jokes, made me feel fun to be around. But you'd ask her about certain things, and this wall would go up. She made it clear that there were parts of her you would never be allowed to know. I hadn't even known she and her husband were having marital problems till she told me in her last Christmas card that they were divorced."

I took a deep breath, battling a sense of total despair. "People die everywhere I go, Lauren. I'm the Lizzie Borden of the greeting card industry."

"You can't blame yourself. There's nothing you could have done to prevent what happened."

That was probably true, but my guilt at having been the reason she was here with these women was palpable.

"Did you tell Tommy about the death threat you got yesterday?"

I shook my head. "Not yet. I'd better go down there and give it to the police." I reached into my pocket. It was empty. I hopped up and checked all my pockets. Nothing. "The threat! It's gone! These are the same jeans I wore yesterday. I remember putting it back in my pocket after showing it to you."

"Maybe it fell out when you took them off last night. I'll go search our bedroom."

She rose as I continued, "The keys, the note, my shoes. Someone's taking my stuff. Somebody is—"

There was a firm rap on the door. I swung it open. A pretty, twentyish female officer, her dark hair fastened close to her scalp with half a dozen bobby pins, nodded at me in greeting. "Are you Molly Masters?" Her voice was surprisingly forceful for her size—she was only about five feet tall.

"Yes." As I answered I was aware of the sounds of the children running into the room behind me.

"You found the body, right?"

I nodded as she said, "I'll need to talk to you privately." She looked at Lauren. "You can stay here with the children. An officer will be up to speak with you shortly." She gave me a rather cold smile, then said, "Want to come with me, please?"

Before I could react, a child's arms were wrapped tightly around my waist as Karen squeezed herself in front of me. "I'm coming with you, Mommy."

"Sweetpea? You need to stay here with Lauren. I'll be fine." I tried to give her a reassuring hug, but she gripped me even tighter, shaking her head against my stomach.

"No!" she cried. "I'm not leaving you!"

This was nothing like Karen, never prone to open defiance and not at all a clingy child. She was afraid for me, and I was slowly but surely filling with dread for myself as well. "I'll be fine. Really."

The officer placed a hand on Karen's back and said sweetly, "Your mommy's going to be fine. Why don't you wait here?"

Karen dropped her arms but set her chin. She was determined not to let herself cry, and that sight alone broke my heart.

"Sweetie, I'm not going to let anyone take me away from you. I'm just going to need to be alone with the police to answer questions for an hour or so."

My purse was still on the table and I grabbed it automatically. The officer immediately said, "I'll take that." As I started to hand it over, an unpleasant thought hit me as I recalled how my keys had mysteriously reappeared. I gave my purse a good shake. Sure enough, my efforts yielded a metallic jingle, but my keys were currently in my pocket.

The officer eyed me strangely as she took the purse, and I said, "Could you do me a favor? Could you see if you can find a set of keys in my purse?"

She nodded and fished through the main compartment, retrieving an enormous set of keys on a chain adorned by a pair of wooden dice. "These the ones you're looking for?"

They weren't mine, but I knew immediately whose they were. "Yes. You can just put them back in my purse."

Someone was framing me for Allison's murder.

I walked beside the officer, feeling as though she were escorting me to a gas chamber. She instructed me to get into a cruiser—a white four-door with the yellow-and-blue official sheriff's band around it. This car was parked at the end of a string of four police cars behind the fire truck and Tommy's car. She closed the door behind me, told me she'd be with me in a couple of minutes, then tossed my purse into the trunk.

Tommy was nearby, perhaps on his way back up to the cabin

to check on Lauren. He changed directions and came over, crouching to eye level with the car window.

"Why are they putting me in the patrol car, Tommy? What about all the other women? One of them killed her."

"They'll probably bring everyone in. They're gonna have to take everyone's fingerprints."

Just then, a husky male voice called from above us, "I got the shoes that match those footprints by the car." The officer was carrying what looked like a pair of filthy Reeboks. The female officer moved off to meet him partway up the path.

I reached through the window to grab Tommy's arm. "Tommy! Someone's trying to frame me for this murder!"

He furrowed his brow. "What makes you . . . Are those your shoes?"

I nodded.

"Don't mean nothin'. So long as you didn't go leaving your fingerprints on any syringes last night."

I glared at him, irritated at how he'd slipped into his small-town-cop persona, complete with bad grammar. "I'm pretty sure my stash of syringes is still locked up tight."

"Good. So don't worry."

Again with being told not to worry. "Someone stole my shoes from my bedroom last night and grabbed the note out of my jeans. Wearing my shoes, that person injected Allison with a lethal dose of poison, while she was behind the wheel of my car. Then the killer put my keys back in my purse, along with Celia's keys. I don't know about you, but I think a little worrying is entirely appropriate!"

"Molly?" a voice trilled from below. I recognized Celia's officious tones and braced myself. The five women were bunched together on the path, flanked by two middle-aged men in sheriff's uniforms. "What's going on? These policemen claim that Allison is dead!"

One of the officers said, "We're going to take you all to the

Boulder County Justice Center, ladies." He instructed Julie and Celia to get into the car with me. Celia, who sat beside me in the middle seat, looked more annoyed than anything else. Julie had been crying.

The female officer got behind the wheel. "I'm going to have to ask you not to talk to one another."

We made our way down the steep, winding road through stratified layers of red-brown rock on either side. Deep, dark green pines above the rock rose in sharp contrast with the cloudless azure sky. The tranquillity surrounding me just made my internal uproar all the worse to bear.

Maybe Allison knew all along that someone was out to kill her and so had pocketed my keys, planning to leave. The washed-out road had interfered with that, but she'd figured she'd be safer driving off and waiting for the road to reopen than spending the night with the killer. Only she didn't make it.

We rode in silence for as long as I could bear. I didn't have anything to hide, so there was no point in my keeping still. "You were sharing her room last night, right, Celia?" I asked.

The muscles in the back of the officer's neck seemed to tense, but she made no move to interrupt us.

Celia shook her head. "I was supposed to, but there was a leak over my bed, so I slept on the living room floor."

"Three of you were in the living room, in front of the only door. You never heard her leave?"

"No," Celia said. "I remember when she returned from your cabin last night, though, because she tripped over me."

"I didn't hear her leave, either," Julie said. "She was definitely gone by the time I got back from my jog at seven. I peeked in the room to see if she wanted some coffee. The room was empty. I assumed she'd gone out sometime during my jog, but the window was wide open, so maybe she'd gone out the window."

"Don't be ridiculous," Celia snapped. "Why would she climb out the window when there was a perfectly good door?"

Julie turned her face and didn't answer. I got the impression that the officer was making careful mental notes on all of this.

"Julie, who else was in the living room?"

"Nancy."

"Did the bedrooms have—"

"Are we playing Twenty Questions here, Molly?" Celia interrupted. "Allison was my neighbor. I loved her dearly." She dabbed at a nonexistent tear. "I don't want to even think about this dreadful tragedy, let alone discuss it. Besides, the officer instructed us not to talk."

Not believing her show of grief for an instant, I clenched my teeth and said, "Sorry." I stared out the window. A flash of color caught my eye and I recognized it as a mountain jay, with its regal black tufted feathers that suddenly merged with brilliant blue at the base of its neck. It was so peaceful here, no traffic, cabins set way back from the road, their dark brown tones blending into the woodside. Ironically, these mountains were where I always used to go when I needed to relax and get my thoughts in order. There was no opportunity for that now.

We reached the northern outskirts of Boulder half an hour later. The road was now less steep and the houses and traffic considerably denser. Our course took us down the west side of town to the Justice Center, an imposing, monolithic red stone structure incongruously set alongside the beautiful, meandering Boulder Creek.

The officer pulled up in front of the building and opened my door first. We all got out as a second vehicle was pulling up with Nancy, Katherine, and Lois in the back. Though I felt foolish, I wanted my purse, needing to hang on to something familiar. It felt as though I were being led to slaughter and, by God, I wanted my blankee. As I'd suspected, the officer started to usher us toward the courthouse without getting my purse out of the trunk, so I asked her if I could have it.

"I'll be sure to give it to you before you leave," she said in a tone of finality.

"You can search it if you need to, but please, at least let me have my drawing pad and pencil. It's got a really dull point, so it's not dangerous."

"Why do you want it?"

"I'm an artist, a cartoonist actually, and I've gotten so used to having a drawing pad and pencil that I feel naked without them."

"Sorry, you'll just have to feel naked till we're finished with the interview."

"Well, at least that will make the strip search go faster," I grumbled.

"Strip search?" Celia shrieked. "They're going to strip search us?"

The officer chuckled, and I felt enough of a kinship with her to make me all the more determined. "It might help me explain better if I can draw while I talk. How about one sheet of paper and a crayon?"

She hustled us toward the lobby, saying, "I'll think about it."

Celia walked beside me, her arms tightly crossed. I asked, "Did your keychain have a zillion keys on it?"

"Yes. They're to the doors of the office building I own. Did you find them?"

I nodded. The officer did a double take at me but said nothing.

What followed was nearly as unpleasant an experience as I could imagine. After having my fingerprints taken—which was done electronically, a process not unlike photocopying one's hand—I was deposited into a tiny room with two hardback chairs and a large mirror, which was definitely one-way glass. I sat in the chair and thought about Allison, trying unsuccessfully to block out the horrid image of her dead body. At length, the female officer entered the room, handed me my sketch pad and pencil and said, "I'll be with you shortly," then left again. I was well aware that she was playing a psychological game—watching me through the glass to see if I'd try to stab myself with my pencil or attempt suicide by paper cut. But sketching truly did help me pass the time.

Desperately seeking a sleuth of my own, I wound up calling on the ghost of a famous fictional one. I drew two little boys, one slightly taller and older-looking than the second, who's wearing a Holmes-like cap and cape, but his toy meerschaum pipe is blowing bubbles. The older boy says to him, "Are you in preschool or elementary school?" He answers, "Elementary, my dear Watson. Elementary." The caption reads: *Sherlock Holmes: The early years.*

The female officer finally returned, but she immediately Mirandized me, which had the effect of causing my stomach to leap into my throat. She asked preliminary questions bent on establishing my identity, address, and so forth, then asked me to tell her "in my own words"—as if I'd use anyone else's—what happened starting with when I first arrived at the Red Fox Resort.

She stopped me when I related how I'd found the threat in the salad bowl and asked me to repeat the exact phrasing of the poem. Then she asked, "And what were your first thoughts when you received that note?"

"That I should get the heck out of there."

"You didn't tell anyone else what the note said?"

"I thought it was a sick joke. I told Allison and Lauren Wilkins, right before we went to sleep. I was planning to tell everyone else, as soon as we were set to leave. Then the road was blocked and there was no way to leave, so I decided to tell only people I felt I could trust about the note."

"And how did Allison react when you told her?"

I shrugged. "She pretended not to care. Told me that it was just a prank, which, like I said, is what I'd thought myself."

"What happened after you found this note?"

I launched into a description of trying to get access to a phone and to contact the owners, waiting out the storm, and Allison sharing a bottle of wine with us.

"And you say that was Allison's wine bottle, right?"

"Yes, and I only had about a third of a glass."

"Did you feel okay after drinking it?"

"No, I suddenly felt exhausted. So were Lauren and Allison."

"Did you help Allison into bed?"

"No, she wasn't *that* out of it."

"What shoes were you wearing?"

"Size seven Reeboks. But this morning, they were missing."

"No chance you left them outside?"

"None."

"Have you had cause to handle a syringe lately?"

"No, never."

She paused and studied my face for a long moment. "Any explanation of how your prints got on the syringe we found in your car?"

Chapter 5

I Feel Your Pane

The revelation was so shocking, I felt faint. "My prints were on it?" I murmured.

" 'Fraid so."

"That isn't possible! I never . . ." I let my voice fade away. The same person who'd put my and Celia's keys into my purse and took my shoes must have pressed the syringe into my hand as I slept.

The door opened and a second uniformed officer—this one male and muscular—entered. He introduced himself, then said, "Tell me what happened, Ms. Masters. From the beginning."

I went through the whole story, this time starting from my initial fateful decision to host a greeting card retreat. Afterward, he asked me a few more questions, which I answered to the best of my ability despite a ringing in my ears. My head felt as if it would explode.

Then at last he was through and told me I could go home, as long as I stayed in Boulder. His parting words were "You might want to speak to your lawyer."

I was too scared and shocked to ask how I would get home, but the female officer told me to "hang on a moment," and soon returned with my purse, from which she said they'd taken the key to my rental car, which they were impounding, and Celia's keys, which they'd returned to her. She was closely followed by

65

Tommy Newton. I was so relieved to see his friendly, freckled face, it was all I could do not to cry.

Tommy led me across the small parking lot crowded with the white sheriff vehicles to his blue two-door. He told me that Lauren had taken the children back to my house, and I mindlessly gave him directions on how to get there.

How could all of this have happened? This was supposed to be a brief, joyous return to my beloved home in Boulder, with a simple little greeting card workshop in the mountains thrown in for fun and profit. Now, all of a sudden, a longtime friend was dead and one of five women who barely knew me had framed me for her murder.

Tommy sat with his hands on the steering wheel, but made no move to start the engine. His face looked grim. Finally, he faced me. "Listen, Moll. You know we kid each other a lot, but I'm gonna tell it to you straight. Things don't look so good for you, and I haven't got any pull here whatsoever."

I nodded. "Can you at least request a copy of the police reports?"

"Can always make the request. Doesn't mean I'll get anywhere, though. What all are you interested in knowing about?"

"The autopsy results. And the test results on the residue, or whatever you call it, from the bottle of wine we drank last night."

"Autopsy won't be complete till tomorrow at the earliest. Even then, I won't have access to it. It's gonna be critical to their investigation that they keep that report confidential."

"But you're a police sergeant."

"Don't matter. There's gonna be a key fact or two about this case that the investigating officers keep to themselves, so they can guarantee only one other person on the planet knows it, too."

"The killer?"

He nodded. "Providing, of course, it was murder and not suicide or an accidental OD. My guess is they'll keep a lid on the precise spot on her body where she was injected. Or maybe the actual substance she was injected with."

My stomach lurched at my imaginary vision of Allison getting a poisonous injection jabbed into the back of her neck. "Come on, Tommy. You know as well as I do she was murdered. I never touched that syringe. My shoes were next to my bed when I went to sleep last night, not half-buried in the woods. And the threat was in the pocket of my jeans in my bedroom. For this to have been anything but murder, I'd have to be either a raving maniac or a compulsive liar."

He fastened his seat belt, started the engine, and pulled out of the space. "Never knew you to lie. Not so sure about the ravin' part."

I let his wisecrack slide, automatically checking to see if the road was clear for his right turn out of the lot. It was, and we headed east and away from the mountains.

"What about the contents of the wine bottle? Surely I have a right to know about that, don't I? After all, I drank the stuff. So did Lauren. What if we need to have our stomachs pumped?"

The muscles in Tommy's jaw tightened. "They did a preliminary analysis on the traces of wine still in the bottle. It had what they call 'roofie' in it. Knocks you out pretty fast and causes short-term amnesia. Gotten to be a rampant problem on college campuses these days. A guy can slip it into a girl's drink, she passes out stone cold and doesn't wake up till morning, no matter what the guy does to her while she's asleep."

"Oh, God. That's hideous!" By the time Karen was off to college in the not-too-distant future, would we have to warn her not to ever leave her drinking glass unattended? I shuddered, then another thought occurred to me: Katherine taught at C.U. She could have ready access to a prevalent campus drug.

Tommy growled, "Doesn't make me too happy to think about Lauren bein' so vulnerable last night."

My immediate reaction was: *Forget about your girlfriend! I'm the one who's being framed for murder!* But I mustered a reasonably calm voice and said, "This wasn't a case of date rape. The only male around us was the cook, and he couldn't have been involved in any of this. It was definitely one of the women in our group who slipped me that death threat, and the cook was never near our cabins." I hesitated. "Was he?"

"He has a one-room apartment in the attic above the lodge. Claims he was there all night. No one heard or saw him in the immediate vicinity. Odds are, he's telling the truth."

"Turn left here," I mumbled as we neared Twenty-eighth Street. My thoughts had focused on the wine bottle and the image of it nestled in the weeds near the path. "Tommy, whose fingerprints were on the bottle?"

"Just Allison's. And yours."

"Mine? But that—Oh. I picked up the bottle this morning when I found it." I punched my thighs in frustration. "Damn it! I wish I hadn't done that!"

Tommy raised a corner of his lips but said nothing.

"The bottle had already been opened when Allison came over to our place last night, but it looked full. She said nobody wanted any in the other cabin. Any one of them could have drugged the wine while Allison was out working on the fuses. Do we have any way of knowing when that bottle was first opened?"

"We?" Tommy repeated. "Believe me, Molly, I'll do everything I can to exonerate you, but that means you keep your distance from this case. You go talking to the other women in the cabin, you're gonna get yourself dug so deep, we'll need a miner's permit to get you out. You and I are not doing a . . . a Starsky-and-Hutch duet here. You got that?"

"That old show was the best analogy you could come up with? Which role did you have in mind for me—Starsky or Hutch?"

"You're the bimbo they have to rescue," Tommy muttered.

If he hadn't been driving, the urge to hit him would have been irresistible. "And *you're* my hero? Ha! Talk about bad casting."

"Right now, I'm the only thing you got goin' for you, so don't push it!"

His words zapped whatever hope I had of trying to keep myself from lapsing into despair. "I never thought I'd say this," I murmured, "but I just want to go back home to Carlton."

"You're not s'posed to leave Colorado till they clear you of all charges."

That had better happen soon, I thought. I was matron of honor in Lauren and Tommy's upcoming wedding, and I needed to review applicants for a scholarship program I ran every year. We drove the rest of the way in silence, save a couple of directions, and soon turned into my north Boulder neighborhood of large homes on oversized, well-maintained lots. The foliage was so much sparser than I'd grown used to in New York, allowing an uninterrupted view of the Flatirons—a series of rock faces in the shape of irons, which graced the base of the mountains due west of Boulder.

The house was deserted. I felt disconcerted as I walked inside, as if I were returning from a stay in the hospital. When we'd moved originally, we'd always expected to return shortly, so the house was fully—and yet impersonally—furnished: mostly bare walls, no bric-a-brac. For a brief, horrible moment, I had a sensation of returning as a ghost to view my pitiful possessions, as if these few rooms were the sum total of Molly Masters's life.

The screen door creaked behind me. "Where is everybody?" Tommy asked.

"They must have walked down to the park. It's just—"

"Mom's home!" came Karen's distant cry from outside.

Fear gripped me so tightly I could barely breathe. I could not let myself get arrested! My children needed me!

One after another, Rachel, Karen, and Nathan barged in, the screen door banging behind them each time like a gavel. The last inside, Karen ignored Tommy and set our old basketball on the floor beside him. "Mom!" she said, panting, her hair in damp clumps. "I dribbled the whole way home!"

"You're supposed to keep your lips closed when you drink," I said.

She giggled and rolled her eyes. "I meant with the basketball."

"Oh, right. Silly me."

"I won a game of HORSE," Rachel announced, casting a glance over her shoulder to make sure Tommy'd heard.

"She cheated!" Nathan growled. "She skipped the letter *r*. And I'm not a hose!"

He and Rachel bickered for a moment, then she stormed off to the backyard. The fact that Karen stayed put and steered clear of the debate indicated to me that Nathan was probably right, but Karen didn't want to betray her best friend in favor of her little brother.

Lauren entered, still limping slightly, once again out of breath, with her round cheeks pink with exertion. She gave Tommy a quick kiss, then turned to me. "How'd it go?"

"Not great." I glanced at Karen and Nathan and didn't continue.

With an exaggerated sigh, Karen said, "Come on, Nathan. Let's go play on the swing set. Mom doesn't want to talk in front of us."

Tommy and Lauren sat on the loveseat in our living room and I filled Lauren in on what had transpired. I told her that the wine we'd drunk had been doctored, which gave the killer the opportunity to press the syringe into my hand so my fingerprints would be on it.

Lauren looked at Tommy. "Why would someone take a risk like that? If Molly or I had awakened, what could they say they were doing? Sleepwalking with a syringe in their hand? And the three of us were alone. The killer couldn't even know that we'd been drinking the wine, too."

Tommy said slowly, "Maybe if you woke up, there would have been more than one victim."

On that somber thought, I glanced at my watch. "I have to go call Jim and let him know about this."

I stood in the kitchen by the one phone I'd brought with me, which had a built-in portable fax–answer machine. One of the downsides of running a financially precarious freelance business: There's no such thing as leaving your office. Tommy didn't get the hint that I'd like some privacy, but Lauren stood up and said, "Come on, Tommy. I'll show you our room downstairs."

I dialed the emergency contact number my husband had given me. After several minutes, he was located, and he greeted me with "Sweetie? What's wrong?"

To my frustration, the sound of his voice instantly put me on the verge of tears. I managed to clear my throat and say, "The class didn't go quite as well as I'd hoped. One of the students was murdered. My friend Allison Kenyon."

"Good God! Allison? You mean that woman you used to golf with? She was murdered? Oh Lord, Molly. Not again. How?"

"Poisonous injection. Late last night."

"Gee-zeus! Do the police have any suspects?"

Imagining his reaction, I winced and closed my eyes. "Well, one. Me."

"Is this . . . What the . . . Molly, why . . ." He paused. "I'll be on the next flight from Dallas." He hung up.

Too drained to do anything else, I sat on the floor and leaned back against the cabinets. My dear, sweet husband would be here in a few hours. Would that help matters or only make them worse? It was bad enough to have to cope with the absurd notion that some virtual stranger had framed me for a murder. When Jim arrived, I'd share his frustration and futility, as well.

Tommy's heavy footfalls were unmistakable as he trudged

up the stairs and out through the front door. A moment later, Lauren entered the kitchen and gave me a sad smile when she spotted my ignoble seat on the linoleum. "Everything okay?" she asked.

I nodded.

"Tommy and I are going to make a run to the grocery store."

"Thanks." I rose, intending to get my wallet. "I'll stay here with the kids. But let me—"

Reading my mind, Lauren held up a palm. "Tommy and I will pay for everything."

I brushed my dark bangs out of my eyes. "That's not necessary." I stared at my hand, which was trembling as if with a life of its own.

"You can handle this, you know. Whoever did this made a big mistake when they chose to frame you."

I meant to thank her for the vote of confidence, which felt unearned, but she left too quickly. My mind seemed to be operating a half second behind the rest of the world. I checked on the children, playing on the wooden swing set in the backyard, then sat in the living room and went to my usual salve: my drawing pad.

Though a perverse character trait, it cheers me to make fun of my duress, so I played around with puns about being in pain. I wound up creating a cartoon in which a man, dressed in a workman's uniform, says to an angry-looking woman, "I realize I charge a little more than other companies, but you see, I not only repair your window, I feel your pane."

The doorbell rang. To my complete surprise, it was Julie the aerobic dog breeder, and she had an enormous golden Labrador with her that looked at once in need of aerobics and overexerted. The dog was strikingly plump, yet was panting so hard I thought the poor thing might collapse.

"Hi, Molly. I tried to call you to say I was coming, but your phone was busy. This is Teak," Julie said. "Do you mind if I bring her in?"

"No, but why is she panting like that? Does she need some water?" I opened the door wide and they both stepped inside.

"She's going to have puppies in a couple of days, and I'm afraid to leave her home alone in this state."

"So you put the poor thing into the car and brought her to my house? Why?" The dog waddled past us as we took seats in the living room. Judging from the jingles of her collar, she'd headed into the family room off of the kitchen.

"I had to tell you something important. I was afraid to let it wait. Molly, I think you're being set up."

It gave me a small measure of relief that someone else could see this, as well. "That's my impression, too."

"Celia told me about how both sets of keys were found in your purse this morning." She lifted her voice at the end as if this were a question. I nodded, and she went on, "I thought I should tell you something right away."

I waited, but she didn't continue. Thinking how this reminded me of conversing with one of my children, I prompted, "Go on. What?" The back door squeaked. A moment later there were the soft quick thuds of sneakered feet.

"Mom?" Nathan called. "Is there anything to drink?"

"Water."

"That's *all*?"

"Unless you want to dissolve Cheez Whiz in it." Under my breath, I said to Julie, "My children are going to be thrilled at having a dog here, however briefly."

"What type of dog do you have?" Julie asked, with that presumptuousness of true dog lovers: the concept that everyone wants—and should own—a dog.

"Oh, boy! Nathan, Rachel, look!" Karen called. Then came the clatter of running feet, as they charged down into the family room.

"We just have guinea pigs. A neighbor in Carlton is taking care of them."

"Whose dog is this?" Nathan called. "It looks sick."

"She's not sick. She's pregnant, so leave her alone." I looked at Julie, who, for someone who "couldn't wait" to tell me something urgent, now seemed to be in no hurry. "You were saying—"

"Eew! What's she doing?" Karen cried. "Mom? You'd better come here!"

"Uh-oh. I'll bet it's time," I said to Julie as I raced into the family room, battling visions of permanent carpet stains. At least the carpet was already brick red.

Julie raced to the middle of the room, then crouched down and cooed, "Come here, Teak." Teak snarled at her. "Uh-oh," Julie said. "She doesn't want to be moved. I never should have brought her."

Rachel was looking truly frightened by the commotion and had slunk away, her eyes wide and her hands covering her lips.

I needed blankets, towels, cleaning supplies, a veterinarian. Thanks to our current transient state, my options were limited. "Karen, quick. Get the pizza box out of the garage. We'll try to slide it under her."

"She's gonna have puppies in a Dominos box?" Nathan asked in disgust.

"Well, it's better than on our carpet." In a flash, Karen returned. We pulled the corners of the box apart and I tried to coax Teak into allowing me to slide it under her.

"No time to be polite," Julie said and lifted the back end of the dog just far enough to shove the cardboard underneath. She sat back on her knees, then turned to me. "Anyway, Molly. The thing is, Celia had her keys all along. Or else, she had your keys. At any rate, I saw her putting some keys in her pocket after the lights went back on. I said to her, 'Oh, great. You found your keys.' But she just looked at me as if I were crazy and said, 'No, I didn't. What are you talking about?' So I said, 'I just saw you put a set of keys into the pocket of your skirt.' To which she said, 'No, that was just some change. My keys are still missing.' "

She widened her eyes and spoke with such enthusiasm, she seemed to expect me to applaud. I was torn between trying to absorb what she was saying, all the while concerned about the dog giving birth two feet away from her.

"Come on, Rach," Karen said. "We should sing a song to the doggie to soothe her."

"Did you see what the keychain looked like?" I asked Julie. Celia's ring held wooden dice. Mine consisted of two loops on an unadorned metal cylinder, and I'd attached the rental car's ring with its plastic ID tag.

"Eew!" Nathan said, half laughing as he pointed at the dog. "What's that?"

Teak pushed out what looked like a random organ about the size of my fist. "Here's the first puppy!" Julie exclaimed. "Now watch. She's going to eat the placenta."

Grimacing, I said, "I don't think we need to watch—"

While all of us Masterses plus Rachel gasped, Teak bit into the red glob, and out slid a tiny dark puppy that looked a lot like a wet rat. Then, sure enough, she gulped down the nonpuppy part while the three kids giggled and cried, "Eew! Sick!" Yet another reason I'm glad to be a human mother and somewhat removed from the animal kingdom.

"No," Julie said, "I couldn't get a good look at the chain, but I'm sure they were keys. So, she either lied about her keys being missing, or she took yours."

"Um," I struggled to get my mind back in sync with Julie. "That's definitely odd, all right." I believed Julie's version. It would have been in keeping with Celia's super-controlling personality if she'd pretended her keys were missing just to make sure we stayed for the entire workshop. But the road was out.

We were already stranded. Unless those were *my* keys Julie had seen, which Celia had taken prior to learning the road was blocked.

"Wasn't that neat, guys?" Julie said to the children. "It isn't every day you get to watch an animal give birth. She could have as many as eight more."

In a somewhat predictable piece of telepathy, Karen and Nathan exchanged a look, then turned toward me and cried in perfect unison, "Can we keep the puppy, Mom?"

"No. This isn't ours to keep, and besides, I've never wanted any dog bigger than a cocker spaniel. They're too much—"

"Look!" Nathan said, "The puppy's right in the middle of the pizza box. We're gonna have to name it Pepperoni."

Karen giggled. "You don't want to name a dog that!"

"What do you want to call it," Nathan said to her. "Extra Cheese?"

"The puppy isn't ours to name," I interjected, mesmerized at the sight of the tiny little thing already nursing while Teak licked her.

"These puppies are going to be too little for you to take all the way to New York with you when you fly back," Julie said helpfully.

"Hey," Rachel cried, "I think she's having another one!"

"Here comes Extra Cheese!" Nathan cried, excited.

All three kids were now into the spirit of this and chanted "push" at the dog.

"Actually," Julie said, "I do happen to have a cocker puppy who needs a home."

"I really don't think—"

"She's five months old and has all of her shots. She belonged to Allison. Her name's Betty."

"Betty Cocker?" I said. "But surely Richard wants the dog, doesn't he?"

"Richard?" Julie repeated, looking totally confused.

"Allison's ex-husband. I know they're divorced, but that doesn't mean—"

"Richard Kenyon's dead," Julie said. "Surely Allison told . . ." She paused, then told me in a whisper, "He was murdered several months ago."

Chapter 6

Stuck in the Middle with Ewe

"Maybe we should go boil some water or something," I said to Julie to coax her out of the children's earshot. We went back into the living room and reclaimed our seats, though I was now so tense it was all I could do to sit on the edge of mine.

My thoughts paged back through all of my past correspondence with Allison. She'd never given me even the slightest hint that her ex-husband was dead, let alone murdered. "I thought they were divorced," I said quietly to Julie. "In fact, she told me yesterday that splitting with Richard was the best thing she ever did."

"They did get a divorce. They'd been separated for two years and officially divorced last year. Then Richard was killed four or five months ago."

"How?"

"Shot while asleep in his bed. As far as I know, the police still haven't arrested anybody. It looked like a burglary gone bad at the bachelor pad he'd moved into."

"Do they have any suspects?"

Julie shook her pretty head, her blond ponytail bobbing behind her like a palomino's. "Not as of the last article I remember seeing in the *Camera*. Course, I could have missed it. I'm always accidentally using the wrong paper as a tinkle mat."

From the other room, Nathan's laughing voice cried, "Eew! That dog will eat anything!" His voice grew louder as he climbed the stairs toward the kitchen. "I'm getting the Cheez Whiz!"

"Nathan," I called over my shoulder, "leave the dog and our canned cheese alone."

Fighting off the momentary distraction of Nathan's comment, I waited until his footfalls—heavy now that I'd stopped his fun—were heard retreating. "Did they ever rule out Allison as a suspect?"

"According to the papers, the killer was apparently a man. At least, some witness spotted a man running from the building immediately afterwards. Of course, the big rumor was that Allison hired the person. But I don't think anybody knows for sure."

A car door shut just outside, and Julie sat up and peered through the sheer curtains. "Oh, dear. It looks like you have more company. And here my dog's monopolizing everything. I'm so sorry I've inconvenienced you with all this. I was just so anxious to tell you about Celia and her keys, and I thought to myself, I'll only be there for five or ten minutes. What are the odds that Teak will have her puppies then?"

"With the way my luck's been going, it was a forgone conclusion. But don't feel bad. It's been a happy diversion for the children."

The door opened and Lauren and Tommy walked in, carrying groceries in opaque plastic bags.

"Hi, Lauren. Nice to see you again," Julie said, smiling as if she'd just been reunited with a long-lost best friend.

Lauren gave a polite but cool greeting, then glanced at me, as if looking for signs that I was in even deeper trouble. Tommy greeted her with a nod, and we all headed toward the kitchen.

"Mom!" Rachel called. "Come watch the dog have puppies!"

Shopping bags still in hand, Lauren stared at the gathering downstairs. Though Teak looked like a canine contortionist, she was doing her best to lick the puppies' fur as they nursed.

Lauren turned her gaze to me. "You bought a pregnant dog while we were out getting groceries?" She glanced back at Tommy. "I told you we should have chosen a faster checkout line."

"It's my pet Labrador," Julie explained. "I have four bitches that I breed."

Her casual use of that particular word made my skin crawl, the death threat clearly brought to mind once again.

"Do you breed them in your car?" Lauren asked.

Unlike me, Lauren was not prone to sarcastic comebacks, and her warm, ready smile was absent. She obviously wanted nothing to do with Julie.

Tommy leaned against the counter and watched Julie intently as she launched into a profuse explanation about how foolish she'd been to bring Teak with her.

"Uh-huh," Tommy said when Julie paused for air. "Must be missin' something." He casually scratched his freckled nose. "Why exactly did you come here, and how did you get Molly's address?"

That last part was a very good question—one I should have thought of myself. Julie had even said she'd "tried to call" first. But we weren't listed in the Boulder directory and the number here was our former renters'.

"I kind of brought the dog with me in the hopes that Molly might be interested in buying one of her puppies." Julie's perfect smile faded slightly. "I got the address from Allison. When Celia suggested the retreat to me, I tried to speak to Molly about it, to decide if I wanted to go or not, but I couldn't get in touch with her."

"Why would Allison give you this address?" I interjected. "Why wouldn't she have given you my phone number in Carlton?"

"She did," Julie said, her smile taking on a nervous edge, "but by that time you'd already left to come here. So, I asked for the phone number and address where you'd be in Colorado, you see." Her vision darted from me to Tommy and back. In the meantime, Lauren was listening to our conversation while quietly putting away groceries in the pantry behind us.

"Uh-huh," Tommy said. He said that frequently during the course of his conversations. It was something of a verbal nervous tic. "And you came here . . . why? Just to ask Molly if she was int'rested in gettin' herself a puppy?"

"You're a police officer in New York, aren't you?" Julie asked, her pretty features souring.

"Uh-huh."

"I don't think I should be talking to you about this without my lawyer present."

Tommy held out his palms. "Just askin' as a friend of Moll's. I'm not here in any official capacity whatsoever."

"Even so," Julie said frostily. "As soon as I can get my dog—"

"Mom!" Karen called. "Come quick! Teak's having another puppy!"

"This one's going to be 'Anchovy,' " Nathan added, laughing.

"Anchovy?" Lauren repeated.

We all rushed into the family room and watched little Anchovy get delivered. Tommy gasped and started to reach for the dog when she bit into the sac, but Rachel informed him in very authoritative tones not to worry, that this was just one of the things that mother dogs do naturally.

Julie was acting uncomfortable, as if Tommy had truly offended her with his questions. Her attitude surprised me. She had to know that I would tell Tommy exactly what she'd told me anyway. Why she wouldn't simply tell him herself was beyond me. She might have felt as if she were being interrogated. Personally, I was so used to Tommy slipping into his police-sergeant role during personal conversations that it didn't bother me. He was now making a studious point, I thought, to keep the conversation friendly and focused away from the murder.

Teak had a total of four puppies, at least during the two hours she spent in our family room. Julie and Tommy worked in tandem and managed to hoist Teak plus pizza box and puppies up and transfer the whole operation to the backseat of Julie's car. We had no spare towels or sheets to donate to the cause, but Julie remembered she had a blanket in her trunk.

Julie studied me for a moment before she got into the driver's seat. "If you're at all interested in adopting Betty, you can come see her tomorrow. Allison had already bought her from me, but of course I reclaimed Betty once I realized she'd been orphaned. I'd give her to you and your family for free if you promise me you'll take good care of her. She's at my house for the time being. Forty-six eighty-six Cherry Drive. Just on the other side of Jay Road."

That was on the same street as Allison's house, I thought, as Julie continued, "As much as I'd love to, I really can't keep her. I've already got four dogs. If you don't want her, I'll have to put an ad in the paper." She said good-bye to Lauren and Tommy, and to the kids said, "Dogs are children's best friends, you know." She drove away at about two miles an hour.

"Betty's the name of a puppy?" Tommy asked me.

"A cocker spaniel. Tommy, can you get access to police records of an unsolved murder from some four or five months ago?"

"Depends on what kind of records. Might be listed in national records for violent crimes, but the information there's just the bare bones. Whose murder we talkin' about?"

"Richard Kenyon."

"Kenyon? As in Allison Kenyon?"

I nodded.

Tommy rocked on his heels. "That's interesting. You got a fax machine I can use?"

"Of course." I rarely traveled for more than a week without my portable fax machine. Since we'd planned to be at my house in Boulder for two weeks, I'd also arranged with our former renters to keep the phone service active.

"My office can fax 'em to me. Where'd this take place?"

"I don't know for sure, but probably right here in Boulder," I murmured, my attention having been drawn to a sheriff's vehicle parked across the street. An officer was sitting behind the wheel, reading the newspaper. Tommy followed my eyes.

"The police are watching me."

"Don't mean nothin'," he said laconically. "They're just trying to psych you out, watchin' how you'll react. Just don't let it get to you and stay put. They'll realize you're not acting suspicious and leave you alone."

My heart was pounding and my face grew warm with bottled rage and desperation. "This was going to be a vacation for Lauren and me and the kids. I have a dozen friends I was hoping to see. Now, one of those friends is dead, and I have a police tail parked outside my home. Tell me something, Tommy. Under these circumstances, what the hell does *un*suspicious behavior look like?"

He shrugged. "Like I said, stay home."

"I should go offer him some dinner," I grumbled as I went back inside.

Not surprisingly, my entire evening was spent answering the phone so that my neighbors could ask why a police car was out front and friends could discuss the murder with me. Though we'd had no friends in common, the story of Allison's death at my greeting card retreat had spread like an airborne virus. I declined the offers of my three dearest and most loyal friends who wanted either to drop by or to vouch for my character at the police station. There was no need to panic, I assured them and myself. If I needed character witnesses at some point in the future they were readily available. By the same token, though, I didn't want to involve them in this.

During one conversation with a particularly dull and loquacious neighbor, I found myself doodling and hit upon a potential no-occasion greeting card. After several false starts, I sketched an enormous corral crammed with sheep, with just a cat's ears and tail visible from the center of the flock. A thought bubble from the cat reads: Drat! Stuck in the middle with ewe!

Finally, around eight P.M. I unplugged the phone to give myself a chance to put Karen and Nathan to bed. By then, Rachel had conked out completely and Tommy and Lauren were watching television. While I was upstairs, quietly reading to both of my children in my room so as not to awaken Rachel, the doorbell rang. Tommy called up to me that he'd get it. Moments later, we all recognized Jim's voice—telling Tommy how he hadn't expected to wind up in Colorado and so hadn't packed the key to this house—and rushed downstairs.

Jim was nervously smoothing his mustache. Tall, thin, and handsome, he was wearing a yellow Izod shirt and black slacks, neater than his normal weekend attire, because of his having been on a business trip. He probably looked perfectly fine to a stranger's eye, but his face was pale and damp with perspiration. His dark hair seemed to have considerably more white hairs than he'd had a mere five days ago. He knelt, and both kids rushed into his arms, crying "Daddy!" All the while he kept his eyes on me. He rose, still gripping both children so that their legs dangled. He said, "Sorry if I woke everybody. Couldn't find my house key. I rented a car at D.I.A. That took almost as long as my flight from Dallas. Are you all right?"

I nodded and gave him a reassuring smile. Inwardly, my emotions were on a rampage. While my relief at having my husband here was considerable, I felt at once guilty for spoiling his business trip, hateful at whoever had killed Allison, resentful that Tommy was still standing near Jim as if to say, *Now that us men are here, we can fix this mess the little women have gotten themselves into,* and, while I would never admit this aloud, aroused at the concept that my husband had rushed across the country to my aid.

While Jim lowered the children, I fixed a glare on Tommy. He was oblivious. Meanwhile, Lauren, never a slouch in the area of knowing when couples should be alone, came upstairs, said, "Hi, Jim. Glad you're here," grabbed Tommy by the hand, and said, "Good night. We'll see you in the morning."

An hour or so later, after the children had gone to bed and Jim had hastily unpacked, we made love. Afterward, it occurred to me that if Jim's radar for detecting when I was "in the mood" were only half as good when it came to discerning my *other* moods, marriage would be a snap.

After church on Sunday morning, I borrowed Jim's rental car—my own having been confiscated by the police—and herded Karen and Nathan into the backseat. Just as I was backing down the driveway, Tommy, who'd been out to breakfast with Lauren, pulled in. I waited as he parked and trotted over to me.

"Where are you all going?" he asked in a friendly tone.

"We're going to meet Allison's former dog." I paused. "Which is not to say that Allison's dog has turned into a cat, or anything."

"Think that's wise?" Tommy scanned the empty street as he spoke, his freckled hands gripping my car door through the window. "The dog's at a suspect's house. Won't look good, your bein' there and all."

"Surely the police will find it even more suspicious if we act as though we're under house arrest. I'll be with my kids and a puppy, for heaven's sake. What could look more innocent?"

"Uh-huh," he said slowly, eyeing me. "Got that fax you were askin' about." He took a folded piece of paper out of his pocket.

He was wearing the same flannel shirt and jeans he'd had on yesterday. Unlike temperatures in the mountains, the weather in Boulder called for shorts and tank tops, but then I'd often seen him in long-sleeved uniforms on hot, humid days. I glanced at the fax—two paragraphs alongside a small picture of the deceased. I thanked Tommy, stashed the fax in my glove box, and drove off before he could insist upon accompanying us.

Julie's neighborhood was close to mine. Our houses were both in the northeastern outskirts of Boulder where the view of the Flatirons is more distant and the effects of the New Age, granola-crunching liberalism associated with Boulder are more distant as well. After having lived here for almost fifteen years, I knew that my neighbors shared the same general areas of concern as all suburbanites; the setting and climate just happen to be exceptionally beautiful here.

As I wound my way through Julie's neighborhood, I tried to orient myself. She lived a couple of doors down from Allison, who'd said something about Lois's house being nearby, too. And Celia Wentworth, I knew, lived on this street as well. I glanced in the rearview mirror. There were no signs of my police escort, which was, I suppose, good news. We found the address, pulled into the driveway, and Julie opened the door and ushered us inside.

There really was such a thing as love at first sight. One look at the adorable Betty Cocker, and I just knew she was meant to be my dog. She had sad, beautiful black eyes. Her fur was an unkempt sea of soft, red-and-blond fluff that would be the envy of most hair-dye manufacturers. It was highlighted by a little white star on her chest. She saw me and her stubby tail started wagging so hard her entire back half wagged with it.

I decided to call our new puppy BC for short.

The house, like Allison's two doors down, was a large, lovely home that had been built onto its tiny lot as though the concept of privacy were irrelevant. For all of the house's nice features, the fenced lot was small and overrun by her dogs— two Dobermans in addition to Teak and a cocker.

"Betty is the puppy of my pet cocker," Julie explained to the children.

Karen and Nathan sat down, and the puppy, tail wagging, raced between them and took turns hopping into each of their laps and licking their cheeks. We left the three of them to their joy and moved into Julie's cluttered TV room to talk.

"Well, she's adorable, Julie. I'm just worried about how I'll be able to get her back to Carlton. Plus, first thing this morning I told my husband we were—"

"Your husband's here?"

"He got in last night."

"That's the reason I can't keep Betty. My husband's quite a bit older than I am. He came into the marriage with the Dobermans, and the only way we could think to make it work was to keep my dog-breeding business at a minimum and never keep any of our dogs' puppies."

"What does your husband do?" I asked out of idle curiosity.

"He's retired. He just tinkers around all day." She paused and looked wistfully in the direction of the other room, where the children's delighted peals of laughter resounded. "All children deserve to own a dog."

"You don't have kids?"

She shook her head. "My husband's got four from previous marriages. So, what do you say? Will you take her?"

"Jim said he'd have to think about it. That actually means no, but I can always pretend not to have understood. Are you absolutely sure Allison didn't have some niece or someone else to take the dog?"

"I'm sure. When she first got the dog, just a month or so after Richard had been killed, she said to me, 'If something ever happens to me, I guess you'll have to take Betty.' "

"Why would she even think to suggest that?" I asked, thinking out loud. "It's tantamount to buying furniture and telling the salesperson who your heirs are."

Julie merely shrugged, but she averted her eyes as if she knew more than she wanted to share.

My curiosity piqued, I asked, "Did Allison ever receive any death threats, Julie?"

"Death threats?" Julie asked, with not-quite-convincing surprise. "No. Not that she told me about."

"Meaning that she might not have told you if she'd received one?"

Julie nodded, still avoiding eye contact. "There were lots of things we knew about Allison that she tried to keep from us."

"Such as?"

A look of despair flickered across her features, replaced by a vapid smile. "Nothing in particular. Just things, in general. Like her marital troubles. You know."

I nodded, able to tell from Julie's body language that there was no point in pressing—she'd said as much as she cared to on this subject.

The kids and puppy rushed into the room. BC was a ball of canine delight, darting among the four of us. "Can we keep her?" Karen asked.

"If it's okay with your dad."

Karen leaped a foot into the air, hugged the puppy, hugged me, and finally hugged her brother, who said in a droll voice, "Dad's going to say no."

While the kids "walked" Betty up and down the block on her leash, Julie and I tried to jam the dog carrier—a plastic crate with a latching metal grate—into the backseat of our small rental car and still leave enough room for both children. We finally managed.

Though uncomfortable with the subject of Allison, Julie had seemed willing to discuss Richard Kenyon's murder with me. I asked, "What did Allison tell you about Richard's death? Did she ever express any theories?"

Julie stared off into the distance. "She said that the thief who did it was killing his own kind. I asked what she meant by that, but she said something about that being a Pandora's box, and that was all she'd say."

The wording was the same as Allison had given me on the night of her death, so I took Julie at her word. "Did you know Allison and Richard fairly well?"

"Nobody 'knew' Allison. She lived almost entirely within herself." She smiled, which dimpled her cheeks. "I have to get back to Teak and the puppies. She had a fifth puppy after we got home yesterday, and I want to keep a close eye on them all, just in case."

I caught sight of a curtain moving in the house next door, as if someone had been watching us and then backed away.

"Who lives there?"

"Celia Wentworth. She lives in that big house alone." Julie apologized for having to rush off, then did just that.

I was sorely tempted to go next door, not because I relished the thought of spending time with Celia Wentworth, but because the more I thought about it, the more she struck me as the most likely killer. None of the others should even have been at the retreat—and Celia had been the one who manipulated everything so that she could choose the participants.

Her door opened just as the kids neared. Celia trilled, "Molly. Are you adopting Betty?"

"So it appears."

"Oh, you're so lucky. That is just the sweetest puppy. I so wanted to take her myself, but I have a ten-year-old Boston terrier who doesn't get along with other dogs."

Karen, who obviously didn't like Celia at all, was watching her as if poised for flight. Celia donned those sugary tones of hers and said, "Hello, Karen. Nathan. I'll bet you're thrilled to have a puppy."

Karen nodded. Nathan turned his back on Celia and muttered that he and the puppy would go wait in the car.

"Molly, I wanted to apologize for my behavior yesterday. Everything was so hectic and unpleasant, I forgot myself."

She gave me a plastic smile, then returned her gaze to the children. "Oh. You know what? I've got two or three pictures of Betty from when she was first born. Would you like to have them?"

Karen looked at me first to see if I'd object, which I didn't, then said yes. Celia's gesture was, in my opinion, one she needed to make to maintain her erroneous self-image as a thoughtful person.

"Let me get them. Come inside. I'll even give you some doggie biscuits. My Bruno won't eat them, but maybe Betty will."

She pulled open the drawer in the end table beside me and grabbed a stack of pictures. She dropped one in the process, which I retrieved for her. It showed her arm in arm with a dark, handsome, bearded man, at whom she was gazing with unmasked adoration.

"Is that your husband?" I asked as I handed it back to her.

She blushed and snatched the photograph from me. "Who? Oh, the picture? No, no. That was just a friend of a friend. My husband's been gone for almost ten years."

"Natural causes?"

"Yes. Incompatibility is a natural cause. We got married too young."

She gave me two shots of a tiny Betty Cocker. Karen said, "Let me see" and sprang up on tiptoe. I handed them to her.

To my obligatory thank-you, Celia said, "Oh, don't mention it. I truly am sorry for everything about this past weekend. If only we hadn't gotten our signals crossed, none of this would have happened. Allison might still be alive."

Perhaps inspired by the mention of Allison, a shocking realization hit me. We said a hasty good-bye—Karen accepting an open but full box of dog biscuits—and got into our car.

The children bickered over who got to hold the dog, but I was too preoccupied to intrude. I grabbed the fax in my glove box and stared at the photograph. The caption below the picture read: *Victim Richard Kenyon.*

It was the man in Celia's photograph.

Chapter 7

In Sickness and in Health, With Puppy or Without

We headed home, our newest addition whining and yipping in the backseat. Karen was thrilled and all but crying with her delight. Beside me, Nathan sat with his arms crossed, angry that he'd lost the battle to be Holder of the Dog. I knew Jim would be less than delighted that we went out and got a puppy without his consent.

My thoughts—a veritable froth of questions about Celia's relationship with Allison's late ex-husband, plus rationalizations and excuses about the puppy—were interrupted when Karen asked, "Why does that lady always talk to us like we're two years old?"

"Which lady? Celia Wentworth?"

"Yeah," Karen said. Through the rearview mirror, I could see her nodding, ignoring BC's attempts to lick her chin. "She acts so nice around me and Nathan it's like she thinks we're great, then two seconds later, it's like we don't even exist. And she wears so much perfume you can barely breathe."

"I'll bet she poops," Nathan growled.

I had no response to that remark and merely gripped the steering wheel tighter.

"I'll bet Betty poops in the house when we're not home," he went on, still surly.

Relieved that he meant the dog, I answered, "Julie said that BC is housebroken."

"What does that mean? That she already broke somebody's house? I'll bet she jumps on the table and eats our food right off our plates."

"We'll train her not to do that."

We pulled into the driveway, and Nathan said under his breath, "The dog likes Karen more than me." Nathan's lower lip was quivering with barely controlled despair.

"Tell you what, Nathan. You can be the official dog trainer and train BC to stay off the furniture." I operated the garage door opener, and we parked.

For a moment, none of us moved, except BC, who, desperate to get out of the car, was a flurry of furry motion in Karen's arms. "Do you think Dad will be mad that we got a dog?" Karen asked.

"I think your dad knows me well enough that if he really didn't want us to get her, he would have come with us to prevent it."

Although that sounded good on the surface, much of the reason he hadn't come was because he'd awakened with a low-grade fever. No sense worrying Karen unduly, though. We got out of the car, and the dog immediately dashed toward the door. The sight of her back end brought to mind an old Datsun of mine, which was missing one windshield wiper. The remaining metal stub would flutter back and forth madly, just like BC's tail.

What I needed now was a battle plan for presenting the news of my impulsive decision to Jim as gently as possible. "Okay. Let's leave BC in the garage while—"

My plan was foiled at its onset when Jim opened the door for us. BC rushed at him, licked both of his bare shins—Jim was wearing shorts and a T-shirt—then darted past him and into the house.

Jim's expression was abject horror.

"Daddy!" Karen cried, hopping with excitement. "Look

what we got! Her name is Betty Cocker. Only Mom calls her BC for short instead of Betty cuz she doesn't want to confuse anybody named Betty in the neighborhood." She ducked under Jim's arm, and daughter and dog tumbled into a joyful hug on the family room floor. Nathan, still in the garage with me, was keeping a watchful eye on his dad. Nathan put his hands in his pockets and took a circuitous route around his father and into the house.

Jim stepped toward me, the door banging shut behind him. "Molly! I said I needed time to think about it!"

"I know. I'm sorry. You can still think about it while you're getting to know her. I've told the kids we'll take her back if you say no."

"Oh, sure. Let *me* be the villain and wrench her out of Karen's loving arms." He yanked the door open and stormed inside, leaving me to stare after him.

Karen wrapped her arms around Jim's legs before he could pass. "Please can we keep her, Daddy? Puh-le-e-e-e-ease?"

Jim sighed, then sent dagger looks over his shoulder at me.

I gave him a sheepish smile. "Isn't she cute?"

Justifiably, he simply glowered at me. In the meantime, BC rolled over onto her back and looked at Jim expectantly.

"She wants you to rub her tummy. I know it was absolutely reprehensible for me to get a dog without your okay. But let's remember that we did agree we'd get a dog as soon as Karen turned ten, which was four months ago."

BC, her shiny black eyes focused directly on Jim, was smiling up at him, pawing the air playfully. Jim bent down to rub Betty Cocker's tummy, sealing his fate.

"It isn't BC's fault her owner died. She's a puppy orphan. How could I refuse?"

Karen, still on her knees, said, "Daddy? If we keep her I'll do everything. I'll brush her. I'll pick up after her. I'll feed her."

"Plus Julie gave me the portable kennel where she sleeps at night and a week's worth of puppy food," I added.

Karen was now gesturing emphatically at Nathan for him to join her in pleading with their father. Nathan stopped his nervous pacing long enough to announce, "And Mom says she's a housebreaker!"

Jim rose. "All right. But it's up to your mom to figure out how we get Betty Cocker back to New York with us."

The children's cheers were halted when Jim said sternly, "Just remember, though, this dog belongs to you two. That means you have to do all of the work, and I'm not lifting a finger to help."

Jim was busy puppy-proofing the fence when the shrill ring of the phone broke the silence within our house. Lauren, Rachel, and Tommy had gone to a matinee, and Karen and Nathan were outside playing with BC. The voice on the other side of the phone wasted no time with a preamble.

"Molly, this is Lois Tucker. I just got off the phone with Julie. She told me you have Allison's puppy. That dog is mine."

"Yours?" I repeated, too surprised to say anything else.

"That's right. As Allison's best friend, she would have wanted *me* to have Betty, not you."

Lois considered herself to be Allison's best friend? If that were true, why hadn't Allison said two words to her on the retreat? Why had Lois acted so indifferent to her "best friend's" death?

Through the sliding glass door, I could see the children laughing as they played a game of tag with BC. "Lois, I'm sorry if you feel you should have gotten the dog, but Julie gave her to me. And since Julie bred the puppy in the first place, it seemed reasonable that she had the right to select the new owner."

"I spoke to Julie, as I already told you. That's how I got your number. But I don't happen to agree with Julie's assumption or yours, and I want that dog. Maybe we should take the matter to small claims court and let a judge decide."

Go before a judge over ownership of a puppy? What is wrong with this woman? Surely a judge would rule in my favor, but my faith in the judicial system nowadays was not what it once was. "Lois, my kids and the puppy have already bonded. It would break their hearts if—"

"You should have taken that into consideration before bringing her home and acting like you owned her."

I took a deep breath and counted to ten. "Could we discuss this face-to-face?"

"Fine. But you'll have to come here immediately. I've got an electrician coming over this afternoon, and I want you out of here before then. As a matter of fact, Allison was supposed to come. We were such good friends, she used to do work for me for free. Now her partner's going to have to do it, and I'm stuck with the tab."

"I met him once," I said, trying hard to turn the tone of this conversation into one less vitriolic, if not friendly. We'd once bumped into each other at a golf course in Longmont. "Joe something."

"Cummings," Lois promptly answered. She told me her address. With only a brief hesitation—during which I considered but then dismissed Tommy's latest instruction to stay home—I said I'd be right over. This, after all, was an emergency. If we lost the puppy now, my children would be devastated, especially Karen.

Jim had plopped down on the couch toward the end of my phone conversation. He was coughing and wheezing. I gingerly sat down beside him and rubbed his shoulder.

"Are you still angry about my getting Betty Cocker?"

"You should have discussed it with me first."

My spirits sagged. "Well, we may not get to keep her anyway. I just got off the phone with a woman from that retreat. She wants BC."

"Well, she can't have her!" Jim tensed and furrowed his brow, his attempt at a shout only making his voice froglike. "Who is she? Does she have any right to take her?"

"I doubt it, but she seems to think she has. I'm going to go talk to her now."

Jim lapsed into a brief coughing fit, rolling his eyes afterward. "Threaten her with me, if you have to. Tell her we keep the dog or I breathe on her."

I felt his forehead. My temperature-taking skills were well honed from ten years of checking children's foreheads: He had a fever of around a hundred and one. I gave him some ibuprofen, warned Karen and Nathan to be considerate and quiet around him, then took off, feeling a heavy dose of guilt. I promised myself that if I could just get out of this without being arrested for murder, I was going to be a better wife. Some vague memory of having made just such a promise once or twice before tugged at me, but I ignored it.

I waved and smiled at a police car that was puttering past my house in the opposite direction. I watched through the rearview mirror as he pulled a U-turn. That was illegal, but this was probably not the time to make a citizen's arrest. Plus, having a police escort might give me some clout with Lois. The officer drove right up on my tail, then suddenly sped up and crossed the double yellow lines to pass me, putting on his siren as he went. So much for my clout.

If I was lucky, Allison's partner might arrive soon. I'd like to know what he thought about Allison's ex-husband, and especially his murder. The two murders could be related, and if so, the fact that Celia had posed so lovingly with Richard was an interesting development.

Lois didn't answer the doorbell. I was starting to worry I had the wrong address when an old tan pickup truck pulled up and Joe Cummings stepped out. He looked exactly as I'd remembered him: tall but somewhat paunchy, with wavy white hair and broad features that seemed to bear a look of happy surprise as their regular expression. He was in his late fifties or early sixties. His navy blue work pants were two inches shorter than his bowed legs and revealed frayed running shoes of an indistinguishable color.

I trotted down the porch steps toward him. "Hi. You're Joe Cummings, aren't you? I'm—"

"Molly Masters? You're the woman Allie was spending the weekend with, aren't you?"

"Yes. Only—"

He took my hand in both of his damp, fleshy ones and shook it vigorously. "Well, hello there, Molly. You know, skinny little thing like you could be a good electrician. You could crawl into a whole lot of holes."

"Yes, and I've been known to dig myself into them. I was wondering—"

"Your hands would be good for wiring. Too small for plying, though."

"Why would I want to ply my hands?"

"I mean for using pliers. Got to have good, strong hands." He'd peered straight into my eyes as he spoke, but now he lowered his gaze and shook his head. "Allie had incredible hands. She could crack a walnut, just by giving it a good squeeze."

"She could?"

He chuckled. "Course not. When you get to be my age, you're entitled to your minor exaggerations." Joe suddenly furrowed his brow and pointed at me. "Did you kill Allie?"

"No! She was my—"

"Do you know anything about wiring?"

"A little." I knew that wires were long and thin and carried electric current. "Why?"

"This job'll go a lot quicker with two, and I hate to ask the customer to help. Kind of shakes their confidence." His smile quickly faded, and he said wistfully, "I can't believe she's really gone."

I'd come to realize that if I hoped to get any information from this man, I'd have to limit his ability to interrupt me. In one breath, I said, "Neither can I. Yet the police seem to think I'm their prime suspect. That's why I wanted to ask you about her, about what was going on with her and her ex."

"Richard?" He shook his head. "Most mismatched marriage you can imagine. Here Allie was this bright, thoughtful, loyal gal who'd never say a bad word about anybody. Richard was only happy when he was hurting people. Meanest bastard I ever—"

He broke off as Lois Tucker threw open her door. She was still wearing the same black sweat suit she'd worn last Saturday, but now her dark hair looked recently washed and curled, and she'd put on makeup. Her smile faded a little as she looked at me. Then she waved and said, "Aren't you ever coming in, Joe? I baked a batch of your favorites—double-chocolate brownies."

"Sounds delicious. Be right there, soon as I get my tools." He rolled his eyes as he turned. "Glad you're here. The wife'd kill me if she heard tell I went to Lois's house alone. Been after my tail for five years now, ever since me 'n' Allie did our first rewiring job here, 'round the time Lois's husband had a fatal heart attack. She's been coming up with odd jobs for me ever since."

"Really? Lois told me Allison used to do work over here for free, because they were friends."

"Friends? Lois and Allison? More like Mrs. Hatfield and Mrs. McCoy." Joe flipped open a metal box built into his truck bed. He stuffed his arm through a white coil of electrical wire till it rested easily on his shoulder, then hoisted up a large tool-box as if it were empty. "Wait'll you get a load of her house." He gestured with his chin at an aluminum ladder on the truck. "Bring that stepladder, while you're at it."

Lois cut off Joe's attempt at an introduction with a gruff "We've met." She narrowed her eyes at the ladder I was car-rying and said, "Taking up odd jobs to keep your greeting card business afloat?"

"No," I said, studiously keeping my voice even and refusing to be baited into an argument. "Joe asked if I'd give him a hand, and I said I would."

We went inside—Joe handling his toolbox with ease and me struggling not to barrel into anything with the ladder. My mouth watered at the rich aroma of chocolate, redolent in the cool air inside.

"I understand you changed your mind about the kitchen switch," Joe said to her.

"Oh, yes." She nodded, a Cheshire-cat smile never leaving her face. "I'm sorry to make you take another trip. I just can never seem to make up my mind till I give it plenty of thought." I stared at Lois, incredulous at her flirtatious mannerisms.

Joe shot me a little darting glance that indicated a spot on the wall behind me. I did a double take at the switch plate just inside the door. It held six switches, all bearing tiny dimmers. This could win a Most Obsessed with Electricity award from Public Service. I followed Joe and Lois into the kitchen and was so concerned about scratching her pristine white linoleum that I balanced the ladder on top of my sneakered foot.

Joe pointed at the overhead light and instructed me to "holler when that goes out," then he excused himself out the back door to the circuit breakers.

"This is a lovely home you've got, Lois," I said.

"You're not getting Betty Cocker, so don't bother trying to suck up to me."

The light went out and Lois instantly cried, "That's it, Joe," with childlike enthusiasm. Her expression soured again as she looked me up and down. "Let's just get right to the point, shall we? I'll buy Betty Cocker for two hundred dollars. That's my top offer."

"She's not for sale," I shot back, then reminded myself to stay calm. "Julie's golden Labrador has a new litter." She was already shaking her head, so I quickly added, "Or you can buy a newborn cocker puppy for two hundred—"

"I don't want just any puppy! I want Allison's!"

Why, I wondered, was she being so vehement about owning this particular dog? Could BC somehow identify her as Allison's killer? No, that was impossible. The puppy wasn't there when Allison was killed, and Richard's murder was before BC's time.

Lois curled her lip at me. Her expression warmed as Joe returned. "So, Joe. How's your wife's health lately?"

"Just fine. Thanks for asking."

Her smile faded a little, and she turned her eyes to me and said, "Did you ever meet Allison's ex-husband, Molly?"

I shook my head, surprised at the non sequitur.

"Really? You never met her ex-husband, even though you were so close as to claim her pet. That seems odd, don't you think, Joe?"

Joe shrugged and grabbed the stepladder from me and set it up under the light with one fluid motion. "You're taking Betty Cocker? Good for you."

"Don't you think it's odd that Molly never even met Richard, yet wants his widow's dog?"

"Not 'specially," Joe said as he climbed the ladder and began to remove the glass globe above us. "Allison told me that Richard never hung out with her friends."

"Well," Lois puffed, setting her thick brow, "of course not. Considering the way he used to beat her."

"What?" My voice was shrill. Lois merely smirked at me, so I focused on Joe. "Is that true?"

" 'Fraid so," he answered through gritted teeth, coming down the ladder, glass globe in hand.

A wave of nausea hit me. "My God. I had no idea." I sorted through dozens of images of Allison, and it struck me how she'd always worn slacks and long-sleeved blouses. I'd commented about that only once, when we'd been golfing in ninety-five degree heat with her in full clothing. She'd told me her skin couldn't handle the exposure to the sun.

Suddenly, it felt as though all the clues had been there all along, screaming at me, but I'd ignored them: the secretive, isolated life she led with her spouse, all the walls that would go up when anyone tried to get personal with her, the excuses and demurrals she'd always made whenever I'd suggested the four of us get together.

Lois lifted her chin in smug superiority. "So, Joe, wouldn't you say this shows which of us were Allison's real friends? You and I knew about her and Richard, and Molly here didn't."

Joe snatched up his toolbox with so much force I half expected him to fling it across the room. He gestured with his chin. "She lived right next door. You could hear what was going on. Did you ever try to stop him?"

Lois's face fell. "Nobody did," she murmured. "What was your excuse, Joe?"

He looked stricken but made no reply.

For the next several minutes, I mutely followed Joe's patient and complete instructions about our task, my concern over Betty Cocker overshadowed. We were to run an additional circuit from the kitchen light fixture to a switch plate in Lois's bedroom, so that she could control the kitchen light from her bed.

The three of us went to her bedroom, where Joe replaced one of the four-position switch plates with one that housed six. I despaired of there ever being an opportunity for me to talk privately with him, but then he told me to follow him into the attic.

I'd expected a dark, icky attic like mine, but should have known better. Lois flipped a few switches in the hallway next to the attic stairs, and lights and air-conditioning greeted us. Upstairs, Joe immediately whispered, "I'll do all the work up here. Whatever else you do, don't leave us alone in her bedroom."

I took a seat on the plywood flooring next to the attic entrance, bracing myself so that no matter what shocking news I might hear, I wouldn't go toppling down the stairs. Joe was uncoiling a length of wire from one side of the attic to the other.

He glanced over at me. "I did try to stop Richard, once I found out. One day she was following me down from an attic, and her shirt got caught on a loose nail. That was the first time I'd ever seen poor Allie's stomach. All bruised and welted."

"Did you confront her about it?"

He grimaced. "She denied it, at first. Then I tried to convince her to leave him. Many times. Told her I'd come get her myself. Told her she could come live with me and the missus for as long as she needed to, and I'd protect her from him. She wouldn't hear of it. Said that if I ever interfered, he'd kill her."

"So then . . . *he* left *her*?"

Joe smoothed his fingers through his hair, which only left dusty finger marks. "Allie told me he'd finally decided to move in with one of his mistresses."

"But I heard he was killed in his own apartment, a bachelor pad."

He nodded. "Guess that 'mistress' got wise to him in time. She got out alive."

My teeth were chattering, though I wasn't cold. "But Richard didn't kill Allison."

The muscles in Joe's jaw worked, and he paused from his wiring long enough to meet my gaze. "No, because somebody got to him first. Gave that bastard what he deserved."

Involuntarily, my eyes widened, and Joe read what I was thinking. He held up a palm. "Not me. I never laid a finger on him, I'm sorry to say. Doesn't mean I never thought about it, just that I got too much to lose. The missus. The kids. Grandkids even. But I always thought if I knew I only had one day left on this earth, I'd take that Richard Kenyon straight to hell with me."

His words sank into me. I knew I'd never forget them or his voice. Joe was now stuffing wire down into the hole for the kitchen light. I asked quietly, "Do you think Allison hired someone to kill him?"

He stopped and peered at me over his shoulder. "If you're just asking for the sake of conversation, yes, that's what I think. *And* I think she should have done it ten, twelve years earlier. But if you're asking 'cause you want to help the police find his killer or something, the only answer you'll ever get from me is Allie's an innocent victim. Period."

Were the two murders related? I'd suspected so and wasn't sure if this terrible information had made me change my mind. "From what you've told me, I don't care if they ever find Richard's killer. I do want Allison's killer brought to justice, though."

He nodded and muttered under his breath, "Me, too. Me, too." He crossed the attic and began to push wire down through a second hole. "Molly, take a flashlight and go into Lois's bedroom. Shine the beam into that spot where the switch plate's going so I can eyeball it from up here. I'm going to drop the wire down to you, and your job's to grab the wire and pull it down till I tell you to stop. Think you can handle that?"

This had all the intellectual challenge of lacing one's shoes, but I merely nodded and climbed down the rickety stairs.

Lois met me on the bottom step. "Is Joe coming down yet?"

"Not until I've pulled on his wire."

A regrettable double entendre, I noted silently, not lost on

Lois, who blushed. She narrowed her eyes at me. "Have you decided to sell me Betty, or do I have to sue you for her?"

"No. And if you take me to court over this, you'll lose. Can't you see that?" Lois set her jaw, but her lower lip trembled slightly and I knew my words had finally gotten through to her. She whirled on a heel, and I followed her into her bedroom. In a softer voice, I asked, "Why do you want this one dog so badly?"

She sat on her bed, an antique four poster with one of those white, bumpy cloth covers. "Betty used to bark all day long. Allison would leave her in the backyard and go to work. I'd go over there and bring Betty into my house. Betty was more mine than Allison's, and I want her back."

Uh-oh. This explanation made sense to me, and for the first time I began to believe that Lois might truly care for BC. "How can we solve this, Lois? I can have my husband bring Betty Cocker here, and we can see which of us—"

"No! There's no need to try to let the puppy decide. I'd lose. Every so often, I used to lose my temper over her barking. She's afraid of me."

Why on earth would Lois want a dog that was afraid of her?

She stared at my neck, and I began to worry that she wanted to wring it. She pointed. "That pin you're wearing used to belong to Allison."

I touched the scooped collar of my T-shirt and felt the small pin shaped like a bird. It was a bluebird, not even a half-inch long from beak to tail. Lois, to my surprise and befuddlement, was right. Allison had won the pin at a golf tournament years ago for scoring a birdie. Then, at the same tournament the following year, I'd accidentally struck a Canadian goose that was sitting in the fairway. Allison had jokingly awarded me her pin for "hitting a birdie." I'd fastened the pin to my shirt and kept it there ever since, even during spin-rinse cycles.

"You in position yet, Molly?" Joe called through the ceiling.

"Just a sec," I called back. Though I felt moronic, I removed my pin, which must have been worth all of two dollars, and held it out to Lois. I suspected that Lois wanted to own Betty only as a prize to signal some weird victory over Allison or perhaps over me. If Lois actually cared about the little dog, she wouldn't have frightened her in the first place. "Would you consider a trade? I keep the dog, you keep Allison's pin?"

Lois sniffed, but accepted the pin. "Fine. Have the damned dog. At least this way I get something to remember Allison by," she muttered.

I forced a smile and nodded, though I was mentally playing the theme music for *The Twilight Zone*. Lois had a bizarre obsession for Allison.

She crossed her arms and gave me another visual once-over. "Has Joe talked to you about his wife?"

"He's mentioned her several times, yes. He obviously loves her." I turned and aimed the flashlight at the opening in the wall.

"Bet you think I'm quite the fool, carrying a torch for a married man. You better hope you don't wind up like me—kids grown, no husband, no career, suddenly alone."

"See it yet, Molly?" Joe hollered.

"Not yet." Keeping my flashlight and my vision riveted to the rectangular opening, I asked, "Did you ever talk to Allison about her relationship with her husband?"

"Not really." The wire end popped into view, and as I snatched it, Lois called, "We got it, Joe!"

As instructed, I kept pulling until the order to stop came from on high. That done, I turned toward Lois, still perched on the side of her bed, hands in her lap. "I guess I never really knew her."

"Yeah? Well, I sure did," Lois snapped. Then she tilted her head and said in a voice that was both quiet and heavy at once,

"When Richard moved out, I went over to her house with a bottle of wine to help her celebrate. She just looked at me and said, 'It isn't over. It won't be over till he's dead.' I knew. I knew she killed him."

Chapter 8

That's Not True, Dear

Lois had me positively spooked, but she instantly brightened at the sound of Joe tromping down the attic stairs. On the hunch that she wouldn't mind spreading a little dirt about Celia, I asked, "I heard a rumor that Richard was seeing somebody else."

To my surprise, Lois promptly said, "Cindy Bates, a young tramp who works as a graduate assistant for Katherine."

Joe strode in, all business, not even glancing at Lois, who had now sprawled on her bed in an alluring pose straight from a pinup calendar. "I'll have this wired up for you in a jiffy," he said.

"It was good seeing you again, Molly," Lois said, a strong hint that she wanted me to leave.

Joe shot me a pleading look.

Liking Joe infinitely better than I did Lois, I said, "It was good to see you, too, Lois. I'm just going to watch and make sure there's nothing else for me to do."

"I would think you'd want to go home and get ready for Allison's funeral tonight," Lois said through clenched teeth.

"That's not till seven-thirty," Joe replied, installing the new switch so rapidly he looked to be moving in fast-forward. In no time at all, he had the switch plate back in place and even threw up his hands in a dramatic motion afterward as if this were a timed rodeo event. Within five minutes, we were leaving Lois's house, Joe's hands full of brownies, mine full of stepladder.

Once we said our good-byes, he did give me one brownie for the ride home.

I truly didn't know what to make of Lois, or of Celia's relationship with Richard. I'd been expecting Lois to name Celia as Richard's lover, not some grad assistant of Katherine's.

Though my contact with Lois had been limited, I couldn't understand her and could picture her as a murderer, especially if she thought Allison was a rival for Joe's affections. I could also see Celia killing Allison, perhaps to avenge Richard's murder, if she—like Lois—believed that Allison had killed him. But I didn't have any proof of either theory. The only hard evidence pointed straight to me.

Once home, it made me feel great that someone was this happy to see me. My family, playing a card game, ignored me completely; however, Betty Cocker was so thrilled, she could barely contain herself. In fact, she couldn't; she piddled on the floor.

I was further delighted to discover that my portable fax machine had received an actual job request. My enthusiasm sagged a little when I saw what the job request was for: an editor at a university press in the Midwest wanted a faxable cover sheet for her correspondence.

The next half hour was spent verifying my initial reaction: This was not going to be an easy job. My doodling eventually led to a scene with a man and woman in bed. The man is looking forlorn and says, "I feel like you're so busy criticizing my every word, you're not really listening." The woman says, "That's not true, dear"; however, pen in hand, she is physically editing the man's words above their heads. The caption for the cartoon reads: *One reason that romantic liaisons between editors and authors rarely last.*

I had already realized that there was not a chance this editor would buy this particular cartoon, but I had fun drawing it. Then it occurred to me: This was a *university* press. The best possible place for me to look for cartoon ideas was a college campus. As a bonus, while there, I might be able to get some information about Katherine and her assistant.

Jim was napping on the couch. I called his name quietly. He opened his eyes a slit's worth and tried to look at me, letting out a grunt in partial cognizance.

"I'm going to C.U. to get some ideas for a new assignment I just got. I'll be back in an hour or so."

"Unn-hmm," he said, his eyes shutting.

Well, nobody could accuse *me* of keeping him in the dark. It was his choice to have his eyes closed during my feeble attempts at illumination.

As I backed down my drive, I saw a police car parked in front of the house. After a moment's consideration, I set my emergency brake, got out, and tapped on his window. It was the young male officer who'd found my shoes—which were being held as evidence, so I was perhaps destined to wear Lauren's sandals for this entire trip. Looking wary and perplexed, he lowered his window. I asked him for directions to the English department and parking suggestions. It seemed to me that if he was going to be following me, I should at least know how to get to where I was going.

Taking his suggestion, I parked on the Hill—a half mile or so of shopping area surrounded on three sides by frat houses and the fourth side by Colorado University. I made my way through the pedestrian tunnel that went underneath Broadway, dodging skateboarders and kamikaze bicyclists, and entered the school grounds.

The C.U. campus is a marvelous mixture of old and new architecture. The buildings feature red Spanish tile roofs and sandstone walls, set in mature landscaping. I hoped to soak up the ambience of being back on a college campus, but there wasn't quite as much ambience to be had as usual. There were so few students milling around as I walked the cement sidewalks of the campus that I suspected summer session had not yet begun. This made the prospect of my discovering Katherine Lindstrom at work unlikely, but it was worth a shot. I wanted to ask her about her graduate assistant, as well as what she knew about roofie, the drug Allison, Lauren, and I had all ingested.

In contrast with the bucolic external setting, the interior of Hellem—the language arts building—was cold and cellarlike, with old, oversized hallways. The one or two classrooms with open doors were in need of a face-lift, their tables shabby, the gray-black carpeting worn. Frosted-glass windows on the outside of classroom doors inhibited my view of the offices, but by merely wandering through the halls and looking at nameplates, I managed to find Katherine's office and went inside.

To my surprise, Katherine was there, seated at a wooden desk stacked with papers, a computer terminal blinking away with a screen saver that showed flying toasters. Behind her was a large window, so overgrown with ivy leaves that only a few square inches let any light through. The room was furnished with three tall bookshelves and a pair of tall, institutional gray metal cabinets. Only a battered couch with a bright flower coverlet broke the monotony.

Katherine turned to look at me, her short hair now combed back behind her ears, a pair of glasses with green frames resting partway down her freckled nose. She whisked them off and gave me a nervous smile.

"Why, Molly. To what do I owe this unexpected visit?"

"Hello, Katherine. I wasn't sure you'd be working now. Aren't you on summer break?"

"Yes, but this gives me a chance to get caught up. This time of year, there's nobody knocking on my door to say, 'Professor Lindstrom, what can I do to get an A?' "

I smiled at her impersonation of a meek student, complete with clasped hands and batting eyes. "And how do you answer that question?"

"I tell them a thousand dollars should do the trick. Sometimes more, depending on their grade point at the time."

I laughed, though with her droll delivery and my barely knowing her, there was no way to tell whether or not she was kidding.

"What can I do for you, Molly?"

While attempting to prepare for this question, it had occurred to me that Katherine did not seem the sort to indulge in idle gossip. This made my seeking information from her more of a challenge, but I chose the only tack that seemed even remotely plausible.

"I've been considering for some time looking into getting a part-time position at SUNY Albany. Do you have a few minutes now to give me an overview of what your job entails?"

Katherine raised one eyebrow. "You want to be a professor of greeting cards?"

"Well, no," I said, bristling a little but trying not to show it. "Creative writing was what I had in mind."

"And do you have a Ph.D.?"

"No, but I was thinking of teaching a noncredit course. Or if that didn't work, maybe a position as assistant to some professor. Do you have an assistant?"

"Yes, she does research for me in connection with some articles I'm writing. For which she gets free tuition and a measly few thousand a year."

"What's her name?"

"Cindy Bates. Why?"

"Is she likely to be on campus now? I'd like to talk to her about what she does. Her duties and the like."

Katherine blinked a couple of times, but held my gaze. "I don't follow. Are you interested in obtaining a post-graduate degree?"

"No, but my theory is, if I knew precisely what teaching assistants did, maybe I can get SUNY to create a position for me in exchange for course credits. Kind of like an internment—or rather an internship—and then they'd be more likely to hire me for a noncredit teaching position when one becomes available." Sheesh. That hadn't made much sense, but I'd inadvertently slipped into a throwback to my own experiences of bluffing my way around teachers: Talk really fast and use a whole lot of verbiage.

"Oh, I see." She paused, then added, "I think." She glanced at her watch and rose. "Cindy generally holds court at Buchanan's Coffee Shop on the Hill. Grad assistants don't rate their own offices, or even desks, so they often develop their own ipso facto offices at restaurants. Follow me, and I'll point her out to you. I've got to speak to her anyway to make sure she's begun the project I recently assigned."

We left the building together. The sky was that picture-puzzle cloudless blue, the air hot and dry. I asked her again if she liked her job, and she said, "Yes. Teaching is a bore, of course, but I love my research, especially in summer when I actually have some time to devote to it."

From her haughty tone of voice, it was apparent that her "research" was supposed to be impressing me. I toyed with calling her "Kath," just to annoy her, but realized this wouldn't suit my purposes, so I merely nodded and murmured in the appropriate places as she identified the buildings on this end of the campus and augmented each with some obscure historical fact. She must be dreadful company in a museum—the sort who would stop to read every word at each exhibit and then recite whatever arcana she'd collected.

"You're going to Allison's funeral tonight, I assume," Katherine asked.

"Yes. Did you know that she and I were drugged Saturday night?"

"Drugged?" she repeated, looking sincerely startled.

"My friend Lauren was, too. The police said it was known as a date-rape drug. Ever heard of such a thing?"

She pursed her lips and nodded. "Flunitrazepam," she answered easily, though the word sounded like a foreign language to me. "It's sold under the brand name Rohypnol, hence its street name, roofie. It's similar to Valium, but supposedly ten times as potent. I read an article about it in the *Camera* recently."

"How would somebody go about getting that drug? Here in Boulder, I mean, since I'm assuming that's where it came from."

"I would imagine it would be fairly easy to buy on the street. One could hang out at any bar, or even, unfortunately, at a popular coffee shop on the Hill, and simply ask who might be selling."

We were headed back through the pedestrian tunnel, dodging the very same skateboarders as before, only now my shoe-hoarding policeman was standing at an intersecting sidewalk. I hope it made it into his reports that I'd not only gone exactly where I'd said I would, but had taken his advice on where to park. Katherine gave him a couple of long looks. "That's odd," she muttered.

"What is?"

"That officer's with the sheriff's department. One usually sees only campus cops or the BPD here." I deliberately kept my mouth shut, but she went on, "Is there any particular reason that officer might be watching you?"

I was tempted to ask how she could be so cognizant of policemen's typical whereabouts and their uniforms as to notice this, but then, Katherine would probably have an arrogant answer at the ready. Instead, I told her the truth. "They seem to think I killed Allison."

She froze and stared at me. "I assumed she accidentally died from a drug overdose."

"What made you think that?"

"Allison had quite a drug problem, for a number of years."

Allison had had a drug problem? That was news to me, but so had been Lois's revelation about Allison's hideous relationship with her husband.

"I believe she went into one of those clean-and-sober clinics after Richard had left her. So, when I read in the paper that she died from a tranquilizer overdose, that's what I assumed. The police never said anything that might dissuade me."

We entered the coffee shop, and Katherine led me through what I'd thought to be the entire restaurant, but what proved to be only the front room. "Why do the police think *you* murdered her?" she said in a near whisper as we climbed a set of stairs with open risers alongside the kitchen. There was little to prevent the chefs from looking up Katherine's skirt. Good thing I was wearing shorts.

"Gee. I have no idea. Maybe they don't. Maybe I'm just being paranoid."

She glanced behind us. "Well, if so, part of your paranoid delusion just followed us into the building."

"Let's ignore him."

Katherine gave me a doubtful glance but then turned and scanned the room, which was two-thirds full, all college-aged clientele. Thanks to Boulder's no-smoking ordinance, coffee aroma permeated the place. "Ah, there she is," Katherine said, pointing. "Come on and I'll introduce you."

We approached a gorgeous young thing sitting alone and sipping what I judged from the absurdly small cup to be an espresso. She tensed her shoulders and pushed back from the table, gazing at Katherine with sky blue eyes. She had a perfect complexion that I'd not seen this side of a porcelain doll. "Katherine," she said with a nod, then turned toward me.

"This is an acquaintance of mine. Molly Masters. She wants to talk to you about . . . Well, I'll let her explain it. Did you read through that material I gave you?" Her voice bore an air of superiority that irritated me, even though I wasn't its intended object.

Cindy appeared to stiffen further, giving me the impression she was turning into a mannequin out of awkwardness at her boss's presence. "Yes. I'll have an outline on your desk in the morning."

"Good. I'm heading home, then." She whirled around and said, "I'll leave you two to your discussion," then strode across the room and down the stairs with a self-conscious gait, as if she expected all eyes to be on her.

The instant Katherine was out of the room, Cindy's posture relaxed, and an unspoken *Thank God she's gone*, seemed to hang in the air. I felt empathetic toward her, the result of my own years kowtowing to pompous bosses. "Do you mind if I join you for a minute?"

She smiled and gestured at the empty chair across from her table—a small square made out of flimsy-looking plywood. "No, go right ahead."

I sat down slowly, not anxious to delve into a subject that would be uncomfortable for both of us. "I told Katherine I was interested in hearing about what it was like to be a research assistant. I'd imagine it's a lot like any internship—all of the work with a fraction of the pay."

She smiled. "That sums it up pretty well. How do you know Katherine?"

"We had a mutual friend in common. Allison Kenyon."

Her face fell. "Allison. Yes, I heard about her death. I'm so sorry."

"So am I." To test her reaction, I said, "I guess you know how it feels to have someone you care about murdered."

She looked as though she might be holding her breath, but she said nothing. Maybe it was her doll-like features combined with her youth, but I felt as though I were about to badger a child. Whatever her relationship may or may not have been with Allison's late ex-husband, she hadn't killed Allison.

"I'm sorry, Cindy." I pushed back my chair, expecting her to ask me to leave immediately. "The truth is, I'm trying to find out who killed Allison Kenyon. I came here to ask you what you knew about Richard Kenyon, on the chance that his murder and hers were related. I fed Katherine a line of baloney so I could meet with you under false pretenses."

"Shh." She made a downward-pushing gesture to indicate for me to keep my voice down. "There are three of Katherine's students in here." I automatically glanced around, which was stupid because I certainly wouldn't know her students if I saw them, but I did spot the officer seated in the corner of the far wall. Cindy raised her eyebrows and looked at me as if enthralled. "You're a private investigator?" she whispered.

"No, I create faxable greeting cards. And, at the moment, I'm a suspect."

Cindy had paled a bit and her body language had again grown tense. "You didn't do it, did you?"

"No," I answered a bit more harshly than I'd intended. "If I'd killed her, I wouldn't be trying to figure out who did."

"No, I guess you wouldn't."

"Were you Richard Kenyon's girlfriend?"

"I wouldn't say—We dated for a while when he had separated from his wife. That was long over by the time of his death."

"Really? I'd heard you were living together."

"Only briefly, and before I knew . . . I'd already moved out before the robber killed him. Richard told me he was divorced, but then, just when he'd convinced me to move in, I got a call from his wife. That was the end of my relationship with Richard."

"What did she say to you?"

"She thought I was somebody else at first, which was a big clue that I wasn't Richard's only girlfriend."

"You mean, she called you by someone else's name?"

"Yes. That particular conversation is burned into my memory. Allison sounded totally smashed, slurring her words and everything. She said, 'He'll do it to you, too, Celia. Don't kid yourself.' "

Allison must have meant Richard would beat her, too, but I asked, "Do you know what she meant by that?"

"I assumed she meant he'd cheat on me, too."

"Did you ask Richard about Celia?"

She grimaced and nodded. "He said he didn't know anybody by that name, and I—"

Just then a large black Labrador came galloping up the stairs, an apron-clad employee in pursuit yelling, "Hey! No dogs!" Not surprisingly, the dog charged ahead, massive tail whapping cups off tables while patrons scrambled to steady them. The oblivious, happy beast charged to a table one over from ours, where a young man with droopy eyelids laughed and said in a stoned-out drawl, "Hey, Toby! How'd you get loose, dude?"

The employee gave one glance at the policeman, who rose from his seat and asked the man, "Is that your dog?"

"Yeah." He grabbed the red bandanna that served as a collar and got up on wobbly legs. "Er, I mean no. I'll take 'im outside and see if I can find his owner."

The officer met my eyes as the dog and his immature owner left. I smiled and said, "Hi."

"Afternoon, Mrs. Masters," he murmured as he followed the others down the stairs.

"Wow. He even knew your name," Cindy commented casually.

"He buys a lot of my greeting cards." It sounded as if Allison knew Celia and Richard were having an affair. That had to have been a source of friction between the two women. "I'm trying to find out if Katherine Lindstrom could have been involved in

Allison's death. Or perhaps even in Richard's. What do you think?"

Cindy was leaning back in her chair, studying my features. She seemed to be mulling whether or not to answer.

I went on, "I realize you have nothing to gain by helping me, but could you anyway?"

She raised an eyebrow and said, "Oh, I wouldn't say I had 'nothing to gain,' exactly. Katherine is a bear to work for, and nothing would please me more than seeing her get busted."

"How so?"

She furrowed her brow. "She set me up with Richard. She engineered our meeting each other, and she lied to me about his marital status. She'd asked him to come to her office to speak to her about something, then she claimed to have something pressing come up and sent me to keep him company till she could get free. Then she called and said she couldn't make it at all. Richard and I hit it off, and Katherine told me he was a terrific guy who used to be married to a friend of hers. When I learned later he was only separated from his wife, she said she hadn't been aware of that."

"That was possible," I answered honestly. "Allison wouldn't have been forthcoming with information about the status of her marriage. So maybe Katherine simply felt like fixing the two of you up . . . that you'd make a good match."

Cindy chuckled, but it was without humor. "That would mean she did it for selfless reasons. That simply isn't possible. She matched us up for her own purposes, probably because she knew we'd wind up hurting each other. Katherine doesn't believe in doing anything that doesn't directly lead to her own gain. Nor does she let anybody get in her way."

That was an awfully harsh assessment, and my reaction must have registered on my face, for she explained, "Once this other professor challenged her over a research paper she'd written—said she'd gotten her sources wrong. She obsessed over the guy—eventually located some female student he'd had a fling with. That was it, he was gone."

She rose. "We've been talking too long. It will look suspicious. Please, don't repeat anything I've told you." She rounded the table, but then bent down and said softly into my ear, "If I were you, I'd watch my step around her. If she finds out you're asking questions about her behind her back, she'll find a way to destroy you."

Chapter 9

How Come I Can't Breathe?

"Why does Daddy have to go, too?" Nathan whined. He was sitting on the floor of his bedroom, wearing a maize-colored T-shirt and his navy shorts. "Can't he stay home and watch us?"

"Because she was a friend of mine, It's called paying your respects." I knelt and gave him a hug, forgetting one of the first lessons I'd learned about BC; whenever anyone hugged, she was desperate to join in on it. A flurry of waggy-tail bliss, she leaped onto Nathan's lap and stuck her cold doggy nose in our faces.

Nathan complained vehemently, not enjoying puppy claws on his bare legs. His cries immediately brought both Karen and Rachel running into the room to make sure the dog wasn't being mistreated. This, in turn, caused Nathan to yowl, "Get out of my room! You're supposed to knock first!"

Jim was supposedly getting dressed in our bedroom, but when I went back to check on him he was fast asleep on the bed, despite the children's noisy argument a short distance away. I woke him and said, "Honey? This is ridiculous. You're not going to the funeral in this condition. People are going to think you're next. I'm getting you an appointment with our old doctor instead."

"There's no point in my going to the doctor," Jim wheezed. "He'll either tell me to stay in bed and drink plenty of fluids, or something else I really don't want to hear."

"There's a wide enough range between common cold and deathbed that it's worth taking that chance. Besides, you need to set a good example for our children." My crabbiness was beginning to show. I've long suspected that we are all given a fixed quantity of patience to use throughout our lifetimes; therefore, much of mine is being held in reserve for when Karen and Nathan hit their teens.

Fortunately, the urgent care clinic at the Boulder Medical Center was open till eight P.M. After some whining and symptom exaggerations on my part, the clinic's receptionist told me that they could squeeze Jim in as long as he got there soon. Jim assured me he was well enough to drive and wheezed and coughed himself into his car.

Both Lauren and Tommy wanted to accompany me to the funeral, no doubt in the hopes of keeping me out of trouble.

But with Jim off to the doctor, it was eventually decided that Lauren and I would go alone in Tommy's rental car, while Tommy stayed home with all three children. We fought our way through a handful of inane questions from Tommy about child-rearing rules but finally made our escape.

"It's a shame Jim is so sick," Lauren said while backing down the driveway.

"Yeah. Ironic, isn't it? He comes all this way to protect me and winds up spending his time sick in bed."

"Mmm," she murmured, giving me the impression that her thoughts were elsewhere. She drove us down the Diagonal, a road in which you're tailgated if you go less than ten miles above the speed limit. "Tommy's been a single parent for several years since his first wife died, and yet he was all but panicked when we left."

"He's probably not used to taking care of two girls, though. When are his sons due back from camp?"

"Two more weeks," Lauren answered. She chewed on her lip, a nervous characteristic of hers, and I suspected it crossed her mind that two weeks from now was also their wedding. If I still hadn't been given the go-ahead to leave Colorado by then, she'd have to choose another matron of honor.

"Are you getting nervous about the wedding?"

"My feet are so cold, my toes have frostbite," she answered quietly.

Uh-oh. When things are going badly in my own life, my need for friends to be doing well in theirs becomes all but compulsive. I could advise her to trust her instincts, but which ones? Those that had inspired her to say yes, or those that were causing her trepidation now? Tommy had slowly but solidly joined the ranks of my favorite people. Yet he could annoy me so much that I frequently considered how lucky it was that *we* weren't a couple.

I showed her where to turn, and we pulled into the funeral home. Lauren's face in profile was a portrait of despair, and I could stay silent no longer. "You're not thinking of canceling the wedding, are you?"

She yanked the parking brake on with a vengeance. "I try to imagine myself walking down that aisle, and I just don't think I can go through with it. We'll see how I feel by the time we get back to Carlton."

My chest tightened in alarm. This was going to break Tommy's heart, and Lauren's, too. "You two are right for each other, Lauren. Maybe it's the wedding itself and not the concept of marrying Tommy that's causing your anxiety."

On the verge of tears, she made no comment.

"Just don't make any rash decisions. Things are too crazy right now for any of us to think straight."

"That's for sure," she said in a voice choked with emotion. She fidgeted with the contents of her purse to buy time to collect herself. A minute later, she started to open her door, then hesitated and studied my face. "Are you going to be all right?"

I was so upset at the notion of Tommy and Lauren's relationship falling apart that it took me an instant to remember what she meant; we were about to attend a funeral of a friend of mine. "I think so."

Allison's death had taken on an almost surreal aspect. In the last twenty-four hours, I'd learned that she'd been a battered spouse and possibly a drug user, that she was aware that her ex-husband had cheated on her with her friend Celia, among others, and that this husband had been murdered almost six months ago. It had become impossible for me to believe that Allison had been anything other than miserable in life.

Though Lauren and I had arrived just minutes before the service was scheduled to start, the funeral home was almost empty. By all appearances, Allison had passed through this world as a virtual stranger to everyone—the only exception, to my knowledge, being her partner, Joe Cummings. He and a white-haired woman were seated in the middle of the room. An ancient couple, whom I took to be Allison's parents, sat in the front row. There was nobody else in the seats normally reserved for family. Lauren and I made our way down the center aisle and sat a couple of rows back from the Cummingses and near the center aisle.

Five women—not counting Lauren and me—had the opportunity to have killed Allison. Of these, Nancy Thornton was the first to arrive. She was arm in arm with a short, bald man I assumed was her husband. Nancy's stature—a full head above his—made her shimmering white hair all the more striking. She was the woman in the group whom I knew the least. Getting to know her better was not going to be easy. As a therapist, she would be used to drawing others out but not revealing herself to virtual strangers.

Lauren whispered, "I'm under strict instructions from Tommy to keep you away from anyone who was on the retreat with you."

Nancy met my eyes and I gestured for her to join us. While Lauren and I moved over, I said under my breath, "You're not actually going to do what Tommy wants, are you?"

She chuckled. "No, I'm going to aid and abet you."

As soon as Nancy and her husband were seated, I said quietly, "You remember Lauren, don't you?"

Characteristically, she waited a beat before saying, "Yes. Hello, Lauren." She did not introduce her husband but turned her gaze to me and asked, "How are you?"

"Fine, under the circumstances." My vision was drawn to a young man with a glorious mane of black hair heading down the side aisle. He took a seat a couple of rows back from Allison's parents. He was wearing dark glasses that hid his eyes, his lips set in a sneer that I suspected masked a well of emotion. I did some quick arithmetic. Allison had been forty, and he appeared to be between the ages of sixteen and twenty. It would not have surprised me if this turned out to be Allison's son, whom she'd failed to ever mention to me. I gestured with my chin. "Who's that?"

"Lois Tucker's son, Max," Nancy answered.

He was surprisingly good looking. I peered at him a second time. He had his mother's features, and I realized that, though Lois wasn't an attractive woman, she would have made a handsome man. Bad genetic luck.

"I didn't see her come in," I said, turning to look. A few more mourners had arrived. Celia now sat beside Julie and an elderly man I took to be Julie's husband. Katherine sat alone in the opposite corner. The only other people behind us were a young couple. They were the two sheriffs, now in plain clothes, who'd been investigating the crime. They were both unabashedly watching me.

"I doubt we'll see Lois here," Nancy said. "Even if she does come, she and her son would never come together. Max hasn't lived at home for over a year."

"I'd gotten the impression that Lois's husband died a couple of years ago."

"He did."

"Then where has her son been living?"

"Until a few weeks ago, Max was living with Allison."

"Allison?" I repeated, surprised. Allison lived next door to Lois. That must have been so painful for Lois—her estranged son able to relate to their next-door neighbor, but not to her. Hmm. That could explain some of the bizarre fixation Lois appeared to have had on Allison.

"He had an apartment in the loft over Allison's garage, until last month when he graduated from high school. He shares a downtown apartment with some kids his own age now."

Nancy's husband shushed us as the piped-in organ music grew quiet, and a man dressed in a black suit made his way to the podium. The eulogy that followed was embarrassingly short and generic, but Max Tucker and Joe Cummings were in tears throughout. Afterward, Max all but bolted out the door, then Allison's parents took positions by the exit. Lauren and I were the last in line, listening as those who proceeded us said the same things—a few words of introduction and condolences as the elderly couple nodded, shook their hands, thanked them for coming. When it was my turn, I shook Allison's father's hand. Then I looked into Allison's mother's desperate eyes and knew her heartbreak. I wanted to tell her that no parent should ever outlive a child, that somehow I would make sure Allison's murderer didn't go unpunished. Yet I heard myself mutter the same lifeless phrases everyone else had. She stopped me, pressed my hand between her parchment-dry hands, and said, "Molly Masters. You used to golf with Allison."

"Yes, that's right."

"Allie said you could always make her laugh, no matter what. She used to call you her favorite person."

Stunned, I could only say, "I really liked Allison."

"It's too bad you moved away." She started to cry.

Her husband said, "Let's go, dear," and gently took her arm. "Thank you for coming, Molly," he said to me as he led her outside. I followed, feeling miserable, and yet all the more determined.

Her parents continued past the other mourners, straight to their car. The male and female officers were standing by a maple tree a few feet away, discreetly keeping an eye on everyone. Max Tucker was in the parking lot, struggling to start the engine on a motorcycle.

Certain that Celia would have a considerably looser tongue than Nancy's, I made my way over to where she was standing. To my discomfort and annoyance, she hugged me as if we were the best of friends, mourning the loss of a mutual loved one. Lauren had been in the process of following me, but when she saw Celia's hug, she turned and started speaking with Nancy.

The sound of a motorcycle engine as Max sped away made both of us turn. "Darn," I said. "I was hoping to say something to him."

"You know Lois's son?" Celia asked.

"No, but he seemed so upset, I thought I'd say something . . . motherly to him."

She let out a chortle and said, "Oh, he'd have enjoyed that, all right."

"What do you mean?"

"He has a . . . thing for middle-aged women."

I tried hard to keep my mouth shut. I was only thirty-seven. As long as there were still a few one hundred-and-four-year-old senior citizens out there, I had fifteen years to go until I would consider myself "middle-aged."

"Allison and Max were lovers," Celia said. She pushed against her frosted hair. Her hairspray was so effective, she might as well have been knocking against wood.

"Was this common knowledge?"

Celia flicked her hand at me. "Everyone in the neighborhood knew." She cleared her throat. "Lois absolutely detested Allison for robbing her cradle."

"But . . . why did you invite Lois and Allison to a weekend retreat together, knowing they had this terrible source of friction between them?"

She set her jaw and said through her teeth, "I promised you I would organize your retreat, and I never go back on a promise. You needed attendees. I thought everyone could set aside their petty differences for one weekend."

"You call Allison taking Lois's teenaged son as a lover a 'petty difference'?"

"Yes! They'd had months and months to work out their dispute. How was I supposed to know they still hadn't come to terms with it?"

"Did you *ask* either of them if they had?"

She clicked her tongue. "There's no sense in trying to be civil to you, Molly." She whirled on her heel and marched off, saying over her shoulder, "You're intent on blaming somebody else for absolutely everything."

I stood there gaping at her for a moment, then retorted, too late for her to hear, "Not 'absolutely everything.' For Allison's murder, I certainly do."

"Molly?"

The sudden voice so close behind me made me jump. I whirled around. It was Nancy. Her husband—if my original assumption had been correct—was standing a couple of steps behind her. She smiled sympathetically, the skin around her gray eyes crinkling into attractive laugh lines. "Talking to yourself out loud is a sign of stress. Did you even realize that was what you were doing just now?"

I chuckled in my embarrassment and frustration. "Actually, I was just talking to Celia, who stormed off right before you got here."

She nodded. "I should have guessed. Celia can drive the sanest among us to talking to ourselves."

Nancy's comment reminded me that I had yet to learn how she'd gotten to know Allison and her immediate neighbors. "You don't live in her neighborhood, do you?"

"No, Celia owns the building my office is in, and we both happened to enroll in Julie's aerobics class. That's how Katherine got to know everyone, as well." She turned and spotted Julie across the lawn. "Which reminds me. I wanted to ask her when our next class was." She moved off in Julie's direction while her husband continued on to the parking lot.

Lauren joined me, closely followed by Joe Cummings, along with the petite, sweet-looking woman I'd assumed was his wife.

Joe was now wearing an ill-fitting brown suit, but he still had on the same ragged running shoes he'd worn earlier today. "Well, hello there, Molly. I'd like you to meet my wife, Ruth." We exchanged greetings, and I introduced Lauren to both of them.

Joe held out his hand, which Lauren shook. "Nice, firm handshake," he told her.

"Good hands for plying," I added.

Lauren shot me a questioning look. Ruth said, "Molly, Joe tells me you made an excellent electrician's apprentice. Joe's got to find a new partner—though I don't suppose this is the time to talk about that. I'm so sorry about the loss of your friend."

"Me, too," I answered. "Did you know her?"

She shook her head. "Only met her a couple of times. She was a loner." She gave Joe's arm a squeeze. "I'm going to go wait in the car. No rush, if you want to stay and chat."

"Means I've got all of two minutes," he grumbled.

"Joe, did Allison ever say anything to you about a young man who was living in her garage loft?"

"Lois's son. Allison never liked to talk about him much.

Lois, on the other hand, used to call me and the wife at all hours to insist I tell Allison to get her claws off her boy, or else."

"Did you discuss those phone calls with Allison?"

He nodded. "She was embarrassed. May-December kind of romance, I gathered. Far as I could see, they truly loved each other. And I was all for anything that could encourage her to get away from Richard."

With Allison sexually involved with Lois's teenage son, I could only imagine how angry that must have made Lois. "Why would Lois use Allison as her electrician if—" I stopped, remembering her crush on Joe, which explained why she'd be willing to put herself through exposure to Allison just to get to him.

"I always suspected Lois had some pull on Allison," Joe said, "as though she were blackmailing her."

"What do you think Lois could possibly blackmail Allison for?"

He shrugged, seemingly all too aware of the possibility somebody might overhear. I looked over and saw that Nancy had left, but Celia and Julie were engaged in an intense conversation. Julie headed our way just as Joe said his good-byes and rushed off. She wore a brilliant smile, sandals, and a black cotton knit dress that was really just a T-shirt. If she raised both arms, the hemline would be above her panties. Watching her approach, it occurred to me that I'd yet to see her in anything that didn't appear to be two sizes too small.

"Hi, Lauren. Hi, Molly. How's BC doing?"

I smiled. Though Julie was not a great dresser and was too terminally perky for my taste, I owed her a tremendous debt for giving me my wonderful new puppy. "She's great and just adorable. Thanks."

Julie clasped her hands in a youthful gesture of happiness. "Do either of you do aerobics?"

"I don't," I answered promptly. "I'm not sure about the dog."

"No, no, I meant you and Lauren. I'm holding a special class tonight in Allison's honor, after closing."

"After closing what?" Lauren asked.

"The studio. I know it sounds strange, but it's the best way for me to get sadness out of my system: exercise and sweat it out. And, see, normally, this is right when we'd be having a class, but I'm here instead. I'm the manager, so I can keep it open late for a private party anytime I want. So, what do you say?"

"Sure. I'd love to go," I lied.

I widened my eyes at Lauren, who took the hint and said, "So would I. So, um, we're going to be exercising at what time tonight?"

"Nine-thirty. So you'll still have plenty of cooldown time, too, before bed." Julie grinned and gave us a gung-ho fist pump. "I'll call Lois, and we'll see if she'll come."

Lauren grimaced and grabbed my arm the instant Julie was gone. "Tell me. Why are we doing this?"

"So I can get more information about the murder."

"Ah, yes. Interrogation during exercise class. And a-one and a-two and are-you-a-killer?"

"Is that going to be too hard on your twisted ankle?"

"My ankle? No, it barely even . . . I mean, yes." She suddenly feigned a bad limp and cried, "Ooh! Ouch!" with every step as we made our way to the car.

We rushed home and checked on our significant others. Jim was on antibiotics. The children and puppy were on the couch in front of the TV. I booted BC off and told the children they needed to train the dog to stay off our furniture. In the meantime, Tommy and Lauren got into a whale of an argument and discreetly moved it to the guest room downstairs.

Not actually owning a leotard, I changed into shorts and a T-shirt. I tucked the kids into bed and grabbed my keys. To avoid embarrassing Lauren and Tommy by interrupting their disagreement, I decided to wait for fifteen minutes in Jim's rental car. If Lauren didn't come by then, I would go alone. In just under that time, she came out and got into the car, but she had been crying.

We took off, and I said gently, "Want to talk about it?"

She shook her head.

Twenty minutes later, after all of eight minutes of aerobics, I was gasping for air. Then, to break my heart, Julie announced, "Is everybody all warmed up? Ready to do some aerobics?" And I realized that we'd merely done the stretching portion. Class was yet to begin.

Nancy, Lois, and Katherine were there, but Celia was missing. Julie flipped on a tape player and started some song that was way too fast for me.

"Go for the burn!" Julie cried over the energetic rhythm of the music. "Let's do it for Allison!"

A memorial aerobics class? Though I'd come to realize how little I'd really known about Allison, I was sure that, were she able to see us, she'd get a good laugh out of this.

Lauren was doing fine, but by now I really and truly hated Julie. She was wearing wrist and ankle weights, which was apparently all that kept her from perkying her way into outer space. She kept bouncing around, calling out, "You can do it, Molly!"

Which was not true. I was thoroughly defeated by a step called the "grapevine," a sideways step in which I promised myself that if I could just figure out which foot went in front, I'd grapevine right out the door to the car.

Julie trotted past me and cried, "Move those arms, Molly! That's what gets the heart pumping."

"It *is* pumping. I can tell I'm not dead 'cause I'm in pain!"

My mind started to hallucinate images of greeting cards. I pictured a woman sweating, tongue hanging out, crying, "If this is supposed to be *aerobic* exercise, how come I can't breathe?"

I survived the class by doing the motions only when Julie was looking at me and gasping for air when her back was turned. At the end of class, we had a "cooldown period," which in my case consisted of lying on my back, panting, and trying not to whimper. Afterward Julie said, "Sorry that wasn't much of a workout, guys. My heart wasn't in it. I'll make it up to you next time."

Lois came up to me and offered me a hand, which I accepted. She pulled me to my feet in one clean-and-jerk motion. "Molly, for a skinny person, you're sure in rotten shape."

"Thank you very much. I've been spoiled by all that oxygen in New York."

Lauren had fared considerably better than I but was still red-faced and sweaty. We all headed to the women's locker room, never a place where I feel comfortable—having been permanently damaged by the experience of being the last girl in my entire high school graduating class to get a bra.

"I was expecting Celia to be here," I said to Katherine, who was using the locker near mine.

"As was I," Katherine said. "She's usually the de facto captain of our little group. Something must have come up."

Julie, totally nude, strode past us, drying her hair. It was truly demoralizing to see that her breasts, despite their size, were every bit as perky as her personality. She grinned at us. "There. That feels better."

I didn't even want to ask what she was referring to, but moments later she had pulled another long T-shirt over her head, stepped into some flip-flops, and was apparently fully dressed. She couldn't tuck this "dress" into her panties, for she wasn't wearing any. Hope she didn't have to sit on a vinyl seat anytime soon.

"I've got to return a couple of phone calls, then I'd better lock up. I need to get home to the pups."

"See you in the sauna," Katherine said to no one in particular.

Within a minute, Lauren and I were alone in the locker room, the others apparently having a regular routine of exercise half to death, then head to the oven for some slow roasting.

"I suppose that means you want to go to the sauna, too, right?"

"I wouldn't say I 'want to,' exactly."

She nodded and led the way. "Wow, this is fun," Lauren said to me. "Next time, let's just hire someone to beat us with a big stick, shall we?"

Katherine, Nancy, and Lois were already seated on the red-wood benches in the sauna. Nancy moved over, and Lauren and I joined them. No one spoke. "Whew," I said to break the silence. "It's like a sauna in here."

Nobody laughed.

"I can see how your particular brand of humor could translate well into greeting cards," Katherine said in that affected drawl of hers. "It would be the equivalent of primitive art." She gave me a haughty look, having essentially slapped me in the face with a duelist's glove.

In as casual a voice as I could muster, I said, "Thanks. And does being judgmental help or hinder you in your teaching career?"

Katherine shot me a hateful glare but said nothing. Beside her, Lois smiled almost imperceptibly, and Nancy stiffened, as if poised to slip into her calming therapist role.

Lauren cleared her throat, then asked, "So, all five of you used to come to this particular class?"

"Yep," Lois said. "We had a pact. It was Celia's idea. We would call and urge each other to show up, because we all hate the class so much."

After a pause, Nancy interjected, "If any one of us chooses not to come, then she has to drive everyone here the next time."

Their carpooling explained why there were only two cars in

the parking lot when we arrived: one for Julie, and one for Katherine, Nancy, and Lois.

"Celia will be driving next time," Katherine said. Her eyes were shut. She had perhaps decided to let our little exchange pass. Then again, if her grad assistant's assessment of her personality were accurate, she'd merely granted me a temporary stay of execution.

Julie poked her head in. "Hiya, girls. Having fun?"

"Sure beats your class," Lois murmured.

Julie giggled. "Listen, whoever is the last one out? Don't forget to turn the sauna all the way off. Okeydokey?"

Julie left. In an innocent voice, I asked, "Were you at Allison's service, Lois? I didn't see you."

"No, something came up." She clenched her jaw, but almost as if she couldn't quite help herself, she asked me, "Was Joe there?"

"Yes, with his wife," I answered. "She seemed very nice."

"That's enough hot air for me," Lois said, promptly getting to her feet. "I'm going to take a quick shower before I leave."

"Me, too," Nancy said. She rose, but hesitantly, looking from Katherine to me as if unsure whether or not we should be left with just Lauren to intercede.

Lauren said, "Actually, this feels kind of nice. I'm going to stay put for a few minutes."

"Nancy, don't we need to be out of here soon so Julie can lock up?" I asked.

"No, you just need to flick on the alarm switch by the front door and make sure the door is shut securely. It'll lock behind you."

Katherine stood up, holding her towel close around her chest, and followed Nancy out. At the door, she turned back, looked at me, and said, "Don't stay in here too long. The effects from the heat have a way of sneaking up on you when you least expect it."

I smiled and nodded. "Thanks for the tip."

"Don't mention it," she said as the door shut. "Have a nice night."

After several seconds, Lauren turned to me and said, "That was creepy. Did you do or say something to her to tick her off?"

I widened my eyes and put a hand on my chest. "Who, me?" Lauren smiled, and I answered truthfully, "Not that I know of, other than using my writing skills for greeting cards rather than literature."

I already felt uncomfortably warm, but sensed that Lauren wanted us to hang out and chat before we had to go home. It was, at least, wonderfully quiet where we were.

After a long pause, Lauren said, "Tommy said he was going to check into a hotel."

"I'm so sorry."

"He thinks I'm stalling on the wedding."

"And are you?"

"Yes. But not because I don't love him. I'm just not sure I can go through it all again. I'd rather stay single than wind up in another bad marriage." She sighed and looked at me for a long moment, then asked the question I'd been dreading. "What do you think I should do?"

"I think you should decide once and for all whether you're happier and generally better off with him or without him, then act accordingly."

"That's just it. Most of the time, I am happier when I'm with him. But not always. If we keep dating but never get married, I can still have my time away from him, so that we don't get stale."

"Oh, so you don't think forty years or so of dating the same person is going to get stale?"

She laughed, but instantly grew sad. "I keep thinking that if this were right, if I were meant to marry Tommy, I'd know it. I wouldn't have these doubts."

"Lauren, all I can say is you're a thoughtful person, and you make good, smart choices more often than not. Doubts might be a natural by-product of your personality, not of the decision itself."

There was a metallic click from the vicinity of the door. Lauren sat upright. "What was that?"

"Must have been something expanding from the heat, or a board settling." I was a trifle on edge, but I assured myself I'd spoken the truth, though I also sounded like my mother. Every time there was a strange noise in our house she claimed it was just a board settling. I'd grown up half expecting to come home one day and discover that our tri-level had settled into a ranch home.

"I think Julie killed Allison," Lauren said.

"What makes you think that?"

"Just a feeling. Intuition, I guess. At any rate, I hate her guts. Which are probably pumped as full of silicon as those boobs of hers."

"You think they're fake?"

"Oh, there's no doubt about that. It's just a question of what she's stuffed 'em with: silicon or helium."

I stood up and glanced at the thermostat, which read one hundred eighty degrees. "Well, listen, I'm getting dizzy. I'd better get out of here before I faint." Lauren, too, rose and pushed against the door. It didn't budge.

"The door seems to be stuck," she murmured, and shoved against it with her shoulder.

She turned back to me, her eyes wide with fright. "Molly, we're locked in here!"

Chapter 10

Is Everything a Joke to You?

I had to try for myself to open the door, even though there was nothing to operate—the door was supposed to simply push open. What did I expect? That Lauren had pulled instead of pushed? Indeed, the door didn't budge.

"It's locked, all right." My heart started thumping. Holy shit! We were trapped inside a cedar-paneled oven, set to slow-bake like a rump roast! I smacked my fist on the door.

Lauren and I pounded and yelled for help. Somebody wanted to kill me. My best friend was going to die, too, just because she was with me.

My mind raced through the mostly unanswerable *hows*, *whos*, and *whys*, but one name stuck. *Katherine*. Her parting words about the dangers of heat had all but shouted that this was her doing.

I had to actively work at blocking out the fear of how excruciating my immediate future might be. I had to keep myself together. If I flipped out, Lauren would too, and we had precious little time and energy as it was. None could be wasted on tears or histrionics.

My forearms and fists aching from my fruitless blows, I said, more to myself than Lauren, "I knew I shouldn't have come in here! I've always hated saunas. Why on earth do people want to subject themselves to intolerable levels of heat?"

Lauren continued to pound on the door and yell after I'd

stopped. There was nothing but dead silence whenever she paused.

In the meantime, I studied the heater, hoping to find an emergency shut-off valve or on-off switch. No such luck. The unit was enclosed by a sheet-metal cover. There were probably some controls in there someplace. "Story of my life," I muttered. "I never have a Phillips-head screwdriver when I need one. I'm really sorry about this, Lauren. This only happened to you because you're with me."

"But *how* could this happen? I didn't even see a way to lock this door when I came in."

"I did. It's a deadbolt, operated by a key. Though the key wasn't in the lock when we came in."

Lauren knocked on the door another four or five times, then sighed and turned toward me. Her hair was damp with sweat, and her face was bright red and shiny. "The rental car's out front. Sooner or later somebody will spot it, figure out that it's suspicious, and come looking for us. And there's got to be somebody left in the shower or dressing room. If I keep knocking—"

"The walls and doors are too well insulated," I told her. "*I* can barely even hear you from in here."

"We've got to do something to get out!" Lauren cried.

"Let's not lose our cool. So to speak."

Lauren glared at me.

I held up a palm in unspoken apology. We'd been friends for so long, she knew that my tendency to crack jokes during bad situations was almost compulsive. I flashed on an idea for a cartoon—more a fleeting hallucination than anything else. A male clown is holding out a bouquet of droopy, wilted flowers to a female clown, who says to him, "Is *everything* a joke to you?"

I took a swipe at my wet forehead with an equally damp—and still aching—forearm. How long could we stay conscious under these circumstances? I doubted it would be for much more than thirty minutes. I was already miserable—thirsty, exhausted, feeling as if every breath was an effort. My face was so hot and painful that I half expected to have blood dripping from my pores.

"Okay, Lauren. Here are our choices. We try to conserve our energy and hope somebody comes and saves us. Or we grab a batch of the rocks out of the sauna. Bundle them into a towel. Make as loud a racket as possible by smashing that against the door. If somebody's still here, they'll hear us."

"Well ... whose towel were you planning on using for Plan B? That's going to influence my vote."

"Please, Lauren. This is no time for modesty."

"Maybe not, but if I'm going to die anyway, I'd much rather have a towel covering my body."

Buck naked and dead from heat prostration in a health club sauna was hardly my fantasy of how I wanted to leave this earth, either. But, never being one to go quietly, I dropped my towel. "We have to use both towels." I spread mine flat on the floor. "I need yours as a potholder to get the rocks."

Lauren obliged and I scooped handfuls of the rocks out and piled them into my towel. Every time I bent over the heating unit, I got a blast in the face of even more intense heat. I worked fast, spurred by the knowledge that each passing second brought us closer to heat prostration and further from the likelihood that anyone still remained in the building. The resulting bundle of stones was roughly the size of a large melon. Lauren's towel was frayed enough that she managed to tear off an inch-wide strip, which we tied tourniquet-style just below the rocks.

I took a couple of turns with our contraption, gripping the bottom of the towel and swinging it with an overhead tennis serve motion. Despite our dire circumstances, Lauren, prone to nervous giggles, started to laugh.

When I glanced back at her, she said, "You look really silly."

"Lauren, if we get out of here, don't you ever, *ever* describe this to my kids."

"Don't worry," she said, laughing all the harder. "We're never going to get out of here."

She held out her hand, and I surrendered my place to her. Using both hands, she twirled it lasso-style, stepping into the door with each revolution. This made so much noise that if anybody were actually in the building, they would have heard.

Nobody came. Either we were alone, or whoever remained was the same person who had locked us in here in the first place.

Already horribly light-headed, I had to lie on the floor. My words coming out in breathy pants and semislurred, I muttered, "The original Olympics were performed in the nude. In fact, this was one of the events—the Rocks-in-a-Towel-Door-Banging competition. Carl Lewis holds the current record."

Lauren's cackle was halfway between tears and laughter. "That's not really funny. My mind's just mostly gone." She took another swing at the door, then had to put her hand on the wall to steady herself. "Oh, shit. This really sucks." Now she was on the verge of full tears.

With effort, I dragged myself to my feet again and took the towel, and we traded places. I knew I could only manage a few more hurls against the door. My vision started to go gray and I almost passed out. Death by sauna had never occurred to me as a possible fate—not even during my teen years when I'd spent a shameful portion of my daydreams imagining how devastated my parents and friends would feel over my death.

"Moll? You've always been the greatest friend I could ever imagine."

"No, *you* are." My head and especially my face were pounding so hard that the pain was excruciating. My tongue felt swollen and it hurt to swallow. About to keel over, the thought of Karen and Nathan came to me, their image so strong I could almost feel their arms around me, hugging me. I couldn't die. My children needed me.

At the very least, I was going to collapse against the door, making some noise as I died. I lashed the rocks against the door repeatedly, pausing for a few seconds each time.

In my current state, I couldn't tell if this was a hallucination, but I thought I heard something on the other side of the door.

"Lauren? I think someone's coming," I muttered.

She raised her head a little. "Are you sure?"

I sank to my knees and shook my head, too exhausted to speak. There was a click that sounded as if the heater had been shut off. Shortly afterward, there was a distinct rattling at the lock. An instant later, Julie threw open the door.

"Oh my gosh!" she cried. "The door was locked! What happened?"

I felt even worse than I had immediately after childbirth and couldn't answer. She grabbed me and all but dragged me into the shower, then turned cold water on full force. The sudden blast of freezing water was so painful and shocking, it felt as though the force of a lightning bolt had thrown me through a plate-glass window. I was too busy trying to survive the experience to do anything but stumble back against the wall.

Julie returned moments later with Lauren, whom she forced into the large shower beside me. I had recuperated enough to be able to stand upright and step away from the stream of freezing water. Cupping my hands, I drank as greedily as if I'd crossed the Sahara.

From a short distance away, Julie chewed on a fingernail and watched our every move. She seemed terribly flustered. "Maybe I should call nine-one-one. They could give you an IV."

"I think I'm all right. Lauren?"

She nodded, still in the direct stream of the shower. After a moment, she said, "I'm okay."

I grabbed a towel, wrapped it around me, and slumped onto

the nearest bench. After a few seconds of breathing heavenly cool air, I had the energy to speak. "How could someone get the key to the sauna?" I asked. "It wasn't in the lock when we all went in there."

Julie paced in front of me, as anxious as a caged tiger. She still wore the simple pullover and sandals she'd put on after class. She shook her head, her eyes so wide they were almost goggly. Her hands trembled as she fidgeted with her bangs. "I have a key on my chain, which I keep with me. There's another one under the tray in the cash register, but we never use it. Only our employees even know it's there. As far as I know, those are the only keys. The lock was empty when I found you." She said the last sentence over her shoulder as she sprinted toward the door. As it swung shut behind her she called, "I'm checking to see if the key's still in the register."

"You okay?" I asked Lauren gently as she turned off the water. Still so red that she looked sunburned, Lauren wrapped herself in a towel and lowered herself stiffly onto the bench next to me.

She nodded but sat slumped over, elbows on knees, with her eyes closed. "Remind me to get on a scale before we leave," she murmured. "If I lost a couple pounds, at least some good's come from this."

Julie dashed back into the room and announced breathlessly, "It's gone. The key's gone."

"Do you lock the sauna every night?" I asked.

Arms tightly crossed, she resumed her pacing. "We never lock it. Except when it's under maintenance, something like that. That key could have been gone for weeks with nobody noticing."

"We have to call the police," I said.

Julie stopped in front of me, clutched her hands, and pleaded, "Do we have to report it?" Her eyes started to fill with tears. "I'm going to get fired over this. Once we report it to the police, our insurance rates will quadruple. The owners will turn around and sue us."

With a look of anguish, she paused and took a seat between Lauren and me, then covered her face and shook her head. "Oh, listen to me. I'm so ashamed. You poor people were nearly killed."

"Right," I said. "I'm sorry, but I can't just say, 'Oh, well. We lived through it, so let's not make trouble for you with your boss.' The police might be able to catch the person who did this."

Julie sagged a little, but nodded. "I never should have taken chances like I have been, letting my friends stay here after me. I always figured, as I long as I take one last swing through the place and make sure everything's okay, what could happen? And now you . . . What have I done?"

"It's a good thing you came when you did," Lauren said.

"Yes, you saved our lives. Thank you." Though I truly did feel immensely grateful, my gratitude was tempered with suspicion. Julie might well have locked us in there in the first place and either changed her mind about killing us or merely intended to scare us.

"I can't believe this!" Julie said, rising. "Who would do such a thing? It had to be one of the women in the class. But none of them would have done it. I mean, yes, we all have our little eccentricities. But to . . . to lock two people you barely know in a sauna. That's so cruel!"

I said nothing, simply stared at her. One of those women's "eccentricities" already included killing Allison.

She said, "I'll go get the portable phone." Julie left the room, heading toward the front lobby. "I'll also go open up the juice bar and get you some drinks."

As soon as Julie was gone, Lauren said quietly, "The last person to leave had to have done this."

"Yeah, but whoever it was would also have made it look as

though she *wasn't* the last one." I stared at the door. "Anybody with a contraband set of keys could have done it. Including Celia, or Julie herself."

Julie brought us the phone and bottles of some lemon-lime concoction. I gulped my drink, then called the Boulder police and explained what had happened. The dispatcher said she'd send someone out right away. Julie seemed reluctant to leave us alone even momentarily and watched us while we pulled on our T-shirts and shorts. I was too fatigued to care about modesty.

Glad to be fully dressed before the police could arrive, we took Julie up on her suggestion to join her at the juice bar and have a second bottle "on the house." This, apparently, was the upside of being slow-roasted in a health club—free beverages afterward.

With Julie playing bartender from behind the counter, Lauren and I sat on the tall wooden stools and accepted our Gator-ades. The counter was in an elongated C-shape on one side of the front lobby. From where we were seated, I could see out over the lot to where our little white rental car was parked.

"I still can't imagine any of my friends doing something like this," Julie said wistfully.

"You must have a different perspective than I do. One of them killed Allison. And I can see any one of them trying to kill me. With the exception of you and, I guess, Nancy, they've all been openly hostile toward me."

"You don't include Katherine in that, do you?"

I nodded, though, until tonight, Professor Katherine had really been more of an intellectual snob toward me than anything else.

"Katherine is just insecure. She's a good person underneath it all. She used to be my sister-in-law."

"She did?" I asked.

Julie nodded. "She used to be married to my brother. They got divorced almost five years ago now."

A black-and-white police car drove up. I was disappointed that a solitary officer emerged. It wasn't that I expected the cavalry to come—the danger was past, after all—but surely a brush with death rated at least one officer per victim.

Julie followed our gazes. "Oh, dear," she said as she hurried over to unlock the door. "Here we go again."

The handsome, thirtyish man in full blue uniform entered, identified himself as Officer Montoya, and asked simply if one of us had "called in a report."

Julie said, "Yes, I'm the manager here, and these two poor folks were locked in our sauna for probably something like twenty minutes or so while I was out on an errand."

"Is the only lock on the outside of the sauna?" he asked.

Still seated at the counter, Lauren and I said, "Yes," but Julie, who was right beside the officer, nodded and immediately began, "I'd left to run to the store. I have a lot of dogs and was low on food. I had to get there before PetsMart closed, but I was too late. It closes at ten. So I went next door to Albertson's." Julie spoke rapidly, gesturing with her characteristic energy. "The only people here, other than these two, were my three good friends. I . . . trusted them to let themselves out. I've done that a couple of times in the past, but I always take a last swing through the place to make sure everything's safe and snug for the night. I really, truly had no way to know anything like this could happen."

The officer waited patiently for her to take a breath, then said, "It'd help me if I could see the layout of the building first, then I'll need to get everyone's statements."

We all escorted him through the aerobics room, sauna, and women's locker room. The locker room had two exits: one into the front lobby and one near the sauna and the exercise room where class had been held.

Officer Montoya asked Julie if she was certain that no one else had been present. She explained that the health club had been closed, as usual, at nine P.M. but that she'd reopened after hours for our special class. Then she gave the participants' names and addresses.

The officer, who had been taking notes as we went, raised an eyebrow when she mentioned it was "a memorial class in honor of Allison Kenyon," but made no comment. Then he pressed a button on his radio, which carried voices that had been sporadically rattling along throughout our conversation and building tour—an annoying buzz that he didn't seem to mind. He spoke quietly into the radio, using some code numbers that clearly added up to a request for additional officers.

He sat Julie and Lauren down at the juice bar and took me to the opposite end of the lobby. I told him what had happened and added Celia Wentworth's name to Julie's list of suspects, with the explanation that she knew about this class and was angry with me. Though I felt a little silly, I explained that Celia could have been keeping an eye on the health club, watching to see whose car remained in the parking lot.

I expected his first question to be: Why would one of these people want to kill you? But instead he asked, "What made you decide to bang the bundled rocks against the door?"

Caught off guard, I hesitated, then answered, "I don't know why I decide to do half of the things I wind up doing. It just struck me as the best way to make noise. I was hoping to rouse the attention of somebody still in the shower."

He nodded. "So the exercise class ended around ten-thirty P.M. How long would you say it was between the time the last person left the sauna and you noticed it was locked?"

"Just a few minutes. No more than ten or fifteen."

"And how long would you say you were locked in there?"

I glanced at my watch, which I'd retrieved from my locker along with my clothes. It was now eleven-fifty. Doing mental arithmetic, I said, "I guess it could only have been fifteen or twenty minutes. It seemed like an eternity in hell, though."

He nodded and said, "I can imagine."

That was, I knew, just a passing comment, but made me tighten my arms across my chest. This was all too raw for me to want anyone "imagining" the particular scene of Lauren and me naked, whirling a towel full of rocks.

He thanked me, then we returned to the juice bar where Lauren and Julie still sat.

The officer took a total of ten minutes getting Julie's and Lauren's statements. We were all set to leave, but, as the saying goes: Be careful what you wish for. Two more police vehicles arrived, including one from the sheriff's department, driven by the petite female officer, whom I was seeing so much of that we should have been on a first-name basis.

Realizing I'd be inordinately late, I asked if I could phone home. Too disoriented to remember my former tenant's number, I called my own eight hundred number, which automatically rang through to that same number. Everybody must have been asleep; my combination fax–answering machine–phone picked up and I had to listen to my own recording for Friendly Fax. I left a message that I was going to be late getting home and not to worry about me. Which was not to say that my family had even noticed I was gone, let alone half baked to death. So much for the thank-God-you're-all-right! telepathy that all my heavy sweating should have earned me.

The officers conferred, and Officer Montoya left. The snatches of conversation gave me the impression that he was going to visit Katherine, Lois, and Nancy, which lifted my spirits. At least the guilty party would experience an anxious moment or two when a policeman knocked on the door.

Another male officer took Lauren into Julie's office to speak to her, while the female officer ushered me back to the same spot in the lobby where I'd given my statement to Officer Montoya. In a matter-of-fact voice, she asked, "Do you think someone was trying to kill you?"

"Yes, and I'll tell you one thing, whoever did it was not thinking logically. If you were going to go through the effort of framing someone for a murder, would you attempt to kill your framee? I mean, wouldn't that defeat your whole purpose in setting the person up in the first place?"

She watched my face for a moment without answering. "So, backing up a little, you think you were framed for the murder of a friend of yours at a greeting card retreat. And you think that the same person who framed you tried to kill you by locking you and another friend of yours in a sauna. Is that right?"

"That's what happened, yes. It's been a lousy week."

She fought back a smile. "Why do you think someone would do this to you?"

"I think I might have unknowingly learned why Allison Kenyon was killed."

"Oh? And why was she killed?"

"I don't know. That's what I meant when I said I 'unknowingly' learned why."

She furrowed her brow. "Oh. I just thought you weren't being clear."

I smiled and couldn't help but think that, under vastly different circumstances, she and I might have been friends. "What I meant was, I've had quite a bit of contact with some of the—"

My story was interrupted by a knock on the door. It was Tommy Newton, looking very worried.

My officer, as I'd come to think of her, went to the door and opened it. I rose and followed, but stayed a step behind her. "I'm Officer Newton from the Carlton, New York, Police Department," Tommy immediately began. "Is everything all right here?"

"Yes, we—"

"Lauren's fine," I answered, over her shoulder. "Somebody locked us in the sauna, but we got rescued in plenty of time."

"Can I speak to her?" Tommy asked my officer.

"She's in the process of giving her statement. If you'd like to wait outside, I'll let her know you're here as soon as she's through."

Tommy shook his head, then turned his gaze to me. "Just tell her that I'll be at the Regency Hotel."

"Oh, for heaven's sake, Tommy. Stay and talk this thing out with Lauren."

Again, he shook his head. "I'd just be taking advantage."

I understood his feelings. He was afraid that Lauren might well act lovingly toward him after the trauma she'd just survived, but that didn't mean they'd resolved their differences. "How did you know we were here? Have you been at my house till now?"

He shrugged. "Parked out front of it, actually. Didn't see your car come back, and finally decided to cruise through the lot." He paused, then said, "Moll, tell her . . ."

He let his voice drift off, and I said, "I will."

Tommy nodded, then returned his attention to the officer and raised his hand as if he were about to tip his cap to her and then remembered he wasn't wearing it. He ran his fingers through his short red hair and said, "Thanks, officer."

She locked the door again, and I said to her, "I don't know why any of this happened. One of the five women on that retreat with us killed Allison Kenyon. One of them also locked us in that sauna."

She held my gaze for a moment but made no comment. Just then, Lauren emerged, and she and I were left alone while both officers escorted Julie into her office to speak to her.

Lauren, frankly, looked terrible, and I suspected I did too. "Tommy was here," I told her. "He said to tell you that he loves you and that he's really sorry about your argument. He can't stand the thought of living without you, and he realizes he's too stubborn and has a hard time expressing his feelings for you, but that that doesn't diminish them in any way. He also said that he's staying at the Regency Hotel."

"*Tommy* said that?"

"That's my story, and I'm sticking to it." I started to head to the ladies room, the gallon or so of Gatorade having worn out its welcome. "I've got to figure out how to go to the bathroom without looking into any mirrors. I've already had enough scares for one night."

When I returned, Lauren was sitting with tears running down her cheeks. She promptly dried her eyes and said under her breath, "This was the last straw. I *gained* half a pound!"

I sat beside her and said quietly, "Would it cheer you up any to know that I just peed out a good five pounds?"

She chuckled and answered, "There's no such thing as a *good* five pounds."

"Probably not in reference to urine, at any rate."

After another ten or fifteen minutes, the police said we could go home. I thanked Julie again for our timely rescue, and we hopped into our car before the officers could change their minds and ask more questions or insist on driving us in a squad car. On an impulse, I took an extra turn to swing through Celia, Lois, and Julie's neighborhood.

"I'm curious to see if there are any police cars still out in front of one of our aerobic friends' houses."

"You don't even know where Nancy and Katherine live, though, do you?"

"No, but we can cruise by the other ones." I pointed out Lois's, Julie's, and finally Celia's houses. The lights were on at Lois's and Julie's, but off at Celia's. This didn't mean anything, since it was nearly midnight, when most folks would be asleep.

I did a double take at Allison's house. "That's really strange," I said, slowing. "The lights are on."

"She probably had them hooked up to a timer system. She was an electrician, after all."

"Oh, of course. That makes perfect—"

Just then, a silhouette appeared in the window.

Chapter 11

Do Not Place Items on Airbags

Surprised by the sight of a figure moving about in Allison's house, I hit the brakes. Lauren had to grab the dashboard, and we were probably lucky that bumping about *inside* the car couldn't trigger the airbags.

I stared at the silhouette in the window, which quickly vanished.

"Did you see that?"

"Yes," Lauren said under her breath, "just before you nearly sent me through the windshield."

I edged the car over to the curb, set the emergency brake, and rotated in my seat to look back at the house. The driveway was empty. None of the lights upstairs were on, just the ones in the front room and on this side of the house, which was probably the kitchen. "It looked like a woman to me. A short woman with teased-up hair. Maybe it's the police officer. No, she couldn't have beaten us here. Maybe it's a tall kid with big hair."

"Molly, I—"

"Look! The lights are going off!" Wanting to see if anyone would soon emerge from Allison's house, I shut off my car engine and headlights. The garage door opened. I gasped and sank down a little in my seat.

Lauren glanced at me but merely crossed her arms and obstinately stared straight ahead. "Molly, you know I love you. But this has been the evening from hell. If you don't get me out of here right away and let me get some sleep, I'm going to have to strangle you."

"I know, I know. I'm being terrible and I hate myself for it, but I just have to see who this is." A badly dented white Toyota Corolla backed down the driveway and drove off in the opposite direction from where we were parked. I never got a look at the driver's face, though my one glimpse of the driver's petite profile gave me the strong impression that it was a woman whose head barely showed above the back of the seat. I also jotted down the license plate number.

As soon as the car was out of sight, I started the engine. "Who do you suppose that could have been? And why would she have access to Allison's garage-door opener?"

Lauren massaged her temples and said evenly, "Maybe it was her sister, or whoever's the executor of her estate."

"Couldn't be a sister. Her parents were her only relatives at tonight's funeral."

"That *was* earlier tonight, wasn't it?" Lauren moaned. "This has been the world's longest twenty-four hours." She leaned back against the headrest, her brown hair fanning across the seat.

"We'll be home soon, and once we get there, I'll wait on you hand and foot. Whatever you want. A glass of wine, a dish of ice cream . . ."

"That's a nice offer, but your cupboards are still pretty bare. Tommy and I didn't buy you any wine. Or ice cream. All I want right now is a prefrontal lobotomy."

I chuckled and said sarcastically, "See? There you go, Lauren. '*I* didn't buy you any wine. *I* want a prefrontal lobotomy.' It's all just 'me, me, me' with you."

Lauren laughed and jabbed me on the shoulder.

Later that night, safe at home and in bed, I was wide-awake despite my exhaustion. Beside me, Jim was groaning in his sleep—his typical behavior when he's sick. Counting a spouse's groans apparently does not work as well as counting sheep. I finally gave up, crept downstairs, and checked on the puppy, who seemed to wake out of a sound sleep the instant I peered through her crate. I let her out for a minute, assuring her that she was a very good dog. She returned to her crate with just a few commands from me, and one small push.

I located my sketch pad. Inspired, no doubt, by my earlier musings about airbags, I drew a pair of old women in the front seat of a car that's been in a fender bender. The airbags have inflated. The face of the woman in the passenger seat is completely hidden by a plate with chunks of cake oozing down the sides. The driver is saying to her, "Why did you have to go and put my cake on the dashboard! Now it's ruined!"

Finally starting to nod off, I went back to bed. Maybe I could send my latest cartoon to the editor of the university press. It was totally irrelevant to her profession, of course, but surely editors drive cars.

"Mo-om!" Karen greeted me the next morning the instant I left my bedroom.

"Wha-at?" I replied, following the sound of her voice, which was coming from the children's bathroom. It took an inordinate amount of time for me to get there. Though the bathroom is only five steps from my bedroom, my muscles were staging an incredibly painful we-ain't-moving! protest after their aerobic workout the night before.

"Look!" she said, pointing at the portion of the floor hidden behind the open bathroom door.

I did as commanded and spotted her toothbrush, lying on its back against the wall. I picked it up for her. "Couldn't you bend over yourself to pick this up?"

"Every morning, I come in here, and my toothbrush is lying on that same exact spot!"

"Really? That must be rather annoying, unless, of course, you want to keep your toothbrush on the floor."

"No, Mom," Karen said in a near shout. "If I wanted to keep it there, I wouldn't be mad about it. Nathan's dropping *my* toothbrush on the floor *just* to bug me!"

"Ah. Well then, it would appear he's succeeded in his goal. But why are you yelling at *me*?"

"Because he's *your* son!"

"Yes, but it's *your* toothbrush. And, knowing Nathan, he's doing it because you aren't putting it away after you use it." Karen folded her arms and glared at the floor, furthering my suspicion that my hunch was correct. Nathan has always been something of a cantankerous neat freak. "So, all you have to do to stop him is to put your toothbrush away after brushing your teeth, which you should do anyway."

Karen stormed past me, crying, "I knew you wouldn't understand!" She slammed her door shut.

"Sweetie?" Jim, his voice still hoarse, called from downstairs. "Is everything all right?"

I left Karen to her pouting and gingerly descended the stairs before answering. I felt a hundred years old. I'd read in the paper recently that old people seldom catch colds. Maybe my body was so prematurely aged as to be immune to my husband's illness.

Jim was at the kitchen table, a bowl of Wheaties in front of him. Though truly a handsome man under normal circumstances, he was not wearing his sickness well. His eyelids were droopy and his nose red. He hadn't shaved. His sandy-colored hair was now mud colored and bore the worst case of bedhead I'd ever seen, sticking up in the back like an Indian headdress. In answer to his question, I said, "Our daughter is a preteen, Nathan's Nathan, and I'm older than germs. Everything's great."

"What does that mean?" Nathan piped up, seated at the table beside his father and eating a bowl of Lucky Charms.

Knowing which part of my remark he'd honed in on, I answered, "That you're one of a kind. It also means you shouldn't toss your sister's toothbrush on the floor."

He grinned.

With visions of him dropping it into the toilet tonight, I realized I should be specific. "You're not to drop her brush anywhere from now on, or you'll have to buy her a new one. It's none of your business if she forgets to put it away."

Nathan had a fit at the unfairness of the concept of having to buy his sister a new toothbrush and eventually stormed off to his room. Jim, watching all of this, met my eyes and smiled.

"Witness the Molly Masters Mothering Method," I said. "When in doubt, tick off your entire family."

"I'm not mad at you."

"It's not even nine A.M. Give it time."

Despite his ill health, Jim launched into a series of questions regarding how much I knew about the status of the police investigation. I had few answers for him, but I did gloss over an account of last night's sauna incident, saying, "Lauren and I got locked in there for a few minutes till the manager let us out." I tried to sandwich that account between tales of my horror at how unpleasant this group of women was—which, since one of them was a murderer, was not much of a stretch.

Jim, however, immediately leaped onto one particular phrase. "What do you mean you were 'locked in' the sauna?"

"Somebody locked the door and we knocked on it until Julie opened it and let us out, so we called the police. By the way, has Tommy—"

"How long were you locked in there? Weren't there any controls on the inside?"

"I don't know and, no, there weren't."

"You could have been killed! Why didn't you wake me up

last night? Just when were you planning on telling me about this?"

I sighed and glanced at my watch. "See? Now you're ticked off at me, too, and not even five minutes have passed."

Lauren emerged from the downstairs guest room, her complexion blotchy and her eyes puffy, obviously from crying. She mustered a reasonably cheerful, "Good morning," which both Jim and I returned.

Jim, seemingly oblivious to her current emotional state, immediately said, "Molly was just telling me about what happened to you last night."

"It was harrowing, but fortunately, we were only trapped in there for—" She glanced at me where I was standing behind Jim's chair. I spread the fingers of one hand, and she continued smoothly "—five or ten minutes. We maintained our dignity throughout. Wouldn't you say, Molly?"

"Oh, absolutely. We kept both our dignity and our decorum. Just lost some sweat. And," I quickly added with enthusiasm, having come up with a positive spin for Jim's sake, "now the police know there's someone besides me doing these evil acts. They know I couldn't have locked myself in that sauna."

I let that sink in for a moment, but if Jim was relieved or impressed by this announcement, he didn't show it. He merely polished off his bowl of Wheaties without comment.

"I don't suppose I slept through the sound of the phone ringing," Lauren said to me, her eyes pleading.

"Shouldn't *you* call Tommy?" I answered. "He did try to see you at the health club, after all." By my book, that was a definite: Tag. You're it.

Lauren merely poured herself a cup of coffee and slumped into the seat across from Jim. "Just because I've delayed the wedding a couple of times doesn't mean I don't want to marry him. Honestly. Here we are, stuck in Colorado, your friend Allison gets killed in our midst, and all he cares about is our wedding date." She glared at Jim. "You men seem to think you're the only ones who have any reason to fear making a commitment. I've been a single mom for three years now. I know all about responsibility and commitment. Just because I wanted to wait a while doesn't mean I never intend to marry him, now does it?"

"Er, no." Jim rose. "You're absolutely right." He gave us a wan smile. "I'm going to go take a shower and get cleaned up." He left the room with purposeful strides. I very much doubted that he had even the slightest idea of what Lauren was talking about, and probably didn't even know that Tommy was staying at a hotel after their argument.

Lauren merely sat there, staring into her cup, forgetting that the point of having a cup of coffee was to drink it. Her expression reminded me of Tommy's face last night and broke my heart. It was never a good idea to meddle in another couple's relationship. Then again, *never* might be a tad strong. After having inadvertently gotten between her and her boyfriend in high school, I actually owed it to Lauren to help patch up one relationship for her. Besides, I couldn't stand to see two people I cared so much about making each other so unhappy.

"Lauren? I happen to know that, here in Colorado, you don't need blood tests for marriage licenses. You can head down to the justice center with a couple of witnesses, get your certificate, locate a judge, and do it all in one fell swoop."

Lauren shot me a furious glare.

"I'm just saying you could have a quick civil ceremony here and then have the wedding of your dreams when . . ." Lauren was clenching her jaw so hard I was afraid her teeth would break if I continued. "I've often wondered where the expression 'fell swoop' comes from," I muttered. "Probably has something to do with birds dying in midflight."

Rachel finally came down to the kitchen, looking groggy. "Hi, Rach," I said. "Is there anything I can do to anger you? I'm

four-for-four right now and I may as well try for a clean sweep."
Rachel merely eyed me suspiciously. In truth, I'd already succeeded in annoying myself into self-imposed silence.

I thought I'd be in for a peaceful afternoon. Karen and
Rachel had been invited to a friend's house down the street. I'd
miscalculated that this left nobody for Nathan to argue with.

However, within a few hours, I'd learned that my having acquired Betty Cocker was a lot like having obtained a second
Nathan. While underneath it all they were both sweeties, it
seemed as though I spent most of the day admonishing one or
the other of them for playing too rough, making too much noise,
or growling at the other. Nathan followed BC around and
grabbed her snout to yank everything she chewed on out of her
mouth. This was a constant avocation, as the puppy was willing
to chew on anything, except the dog biscuits Celia had given us.

In the meantime, Jim was zoned out on TV. Lauren had spent
hours now pretending to read a magazine, but she seldom even
flipped pages. She was lost in her own sorrow while waiting for
Tommy to call. I brainstormed for ideas for my lone job—the
editor of the university press—but was literally "drawing"
blanks.

By mid afternoon, I desperately needed a break and faxed de-
scriptions of all the various cartoons I'd worked on for the last
few days to the potential client. I'd read somewhere that sore
muscles were the result of lactic acid buildup and that, therefore, the best way to ease your pain was light exercise. This was
the same hair-of-the-dog theory that could keep alcoholics
going for years, but at least it was a course of action. Lauren—
go figure—declined my invitation to go for a walk. Jim was
still too ill to join me, and Nathan and BC too involved in a tug-
of-war game.

It occurred to me that I might as well head through Allison's
neighborhood. Maybe then I could bump into Lois or Celia and

find out whether they'd talked to the police about my getting locked in the sauna.

The weather was lovely—cloudless sky, bright but not too hot. It was slightly more than a mile to Allison's house. My muscles were having quite a scream over the concept that any of this was actually going to ease my pain. Each step felt as though I were dragging an anvil. It was remarkable how many muscle groups I'd managed to injure. Even blinking was painful.

I reached the street, wishing I'd simply cut through Allison's backyard. Her house looked completely deserted now. Next door, Lois's front windows and door were open. There was no sign of her, though. Up ahead, Celia was out in her yard, tending to her flower beds. In this bright sunlight, her frosted and teased hair had a cotton-candy sheen. How strange that her heavy makeup never seemed to change, even when she was home alone. She spotted me and leaped to her feet. "Molly! I can't believe you're actually out here! The police came and rang my doorbell last night at an outrageous hour. By the sound of it, someone tried to kill you!"

"Yes, that's true. But I'm fine now."

"What are you doing, walking here all by yourself? If it were me, I wouldn't ever leave the house."

Which is exactly how the killer would want me to act, I thought. "Tell me something, Celia. Late last night someone drove out of Allison's garage. Do you have any idea who that might have been?"

She pursed her lips and shook her head. "That doesn't make any sense."

"Nevertheless, that's what I saw. It was a white Toyota Corolla. An older make." I knew very little about cars, except for those brands I happened to own myself, which was the case now.

"Oh." Celia's eyes widened. "I wonder if that could have been Allison's housekeeper, Maria Chavez. That sounds like her car, anyway. But she wouldn't park in Allison's garage, surely. And what time was this? Weren't you locked in a sauna?"

"It was around midnight."

"I wonder if she's living there. I think I remember that Allison had said something about letting Maria live in for a couple of weeks. But I can't recall for certain. And, surely, now that Allison is dead, Maria shouldn't be there." Celia looked as if her mind was elsewhere. "How do you like my lupines?" She gently brushed her gloved fingertips along a tall hyacinth-like flower.

If she was trying to change the subject for some reason, that wasn't much of an attempt. Her lack of concern about her immediate neighbors struck me as odd. If the victim of an unsolved murder had been living one house down from me, I'd sure want to know why her housekeeper was apparently coming and going at will. "So you think it's possible that Maria's been living two doors down from you, but you don't know for sure?"

Celia gave a little shrug. "Lois's property blocks any view of Allison's house from mine. Yet, I must say, I've never seen any trace of Maria for the last few weeks."

At the sound of a badly tuned engine, I turned, and last night's dented car drove in front of us. "That's the car now," I said.

"Oh, yes," Celia said, waving at a Hispanic woman behind the wheel. "That's Maria, all right."

I watched for Celia's reaction, but she gave none. If uneasy or surprised at Maria's coincidental arrival, Celia was doing a good job of masking it. Was Celia truly apathetic about Allison's housekeeper's comings and goings, or was Celia hiding something? Perhaps it was basic paranoia on my part, but I suspected the latter.

Celia excused herself, saying she had a phone call to make. Maria had parked in Allison's driveway and entered through the front door. She had the garage-door opener in her possession as of midnight. But perhaps she didn't want Celia and other neighbors to see her drive into the garage as if she owned Allison's house. My curiosity was such that I dashed over there as quickly as my aching legs could move. At the very least, even if Maria Chavez was unwilling to speak with me, I could ask to go through the backyard for a shortcut home.

I rang the doorbell and smiled at the attractive, bright-eyed woman who answered the door. "Hello," I said, "My name is Molly Masters. I was a friend of Allison Kenyon's. Could I speak to you for just a minute?"

She gave me a puzzled smile and said, *"No comprendo. ¿Habla usted español?"*

"No, I don't. Do you speak any English at all?"

She shrugged and shook her head, emphasizing our language gulf by rattling off something that I couldn't understand.

Using gestures, such as walking fingers and pointing, I asked, "Could I cut through the lawn to get to the road?"

Maria giggled, said, *"Sí, Señora. Buenos días,"* and went inside.

I let myself in through the gate, though that was almost more trouble than it was worth. The fence was a two rail with a wire mesh attached that I could easily step over. Why would a housecleaner come here at least twice, several days after her client's death? How much cleaning could there possibly be? Maybe she was living here through the end of the month, despite Allison's death. If so, why hadn't she gone to the funeral to pay her respects?

Allison's lawn, a good half an acre or so in size, had been mowed recently, cared for as if nothing had happened. Her housekeeper was apparently coming and going at will. It was as if the house and property were the living body, and Allison had only been the tonsils.

I froze at a sound behind me. It sounded like the growl of a dog or a wolf. I turned slowly. Two Dobermans were on Allison's back deck. Their front paws were on the edge of the deck. The dogs looked all set to spring at me.

"Oh, shit," I said under my breath, my heart racing in abject terror. "Nice doggies. Stay." I tried to back away as smoothly as possible. I had a considerable distance to go till I made it to the road. Even then there was nothing to protect me from getting mauled. Except oncoming traffic.

The dogs watched me take one or two backward steps, then charged. I screamed, whirled around, and ran for my life.

Chapter 12

I Fold

I made it to a tree and swung myself up into it in one motion born out of desperation. I was hanging like a possum, my legs and arms wrapped tightly around the branch. The dogs were leaping at me, growling and snapping.

I could feel their hot breath against the back of my neck. One dog's leap and snap almost got hold of my hair. I pressed my cheek against the bark of the branch and tried to pull myself higher. All I had going for me was that their barks were making a ferocious racket.

The noise had roused Allison's housekeeper, thank God. She screamed to me in Spanish. I could only see her in the corner of my vision. She was standing on the edge of the deck, her hands to her face, screaming. She made no move to charge out and grab the dogs or to go inside to call for help.

I shouted back to her, "Call nine-one-one!" Oh, damn! Why had I taken German instead of Spanish! "Uh . . . *nunez-uno-uno!*"

I couldn't hang on for more than a minute or two. The police would never get here in time.

"No, wait! Call Julie Murphy. Hulie Murphy!"

I tried to turn my head enough to see if Maria had gotten to the phone, but couldn't. Shit! Maria probably didn't know who Julie was. Celia, one door down, didn't even know if Maria was living here!

Rough tree bark pressed against my skin. I clung to the branch for all I was worth, my eyes shut tight. I was afraid to move, even to breathe. My arms and legs already ached with exertion. The dogs barked and snapped their strong jaws, leaping to within inches of my flesh.

My mind seemed to go into a semiconscious state as I clutched the branch. My body was trembling so much, the entire tree seemed to be shaking. The Dobermans' growls and barks grew ever louder. In my mind's eye, their teeth grew longer and sharper as well.

If only I hadn't exercised so much yesterday, I might have had more stamina. Damn! The one time I do something "healthy," and it could cost me my life. I told myself that I could lock my elbows and knees into this position and stay here for as long as it took. However, with a pair of dog jaws drooling for me, I was also saying my prayers.

A minute or an eternity later, I heard a woman's voice from the direction of Allison's house scream my name. Julie, I thought. She hollered, "Peek-a-boo! Tammy! Drop!"

Just like that, the commotion below me ceased. I risked enough movement to allow myself a quick look down. The Dobermans were lying on their tummies, panting sheepishly at Julie, who was fast approaching with a pair of leashes.

"Bad dogs!" she said.

Yeah, bad dogs, I thought, trying not to whimper with exhaustion. Eviscerating me for walking across someone else's yard was a definite no-no! My shoulders felt as though they were about to disconnect. If I let go now, I'd fall right on top of the dogs. A pair of metallic clicks let me know that Julie had snapped the leashes onto their collars.

"You can come down now, Molly."

I tried to loosen my grip with my legs and realized my arms no longer had the strength to support my body even momentarily. "Not without falling flat on my back, I can't."

"Oh, gosh. Just a moment." Julie slipped the loops of the leather leashes over a metal stake supporting a nearby sapling, then ran over and held my shoulders while I swung myself down. The pain from my change of position was so great I groaned.

"Molly, I am so sorry. Somebody must have deliberately opened the gate and let the dogs out. I happened to look out my window at the gate not fifteen minutes ago, and it was closed tight then."

Standing straight up required an enormous effort; my arms and legs wanted to stay locked in place. Every muscle in my body was trembling. It felt like a one-person earthquake. I glanced over at the dogs, lying on the grass a short distance away, looking at me with indifference. They seemed perfectly docile now. "What were they doing in Allison's yard?"

"They must have leaped Allison's fence, but I can't begin to guess why. They've never even been on this side of the road before. And I've never seen them attack someone like this, either. You weren't teasing them, were you?"

"Of course not!" My emotions teetered between terror and rage. "I was simply trying to walk across Allison's lawn!" I took a couple of calming breaths. Having those dogs watch me and their owner from such a short distance away, however, was good motivation to keep my temper in check. "I don't . . ." I paused and lowered my voice. "How the hell did this happen?"

"I'm sorry," Julie said again. "It's just that I'm so . . . surprised."

"I was outside talking to Celia in front of her house just a few minutes ago, and I walked right down your street to get there. The dogs had to have already been on Allison's deck by then, or they must have crossed the street just after I'd passed your house."

"I can't believe they did this," Julie said, shaking her head, her eyes brimming. "I've lived with these dogs for three years now, and they've never tried to hurt anybody. They're really gentle dogs."

"Gentle? They were trying to maul me!" I studied her youthful, pretty face. She shrank back at my words, staring at me as if afraid of what I'd do to her. By all appearances, she was as horrified as I was. "Well, it seems as though you've saved my life twice in less than twenty-four hours. Thanks." Odd, though, that both times I'd been in jeopardy thanks to her: the sauna in her gym and now her husband's dogs. Was that really just a coincidence?

Lois trotted up to the fence along her property, her stiff-legged gait hinting at serious knee troubles. Perhaps she had strained a muscle last night. She hadn't had much trouble moving around during aerobics. "Julie, Molly. What in God's name is going on out here?"

"Somebody let my husband's dogs out of the fence, and they were in Allison's yard. They chased Molly up a tree."

To my severe annoyance, Lois chuckled. Despite the heat, she was still wearing her basic black sweat suit, on to which was fastened the bluebird pin that Allison had given me. Her dark hair had been pulled back into a tight ponytail.

"Where's the woman who cleans Allison's house?" I asked Julie, doing my best to ignore Lois, who'd climbed over the fence and was approaching us gleefully. "Is she still inside?"

"Maria? She drove off while I was running over here."

"What's all the commotion?" Celia cried, rushing through Lois's yard.

Where the hell was everybody while I was clinging to a tree branch for my life?

"Julie's dogs chased Molly up a tree," Lois announced, still smiling.

I watched Lois out of the corner of my vision, hoping the Dobermans would at least growl at her. Instead, they were sitting at attention and eyeing her, their stubby tails wagging, as if expecting her to toss them a treat. "Did Maria call you?" I asked, again directing my attention only to Julie.

"Yes. She just said, 'Come get your dogs right away. They've chased a skinny lady up Allison's tree.'"

"But . . . she doesn't speak English," I protested in confusion.

"Maria Chavez?" Lois said to me. "She speaks better English than me."

"Apparently so," Celia said with a haughty toss of her lacquered coiffure, "since proper grammar is 'better than *I*.'"

"Oh, yeah?" Lois said. "Well, there are a lot of things that *are* better than you, Celia, *including* proper grammar."

Julie retrieved the dogs' leashes and said briskly, "If I don't hurry, I'm going to be late for my next class at the gym." My impression was that she mainly wanted to get away from Lois and Celia and their brewing confrontation as quickly as possible.

Meanwhile, Celia's attention was focused solely on Lois. Celia gaped, putting her hands on her hips. "Why, I never—"

"Good," Lois snapped. "I don't care if you never. Just get out of my yard!"

Celia crossed her arms. "I'll leave your yard as soon as you leave Allison's."

"Oh, yeah? Who died and appointed you caretaker?"

"Allison did, as a matter of fact! She admired my gardening talents! The least I could do was maintain it until the estate is settled. She was my dearest friend!"

"Like hell she was. You just lusted after her husband!" Lois started marching toward Celia.

Celia did a remarkable job of backing up at exactly the same pace. "I did not! You're the one who 'lusts' after Allison's business partner! I had no interest in Richard whatsoever. We were just good friends!"

By the time Lois was to the fence that separated her property from Allison's, Celia was halfway back to her own yard.

"Cut the crap!" Lois snapped. "Friends, my ass! Who do you think you're fooling?"

"Whom," Celia said triumphantly, then turned and kept going toward her own property, nose in the air.

I watched all of this in stunned silence. I'd always assumed my children would outgrow their immature squabbling. Here were two women in their forties acting like four-year-olds.

At the fence, Lois stopped and turned toward me. "Are you all right now, Molly?"

I was surprised she even remembered I existed. I looked at my skinned calves and forearms. "I'm fine. Um, thanks for asking."

Lois stepped awkwardly over the fence, saying, "All the same, come over to my house and we'll dress those scratches for you."

I hesitated, the thought of being with Lois unappealing. However, this would be a rare opportunity to talk to the woman alone. Physically, I was not up for climbing over the short fence and told Lois I'd ring her doorbell.

Maria Chavez's car, I noted as I reached the front yard, was gone. Her bolting under these circumstances gave me all the more cause to suspect that her reasons for being in Allison Kenyon's house weren't aboveboard. My getting mauled by dogs would likely have led to her having to explain her presence to the authorities.

Lois's house and its extraordinary electrical system were still impressive on second visit. I assured her I could minister to my own injuries, if she could just provide the supplies. She sat on the fuzzy black toilet-seat cover and watched as I swabbed my minor scratches with alcohol.

"Has Maria Chavez been living in Allison's house for long?" I asked in a matter-of-fact voice.

Without hesitation, Lois said, "She's *not* living there."

"But I saw her drive out of Allison's garage late last night."

Lois nodded. "I spotted her there, too, just after the funeral. In fact, I called to ask what she was doing. She claimed to be closing up the house, on Allison's behalf. That sounded reasonable enough. I hadn't stopped to wonder about why her car wasn't in the driveway, though."

"Because she didn't want the neighbors to see it there at that hour," I said. "Which still leads me to suspect she has another reason for being there, late at night, which she's keeping secret. Do you know much about her?"

"Not a thing, except Allison raved about her and obviously trusted her. And, again, that she speaks good English."

"Do you know how Allison found her?" I asked, hoping Lois would name some service company that I could simply call up and inquire about her.

"No idea," she answered. Beneath those thick eyebrows of hers, Lois's dark eyes were fastened right on mine. Unlike my earlier, similar conversation with Celia, I was certain she was telling me the whole truth.

"I saw your son, Max, at Allison's funeral," I said, testing her reaction. "He's very handsome."

"Yes," she said through a tight jaw. "Allison thought so, too. As you've no doubt heard by now."

"That must have been awful. I have no idea how I'd handle it if a friend of mine were to . . . form an attachment to my teenage son."

"That's right," she snapped. "You don't know. You couldn't possibly know. I was so mad, I wanted to—" She broke off, then began again, "The truth is, there was a time when I used to lie awake at night, plotting ways to kill her. That is, when I wasn't busy being barraged with images of Allison and my son together. But I didn't kill her. Did try my damnedest to seduce her husband, though. Seems his dance card was overflowing."

"With Celia, you mean?"

Lois laughed and nodded her head. "Celia had the hots for

Richard the very first day she and her husband moved into the neighborhood. That's what drove Celia's husband away, in fact. They didn't last six months here, and, boom, he moved out. Never saw him again. Moved to Michigan, I think."

"Did Allison know about Celia's crush on Richard?"

"How could she *not* know? 'Course, it's not as if there was anything she could do about it. They didn't exactly have an equal opportunity marriage. That's probably what drove her to my Max . . . her urge to get good and even with Richard, I mean. What better revenge against an estranged husband than making it with the kid next door?"

That was one rhetorical question I hoped to never experience the answer to for myself: the you-hurt-me-so-I'll-hurt-you-even-worse game that all too many bad marriages seemed to deteriorate into. I was curious as to how this romance between Max and Allison could have developed. "You home-schooled Max, didn't you?"

"Once he hit his teen years, I sure did. I wanted to keep him away from high school students' preoccupation with drugs and sex." The pride that was obvious in her voice faded as she scoffed and shook her head. "Lot of good that did. He had all that extra time to hang out with the neighbors. Pretty ironic, wouldn't you say? I'd made an arrangement with Allison. She'd agreed to tutor him in science in exchange for his doing yard work. So I brought 'em together."

"He wound up living there, didn't he?"

She pursed her lips and nodded. "Max and I were having a few spats. Just typical family problems. Nothing we couldn't have eventually resolved, if only Allison had kept her butt out of the picture."

She spoke with so much rancor, it was hard to believe she hadn't had a hand in Allison's death. I also couldn't get over the image of the way the dogs had looked at her, as if awaiting a reward for performing their task. If Lois had let them out of the fence . . . Then again, surely she couldn't have guessed I was going to cut through Allison's yard to get back home.

"Where does your son live now?"

"He's eighteen. Thinks he's an adult. He's got a small apartment on Walnut." After a pause, Lois said, "If I had it all to do over again, I'd still home-school. At least I know I'm a decent person with wholesome family values. Take Katherine, for example. She's still teaching, despite her past."

"Despite what past?"

She gave me a sly grin, her thick eyebrows drawn together. "Ah, so you *don't* know everyone's deepest secrets, after all." The smile turned into a snarl, and she added, "Just mine."

"I barely know anything about Katherine. Even less about Nancy. What did Katherine do?"

Lois winced a little as she rose. "Damned trick knee," she muttered. "You wouldn't have to ask, if you'd known Allison better. Katherine told her in confidence, but, of course, she blabbed about it to everyone. You'll just have to find out about it on your own. Maybe that'll make you keep your nose out of my affairs."

Damn! She'd been forthcoming during our conversation. Now all of a sudden, she seemed to resent my questions, even though she was the one who brought up Katherine's past.

She started to walk out, then hesitated at the bathroom doorway. "You're not going to keep assisting Joe, are you?"

"No, I'm not. I seem to keep myself plenty busy, between getting locked in saunas and chased by Dobermans."

She put her hands on her ample hips and studied me, slowly smiling. "The police came by here last night. You *have* been having a bit of a bad time of it in Colorado, haven't you? Has it ever occurred to you that maybe it's time for you to leave?"

She didn't wait for my response, which would have been rife with four-letter words. She merely turned on a heel and left the room.

I caught sight of my reflection in the bathroom mirror and scared myself. My hair was tangled, the rough tree bark had rubbed one cheek raw, my eyes were bloodshot. "That's it. I fold," I murmured to myself, wondering what madman had dealt me these cards in the first place.

A cartoon about poker occurred to me. Maybe, if I never came up with any good ideas for the university press editor, she'd be into poker and would go for this one. Four people, their eyes tightly closed, are sitting around a table. In the center of the table is a deck of cards and four chips. Three of the people say, "I fold." The fourth thinks: Drat! And I had three aces! That's going to be my only good hand all night! The caption reads: *Psychics playing poker.*

I limped out of the bathroom. Lois Tucker was sitting in her living room. To my utter surprise, she was crying quietly, tears running down her cheeks.

Chapter 13

Violets are Purple. Hence the Name

Feeling awkward at witnessing the normally combative Lois's fragile emotional state, I pretended I hadn't noticed. I headed for the door as fast as my sore, injured legs would take me, saying, "Thanks for . . . the antiseptic. I'll let myself out."

"What the hell am I supposed to do now? I love my son. I also love a married man. Neither of them thinks I'm worth crossing the street for. I gave up everything to raise my boy to the best of my ability. And I was a good mother, Molly. Now he's turned his back on me. He won't even let me know his address or phone number."

Unable to think of a better response, I suggested, "Couldn't you go back to work?"

She tsked and rolled her eyes. "Oh, right. I'm sure the world of high tech is chomping at the bit to hire a forty-three-year-old first line manager. It's fortunate that, between my husband's life-insurance payoff and investments, I don't need to work to survive." She crossed her thick arms. "It was so much better and easier when Allison was alive. Then I had somebody else to blame. And to hate."

"Lois, take it from a woman who's just been chased up a tree. Hang in there long enough, and things will turn around for you."

Before she could give some demoralizing response, I

reached the front door and said, "Good-bye, Lois. I've got to head home." And hug my children.

Having lost my eagerness for shortcuts, I left by the front door and started walking down the block. At the end of Lois's front walk, I did a double take at a sedan. The driver was either Professor Katherine Lindstrom or someone who happened to have an identical short auburn bob.

Had Katherine seen me talking in Celia's front yard and let the dogs out, hoping that they would attack me? That was such a stretch. Nobody could have guessed my decision to take a shortcut through Allison's yard and beat me there with the dogs. Only Julie could have controlled those dogs that well—and she was either a very good actress or innocent. Maybe it was just a case of bad luck on my part.

A car was slowing down right behind me. My heart started thumping. It was either an old friend who'd spotted me or, with my luck, some maniac who would be aiming an Uzi at my head.

The car pulled up beside me. "Moll," a familiar male voice called, "get in."

I sighed with relief. Tommy, in his rental Escort, was gesturing at me. I gladly eased myself into the passenger seat. "Where were you half an hour ago when I needed you?"

"Uh-oh," Tommy muttered. "Been gettin' yourself in a fix again?"

"I was nearly eaten alive by Dobermans."

He sighed, then signaled and pulled the car onto the shoulder. He set the emergency brake, turned to me, and said, "Come again?"

"I was taking a shortcut across Allison's yard, and Julie's Dobermans were there—Julie says somebody opened her gate and let them out—and I had to climb a tree. I might never be able to—"

"Is Lauren okay?"

"Lauren?" I repeated irritably. "She's at my place, waiting

for you to call. Not to be self-obsessed or anything, but somebody's trying to kill me! That is, when they're not busy trying to frame me for murder. I could use some help, you know."

Tommy blew out a slow breath. "What all do you need?"

"A bodyguard, for one thing. I also need to know more about Katherine Lindstrom. Apparently she's got a shady past."

Tommy nodded. "I had my people back in Carlton run some background checks on all the suspects. Your English lit professor used to teach at some little-known university in Massachusetts. Her name was Katherine Bennington then."

"Is it true that she used to be married to Julie Murphy's brother?"

He nodded. "Bennington was his last name. Thing is, though, she legally changed her name to Lindstrom. Prob'ly because of her criminal record. Seems your professor had quite a drug problem."

That was a surprise. She had such stuffy, affected mannerisms, it was hard to imagine she was once a druggie. And, come to think of it, this was the second time someone was said to have had a drug problem. Professor Katherine herself had claimed *Allison* had a substance-abuse problem. "So she has a criminal record as Katherine Bennington, I take it?"

He nodded again. "She was into heroin."

"My God. How could she get hired at C.U. with that kind of a track record?"

"Hard to say. My guess is she got herself cleaned up and maybe pulled some strings."

"I'm pretty certain I saw Katherine Lindstrom drive by here just a minute ago. She could have been in the neighborhood, spotted me, and tried to feed me to Julie's dogs."

Tommy swiped a dot of perspiration off his brow. "Or, more likely, it don't mean diddly. She lives just off Forty-seventh."

I glanced over my shoulder in the direction of Forty-seventh

Street, trying to get my bearings. This had been a possible route for her to take back to her house, though not a direct one.

"What makes you suspect her?" he asked.

"If I had to give my best guess right now as to who locked Lauren and me in that sauna last night, I'd say Katherine. We'd just exchanged words, and she implied I should watch myself, or else."

"Implied it?"

"Yes. I don't recall her exact words, but there was a lot of menace there, believe me."

"And we gotta figure that the person who locked you in there also killed your friend. Right?"

"Right." I'd answered automatically but now stopped to reconsider. "Actually, I wouldn't want to risk my life on that assumption." A shiver went down my spine at the thought of how close I'd come to having a Doberman's jaw chomping me. "The thing is, we know whoever killed Allison also tried to frame me. Yet I'm not as viable a suspect now that the police know somebody locked me in that sauna. So it's possible someone other than Allison's killer wants me dead. But that's a real stretch. My greeting card retreat wasn't *that* bad."

"Depends on how many of your lectures they had to sit through," Tommy said. "Tryin' to off you while the police are investigating a murder would be unbelievably stupid, though."

"People do stupid things all the time. Such as insulting the best friend of the loved one you're currently on the skids with."

He winced.

"I'm sorry. I wouldn't tease you about Lauren, except that I'm absolutely certain things will work out between you two."

He gave me a subject-is-closed glower. "So you have no idea who could've killed Allison, right?"

"Right. But I do know this: Lois is slightly wacko and hated Allison for sleeping with her son, yet she also hoards things that belonged to Allison. Lois claims that Allison blabbed to her about something shady in Katherine Lindstrom's past, maybe about her drug use. Katherine's grad assistant warned me to stay away from Katherine, because she has a tendency to destroy her competition." I cleared my throat, and went on with what else I knew about my greeting card retreatees. "Celia Wentworth used to be head-over-heels for Richard, Allison's late ex-husband. She could have killed Allison to avenge his death. Julie and Nancy don't seem to have any motive, but Julie keeps popping up in the nick of time, so there could be something there I haven't discovered yet."

We sat in silence, then Tommy said, "Glad to see that, once again, you're keepin' a low profile 'n' allowin' the police to do their jobs."

"Hey, you asked me if I knew who did it. I'm just giving you a complete answer."

Tommy released the parking brake. "Tell you what. I'll drop you off at home and go pay Katherine Lindstrom a visit."

"She's only met you once. She won't even talk to you."

"Good point. May as well stay out of this."

"Look, Tommy. We both know I'm going to talk to Katherine. So why don't you save us both a lot of grief and take me with you now?"

After some lame protestations, Tommy pulled over again. He whipped out a notepad onto which he'd scribbled addresses and phone numbers, and a cellular phone, which he explained he had rented yesterday. He claimed our incident in the mountains had convinced him to do so, but I'm sure his suddenly finding himself operating from a hotel room had something to do with the decision as well.

Tommy dialed, and a moment later said, "Ms. Lindstrom? This is Sergeant Tommy Newton, Molly's friend from New York." After a pause, he said, "No, she's fine now." Again, he listened, smiled, and said, "You have no idea. In fact, she's had another incident. She's asked me to lend her some professional expertise. I was hoping we could stop by and ask you a couple questions." Tommy then went on to say "Uh-huh" three times, then thanked her, hung up, and pulled a U-turn to head toward Katherine's house.

"Aren't you going to call Lauren?" I asked.

"Maybe later. Not while I'm driving."

I snatched the phone and dialed my home. Jim answered, and I explained how I was with Tommy and would be home in an hour or so; then I asked for Lauren. As soon as she was on the line, I said, "I'm on a cell phone in Tommy's car."

"What are you doing in his car?"

"He ran into me on my walk. Not literally, though. I think he was circling the house, looking for you."

Tommy glared at me. I gave her the number, with the excuse that she may need to reach me, though I secretly hoped it would be Tommy she would need to reach.

"Where are you going?" Lauren asked.

"He's taking me over to Katherine Lindstrom's house, though I didn't exactly tell Jim that, in so many words."

"How is Tommy? Never mind. You can't answer with him sitting right there."

"He's fine. Want to talk to him yourself?"

"No!"

She spoke so loud I know Tommy heard, but I hung up and said, "She's busy right now."

We were soon at Katherine's house, a new townhouse just east of town. She escorted us into the living room portion of what real estate agents call a "great room." It was really only so-so. The upholstery complemented her teal carpeting. I'd pictured her as living in a small house on the Hill, furnished solely with antiques, but I'd been completely off. Not a single piece of furniture appeared to have been made more than five years ago.

Katherine had a full glass of iced tea on the wrought-iron-

and-smoked-glass coffee table in front of her. She offered us some, but we both declined. Though I was thirsty, I'd decided to set a blanket policy of not ingesting anything that came from a suspect's kitchen.

"Am I to gather," Katherine began in a breathy, William F. Buckley affectation, "that the two of you are here because you are presupposing I had something to do with Molly's recent mishaps?"

Tommy immediately asked, "Can you tell me 'bout your whereabouts at two-thirty this afternoon?"

"I was grocery shopping at King Soopers. Was that when Molly had her latest—as you put it to me over the phone—'incident'?"

Tommy evaded the question and asked, "What route did you take home?"

With a tone that clearly portrayed she thought we were ignoramuses, she gave us her exact course, which did indeed cut through Julie's canines' neighborhood.

"That's a rather circuitous route," I said, then shuddered—I was starting to sound like Katherine. I'd meant to say, Whatcha go that way for?

She took a long drink of tea, peering over the rim at me. "Perhaps, but there are fewer traffic lights. Does my choice of roads comprise the entire content of your interrogation, or is there something else that's puzzling you?"

"We know about your drug history," I said.

She returned her glass to its coaster. Only the slightest stiffness in her manner hinted that my question had caught her unaware. "I'm sure I have no idea to what you are referring."

"You served three months in a halfway house in Boston while using the name Katherine Bennington," Tommy stated. "Did you tell the Boulder police about your record?"

"Yes, though I had been led to believe that a press release to that effect was not imminent. Where, pray tell, did you hear this?"

"Like I said, Molly here asked me to lend my expertise. Ran my own background checks on everybody in Molly's workshop."

Katherine gave her short auburn hair a shake before leaning back in her chair. "This is, you realize, thoroughly irrelevant to Allison's death. If you must know, I was arrested a number of years ago for possession of heroin with intent to sell. My colleagues at the university are fully aware of that regrettable transgression, as are the police. Those professionals, apparently unlike yourselves, realize a lot of people do foolish things in their youth. They felt I deserved a second chance, and I daresay I have more than exceeded their expectations."

"You told Allison about this, too?" I asked.

"I don't recall whom I told or did not tell. Rest assured, however, that Boulder is a small town in terms of how quickly news of a personal nature spreads." She pursed her lips and narrowed her eyes at me. "Don't you have anything in your past of which you are now ashamed?"

"Sure. I have things in my present I'm ashamed of."

On the surface, her story sounded reasonable. Yet, why would her first response to me have been to deny her drug history if she didn't care who knew about it? Also, why hadn't Julie—her ex-sister-in-law—mentioned this to me? When I'd told her I suspected Katherine of locking me in the sauna last night, Julie had said only nice things about her.

"I didn't realize you and Julie were once sisters-in-law," I said.

She pursed her lips. "That marriage was, in many ways, a much greater mistake than the error that led to my arrest. In fact, Julie furnished me with my drug supplier."

I gave Tommy, sitting beside me on the couch, a quick

glance. He seemed content to listen to Katherine and me. "We're talking about Julie *Murphy*, right?"

She chuckled without humor. "You sound surprised. Is it because Julie's such a fitness freak that you can't picture her having once had such an unhealthy habit?"

I shrugged.

"Rest assured, Molly, Julie is not as squeaky clean as she now appears. When I met her, she was not only a user, but turning tricks in Boston Common."

This caught me so off guard, my surprise must have been obvious. Katherine smiled at my reaction. She snatched up her iced tea and swirled the cubes before taking a sip. "She's come a long way. I could make a joke about her breeding bitches, but I'll refrain."

There was that *bitches* word again. I felt sure Katherine was lying. "According to Lois, you're the one with the shady past, not Julie."

Katherine studied my face for a moment, then slowly smiled. "Only because I am so much better at respecting Julie's right to privacy than she is mine. She was the black sheep of her family—not bright enough to hold down much of a job, but attractive enough for that not to matter. She worked for a dating service after high school, and one thing led to another. My former husband and I took her in and helped her get a fresh start. However, right at that time, I started having serious health problems and was in a lot of pain. Shortly thereafter, at the age of twenty-six, I learned that I had breast cancer. I had a radical mastectomy. My husband was repulsed and left me, but Julie stayed on. There I was, in physical and emotional anguish. And there she was, with ready access to feel-good drugs."

Beside me, Tommy made a quick scribble in his notebook but remained silent. This seemed too elaborate a story for Katherine to concoct. Yet I'd seen her wearing nothing but a towel last night and had not noticed anything unusual about her breasts. Not that I'd been looking.

"At the time of my arrest, I had purchased such a large quantity of heroin that the police drew the incorrect conclusion that I had intended to sell it. In truth, my intention was to overdose." She set her glass down and leaned forward to stare right into Tommy's eyes. "I made some terrible mistakes. I served my sentence and have paid my debt to society."

"How did Julie manage to get where she is now?" I asked. Katherine raised an eyebrow at me, and I explained, "How did she wind up here in a wealthy Boulder neighborhood, working as an aerobics instructor?"

"After my arrest, I agreed to keep her name out of my legal battles, but only if she would enroll herself in a detox clinic. I never saw her again, until we happened to bump into each other in Boulder, entirely by accident. We both vowed to start our relationship anew and never to speak of our sordid past. That, as you might have surmised, is a pledge that I have managed to keep until just now."

Tommy and I exchanged glances. I shrugged. He rose, and I followed suit. "Thank you for your time, Ms. Lindstrom," Tommy muttered.

"You're welcome." She opened the door for us. "Next time you wish to engage someone in an interrogation, Officer Newton, you might consider, as a matter of simple courtesy, identifying it as such first. Have a nice afternoon."

Much as it killed me to let her have the last word, I was unable to think of a snappy comeback. For one thing, it had been a very trying twenty-four hours, and for another thing, Katherine was right. We left quickly and got into Tommy's car without a word.

"What did you think?" I asked Tommy. "Do you believe her?"

He ran his fingers through his red hair. "Julie Murphy hasn't got as much as an unpaid parking ticket. That's more than unusual for a former hooker with a drug problem. S'pose it's possible, though."

What *I'd* been struck by was how haughty and unlikable Katherine was. "Have you noticed that all of these women are at least slightly off-kilter?"

"Figured that's what comes from hanging with you."

I rolled my eyes but, with effort, let the remark pass. "Do you happen to have Nancy Thornton's number? She's a therapist, after all. She might be willing to give us her professional opinion of these women's personalities. Either way," I added sarcastically, "heaven knows I'm depressed enough to visit a psychologist."

I scooped up the cell phone, and Tommy grudgingly looked up Nancy's office number for me. I told her only that I had some questions about our fellow retreat members.

There was a long pause. Finally Nancy answered, "I have very strict boundaries. I never accept friends as patients. I never discuss my patients with friends, nor vice versa."

I wasn't sure how my questions would fit in with her ground rules. "Okay. Can we just talk about Allison, as one friend of hers to another?"

After a pause, she replied, "That would be fine. Actually, I'm home this afternoon, so this would be a good time."

"Great." I glanced over at Tommy. "Just one thing, though. Would you mind if my friend Tommy Newton accompanied me?"

There was a long pause. "Yes, I would. I said I was willing to discuss Allison as one friend to another—not in front of a police officer."

"You're right. I shouldn't have asked."

She gave me her address on Fourth Street, which was right against the Foothills. Houses there tended to be small and old and rarely came on the market. When I hung up, Tommy grumbled, "What am I s'posed to do? Wait in the car?"

"I could probably catch a bus home."

"With your track record, it'd prob'ly run you over."

"So you'll wait for me? Thanks. I won't be long."

He parked on the street and I walked down her short gravel driveway. Her house was a ranch-style bungalow made of flagstone, with old nine-pane windows and a one-car garage. I rang the doorbell. She was wearing a black muumuu and sandals. My eyes were drawn to her glorious white hair. If I could go "gray" like that, I'd be thrilled, but judging from my mother's salt-and-pepper hair, I was unlikely to be as lucky. Furthermore, since I compulsively plucked out my white hairs, I expected to go gracefully *bald* instead.

Nancy swept me inside with a gracious welcome. Her house smelled of spices and dried flowers. We took seats in her sunroom in the back. I was just about to speak, when the sound of clawed footfalls on linoleum frightened me into silence. I turned and stared at the doorway as an enormous Great Dane loped into the room.

"Oh, great!" I cried. "A Dane!" and flattened myself against the back of my chair.

"That's Faldo," Nancy said. "Don't worry. He's perfectly harmless." Faldo stuck his huge snout in my face and sniffed.

"Maybe so, but I can see he's not toothless." I pushed myself all the harder into my seat.

Nancy snapped her fingers as she got up, and Faldo instantly stopped hogging what little remained of my personal oxygen supply to look at her. "And I can see he's scaring you. Come, Faldo." She opened the back door, and Faldo trotted outside.

Through the window, I watched as a squirrel caught sight of the dog and tore across the lawn. Though no fan of squirrels myself, it was all I could do not to yell, Run, squirrel! Run for your life!

"What's on your mind, Molly?"

"Oh, um . . ." I flinched as Faldo barked just outside the open window beside me—a deep *woof*! that rattled the walls. I took a couple of deep breaths, trying to quiet my pounding heart. *Whether or not Tommy Newton is close enough to hear me scream* was currently on my mind but would not be a good answer. "Did you know that Allison was a battered wife?"

Nancy blinked a couple of times, then said, "I suspected as much, yes, but she always denied it."

"You didn't feel any ethical or moral obligation to pursue it further?"

"More than once I gave her the name of an excellent therapist. Beyond that, I feared my interference might do more harm than good."

"Do you think she killed her ex-husband?"

She lifted her hair off the back of her neck with both hands, then said, "I am not comfortable answering that question."

I could only take that as a yes. "Allison hid her troubles from me the whole time I knew her. When I saw her for the first time in years on Friday, she acted down and out."

Nancy frowned. "She'd been that way ever since the divorce and even more so after her ex's death. I'm sure she felt responsible, especially since the crime is still unsolved. At the very least, she would have been left wondering whether or not somebody killed him to avenge his treatment of her."

Something about Nancy's voice was so soothing that, even with this subject matter, I felt myself almost nodding off. My trance was broken when Faldo growled. I glanced outside and watched Faldo circle the cottonwood. He'd probably treed some poor woodland creature—such as a grizzly bear. "So, you think that's all that was bothering her? Nothing else?"

"No. There was definitely something else, some recent trouble, very much on her mind. I have no idea what that 'something' might have been. Yet that, in my opinion, is why she died."

"You were telling me the other day about how Lois's son moved out. You don't think he could have had anything to do with Richard Kenyon's death, do you?"

She shook her head. "One of my patients lives next door to him. I run into Max quite often."

"You make house calls?"

"No, I run into Max because he's a waiter at the Harvest, where I often have lunch." Her tone of voice implied I should have made that connection on my own.

"Tell me something, Nancy, did you like Allison?"

She tilted her head as she considered the question, then answered slowly, "I suppose the answer is no. She had a well of suppressed anger and resentment. Though she masked it, it made her a difficult person to be around for any length of time."

Interesting, then, that she'd agreed to talk to me about Allison "as one *friend* to another," I thought. "What about the other women in the retreat? Do you like them?"

She grinned and answered, "Some more than others. I'm not very close to any of them, to be honest."

Again, I was momentarily distracted by the sight of Faldo batting something between his paws, but I forced myself not to stare. "Purely hypothetically, if someone my age were to be sexually involved with a friend's teenage son, why might the boy's mother be inclined to collect tokens which once belonged to that friend?"

Nancy laughed in surprise, then shook her head. "Nice try, Molly, but that simply isn't hypothetical enough for me to answer."

"All right, then, how about this one?" Thinking about Katherine and her criminal record, I asked, "Could revenge over someone's having divulged a secret be a motive for murder, even if that secret was all but common knowledge?"

Nancy thought for a moment, looking puzzled by my intentionally vague question. "That would not be what I, or what a rational person, would consider a reasonable motive. That's not to say, however, that the *killer* could not consider it sufficient motivation. I once heard of a man who shot his wife for complaining one too many times about his not putting the toilet seat down."

"Yes, but the difference is, the guy with the toilet seat acted in a moment of passion. Allison's murder was not only planned, but *I* was framed for it. You know the people on the retreat. I don't. You must have an opinion on which one of them did it."

"An opinion? Yes, I most definitely do. But I won't share it with you, Molly, because I could be wrong. I will tell you, though, that if I were investigating this murder, I'd start by looking at the opportunity. Who had the opportunity to set up the scenario in which Allison was killed?"

As the organizer of the retreat, the answer was Celia Wentworth. Nancy was all but telling me she thought Celia did it. I could have pursued that idea further, but Faldo had trotted up to my window. I shot to my feet, wanting to leave before he committed my scent to memory and associated me with a chew toy. "Thanks, Nancy. I'd better run. Your dog isn't likely to jump over the fence . . . or the house, is he?"

"No," she said with a laugh, "And he really wouldn't hurt a fly."

"I'm sure the flies are grateful."

I raced to the car, where Tommy was dutifully waiting. We left Nancy's house and headed east across town. Tommy asked me what I'd learned.

That Boulder's gone to the dogs. "Nancy hinted that she thought Celia did it. I also learned the name of the restaurant where Max Tucker, Lois's son, works. That's kind of on our way."

To my surprise, Tommy said he was game and that he could use a drink anyway.

We soon reached the vegetarian restaurant, which, with Boulder's health-crazed populace, had been a city staple for years. I inhaled deeply as we entered the paneled lobby; the spicy scent from the Harvest's iced tea was unchanged after all these years. The young hostess assured us that Max Tucker was working and agreed to seat us in his section.

At this late afternoon hour, we passed only one table of customers, and we convinced her to let us sit in a deserted corner of the restaurant. She offered us menus, but we assured her we were just here for drinks. After a minute or so, Max sped around the corner toward us, but his pace slowed the moment he saw me.

He quickly shifted his gaze to Tommy. "What can I get for you?"

"I'll just have a beer."

Max reeled off about a dozen names, including a couple of local breweries.

Tommy listened, and when Max was finished, said, "Just give me whatever's on tap."

Again, Max gave Tommy three choices. Tommy sighed. "Changed my mind. Just give me an iced tea."

"Want the house tea, or we also have—"

Tommy raised his hands to cut him off. "Yes. The house tea." Max turned his eyes to me.

"I'm fine." Before he could leave, I said, "I saw you recently at the same gathering. My name is Molly Masters."

"Yeah. I remember seeing you at Allison's funeral."

"You're Lois Tucker's son, right?"

"You know my mom?"

"I'm Sergeant Newton, a police officer from upstate New York," Tommy interrupted. "I'm unofficially looking into the death on the request of Ms. Masters here. Got a minute to answer a couple questions?"

Max scanned the nearly empty room as if searching for an excuse to say no. He sighed. "Just a sec." He left but returned moments later with the iced tea. He set it in front of Tommy and said, "Look. I don't know anything. All I know is, Allison was getting death threats for months. She, like, wouldn't tell the police, no matter how hard I tried to convince her to. That's why I moved out. She told me it wasn't worth it anymore. She said I was, like, bound to find some girl my own age soon, either way. She said she'd rather give me up than risk her own neck."

"How were these threats being delivered?" Tommy asked solemnly.

"Phone calls, mostly. Sometimes notes in her mailbox."

"You ever overhear any of those calls? Or read any of the notes?"

Max shook his head. "Not the phone calls. If I answered, the person would just hang up. I did see one of the notes, though."

"Still got a copy of it?" Tommy asked. While he slipped into his policeman persona, I sat in motionless silence, hoping against logic that Tommy could solve the murder simply by asking Max Tucker the right questions.

"Allison got rid of it right away, but it was unforgettable. It was a poem:

> 'Roses are red
> Violets are blue
> You'll soon be dead
> So the hell with you.' "

I nearly jumped out of my seat, but Tommy calmly asked, "Who'd she think was behind those threats?"

Max drew his eyebrows together as if surprised we didn't already know the answer. "Her ex. Richard Kenyon."

Chapter 14

More Doggone Trouble

Max wiped his palms on his green apron and shifted his weight nervously.

"Richard?" I repeated. "But he's been dead for five months now!"

Max furrowed his handsome brow. He had exceptionally attractive masculine features. In fact, he looked just like his mother.

He glanced to either side, as if concerned that a nonexistent customer might overhear. "Yeah, but Allison believed he and his lover were, like, in cahoots." His expression was contorted in emotional pain. "I wanted Allie to go to the police, but she, like, refused. I should've insisted. Maybe if I had . . ."

"So, you're sayin' Richard's lover continued to send the death threats after Richard died?" Tommy asked.

"Right." Max backed away from our table. "Listen. I really gotta get back to work." He strode around the corner toward the kitchen. Though he managed to incorporate a nonchalant swagger into his strides, he'd clearly lost his cool.

Tommy had a couple of gulps of his tea, then pushed the glass away. "Too sweet," he murmured as he rose, flipping a couple of dollar bills onto the glossy wood table.

We crossed the small parking lot to Tommy's car. He walked at a steady and unfriendly pace, his eyes downcast and his hands in his pockets. That meant he didn't want to talk, but since we weren't a couple, I didn't feel obligated to pick up on his nonverbal cues. "If Richard's one-time lover really was behind Allison's death threats, the most likely candidate is Celia."

"And why's that?"

"Because Celia was his lover."

"Wasn't he also linked with some grad student?"

"That was later. He apparently dumped Celia for Cindy, who claims to have then dumped Richard."

"Guy got around." Tommy unlocked the passenger door without looking at me, then rounded the car.

Once we were inside, I asked, "Have you been able to find out anything about who the Boulder police think killed Richard?"

He started the engine, signaled, and pulled onto the street before answering. I was just about to repeat the question when he said, "From what they told me, some guy in a condo near Richard's overheard him arguing with a woman. The neighbor was a Good Samaritan and went over there, concerned about the woman's condition. Says the woman bolted past him in tears. Definitely wasn't Allison. Few hours later, the neighbor alerted the police when Richard Kenyon was murdered. Far as I can gather from what the officers told me, the gunshot woke the neighbor up. Looked out his window and spotted a man running from the back exit. He was dressed for the weather—stocking cap, winter coat, gloves—and was carrying a partially full pillowcase. The apartment had been ransacked, as if it was a botched burglary."

"Was this witness absolutely certain it couldn't have been a woman, wearing a man's coat and hat?" I asked, thinking about how easily Lois could have pulled off such a ruse. When seen from the back, at any rate.

He shrugged. "Don't even know the witness's name. BPD gives me info strictly on a need-to-know basis, just like they would anyone else."

"You *do* need to know this stuff!"

"Why's that?"

"Because Richard's killer and Allison's killer could be one and the same. And that person could be trying to kill *me*. That's why."

"Uh-huh," Tommy muttered noncommittally. The light was turning yellow and he braked, causing the car behind us to come to a screeching stop.

I gave him a moment to expand on his response, but, to my annoyance, he didn't. "What I'm trying to say, Tommy, is that you're a police sergeant and you're my friend. Theoretically, that means you have a personal interest in my not getting murdered during our joint vacation here."

"That's exactly the point." He tapped the dashboard in front of me with his index finger and added redundantly, "You hit the nail on the head. I got a 'personal interest' in this case. Officers aren't supposed to have a personal interest in their cases. Clouds judgment. You find yourself reacting from emotion, 'stead of logic."

I snapped my tongue in disgust. "That is just so . . . male. Who's to say that because you care on an emotional level you are automatically less analytical and less logical? Maybe the more you care about the victims of a given crime, the more determined you'll be to solve it."

The light turned green. He ignored the honking horn of our tailgater and cautiously eased us through the intersection. "Could be, but I can guarantee you, Molly, soon as I go to the BPD and tell 'em how I *need* to know so's I can help out a friend, they'll be showing me the door."

"Then don't tell them that's the reason. Have one of your officers back in Carlton call and tell them you might have a copycat case."

"You want me to order one of my officers to lie to the BPD?"

My cheeks warmed. "Tommy, in the past twenty-four hours I've been locked in a sauna and chased by a pair of Dobermans.

Color me selfish, but yes, I want you to lie, cheat, and steal if that's what it takes to get me out of this mess."

"And what happens when I need the BPD to take it serious that you need protection? That you're an innocent victim here? How credible am I gonna be when they figure out I'm havin' my men lie to 'em?"

"All right. Never mind. Bad idea." Before he could continue his tirade and say that my emotions had affected my judgment, I opted for a quick change in subjects. "You're going to come in with me and say hi to Lauren, right?"

He shook his head. "Bad idea."

After listening to my report on my adventures with Tommy, Lauren said she wasn't feeling well and went to the guest room. Jim, however, was looking a bit perkier. He asked me how I'd gotten the scratches on my arms and legs, and I told him I was climbing a tree to get away from some nasty Dobermans.

He stiffened. "Dobermans? You were chased up a tree by attack dogs?"

"Yes."

"I thought you were just going for a walk!"

"That was my intention," I said, a little snippily, "but then it inadvertently turned into a dash and a climb."

Jim started to say something, then clamped his jaw shut and massaged his temples. After a brief pause, he said, "Promise me this much. Next time you've got to do anything that might put yourself in danger, let me help."

"You want to *help* put me in danger?"

He dropped his hand and glared at me. "This isn't funny, Molly."

"You're right, sweetie." I gave him a hug. "Sorry." I assured him that I would do a better job at keeping him informed of my whereabouts, and he eventually seemed to relax his guard a bit.

Karen called out from below, where she and Rachel were sprawled in the family room, "Mom?"

"Daught?" I answered automatically. Karen often calls out "Mom?" as a preamble, even when we're alone and I'm looking right at her. I'd recently asked her why she persists in doing so, and she'd answered, "Mom? I don't know." She gets her sarcasm from her father.

"Rachel and I are bored," Karen moaned. "There's nothing to do."

"Why don't you play with the dog?" I suggested.

"She's asleep."

Nathan stormed down the stairs. His narrow shoulders sagged but his dark eyes were flashing with anger. "Look what Betty did." He thrust a slightly gnawed plastic truck into my hands. The bed of the truck was missing, leaving only the base. "She chewed the sides off."

"She made it into a flatbed. It can haul more stuff that way."

"She also chewed up my Legos." He had his deep breathing going, which always means he's stifling tears. "She chews all my stuff," Nathan grumbled, pacing. "She's chewed on everything I brought to Colorado, even my suitcase! I want a new dog. Betty Cocker only likes me because she thinks my toys taste good."

Karen, with Rachel in tow, had run up the stairs from the family room and instantly launched into an argument with Nathan in defense of BC. The time-honored cure-all for boredom: a screaming fight with one's sibling. In the meantime, Rachel looked in BC's kennel in the kitchen and said, "Where is she? She's not in her kennel."

"I let her outside several minutes ago," Jim replied.

"C'mon, Rach," Karen said, raising her jaw in defiance as she slid the back door open. "We've got to go get Betty and protect her from Nathan."

While Nathan complained to me about his sister and dog, the

two girls raced around the yard calling for her. A minute later, her cheeks already tearstained, Karen rushed back inside. "BC's run away!" She leveled a finger at Nathan. "And it's all *your* fault!"

I had the same instantaneous pounding-heart panic that I always experienced whenever my children were missing. I went into the backyard and started calling. As Karen had warned, Betty Cocker was not in the yard.

The female half of our next-door neighbors—an elderly couple whom we'd known for years but had little in common with—heard me and cried, "Oh, Molly. You're not looking for a cocker spaniel puppy, are you?"

"Yes. Have you seen her?"

"She dug under your fence about ten minutes ago." She pointed to a small, but effective, tunnel under the wire mesh in the back corner of our fence. "You should have seen the little thing, digging and digging away for, oh, must have been fifteen minutes or so. Determined little dickens, I must say. You don't own a dog, though, so I thought it had to be someone else's that happened to cut through your yard."

I gritted my teeth. During fifteen minutes of watching her dig, you would think it might have occurred to her to let us know what was happening. "We just got her yesterday morning. Didn't you notice Karen and Nathan playing with her in our yard since then?"

She shook her head. "I'm sorry. I hope you find her and get her back."

No thanks to you, I thought sourly, as I went back inside. If good fences made for good neighbors, apparently both our fence and our neighbors weren't deep enough.

Karen immediately said, "She's gone, isn't she?"

"She tunneled under the fence."

Karen's jaw dropped.

"Don't worry," I automatically said, though I was very worried myself. "We won't have much trouble finding her. She must have gone back to her old house."

"You have to get her back!" Karen said. She turned to Nathan and cried, "She ran away from home because you're so mean to her!"

"That's not true. Nathan, Karen, this is not anybody's fault. I'm going to get Betty back."

"You don't know that," Karen said through her sobs. "Somebody could have kidnapped her."

Or she could have been hit by car, which was my biggest worry. Full of false bravado for the children's sake, I called Julie. She said Betty wasn't there, but she'd go look for her and meet me at Allison's house. I agreed, but asked her to first check to make sure her Dobermans were locked up.

Jim, anxious to help, insisted on driving me, so we left the kids in Lauren's care and took off. The first place BC might have gone was back to Allison's house. Or maybe to Julie's.

Julie was standing in front of Allison's driveway when we arrived. I introduced Jim and Julie briefly while getting out of the car.

"Betty's not at my place," Julie said, "and she's not in Allison's backyard."

Jim said he was going to drive through the neighborhood and promptly took off.

"Maybe she's inside the house. Have you tried the doorbell yet?" I asked Julie.

"Excuse me?"

"The housecleaner, Maria Chavez, seems to be here quite often, for some reason." I trotted past Julie in as quick a pace as my aching muscles could abide and rang the bell. No answer. Julie called Betty's name while I rounded the house to peer through the garage window. Maria's car wasn't there.

"I'm going to start at Lois's," I told Julie. "She wanted Betty in the first place."

"I'll circle the block on foot," Julie said with a nod.

I knocked on Lois's door. Lois swung the door open and stood in the entranceway staring at me, arms akimbo.

"Lois, BC seems to have gotten out of our yard."

"Huh. Dog doesn't like you and ran away, hey? Fancy that. You should've let me have her in the first place."

"Be that as it may, she's missing and I need to find her. Have you seen her?"

"I thought that went without saying. No. Now scram."

Just before she could shut the door in my face, I detected the unmistakable scent of chocolate. I stuck my sneakered foot in her doorway. "You're expecting Joe Cummings again?"

"Not that it's any business of yours, but yes, I am, and no, you can't stay and talk to him."

"Help me find BC and I'll be out of your hair in no time."

She put her hands on her hips and narrowed her eyes at me. "A little bit of friendly extortion, hey?" She pointed with her chin. "Betty's at Celia's house."

"She is?"

"I saw her behind Allison's fence, barking, just a few minutes ago. Celia came out and got her. Took her back inside her house."

"Why didn't you just tell me that in the first place?"

"Because you shouldn't *have* Betty Cocker 'in the first place'! Which reminds me. When are you going to reimburse me for that dreadful retreat?"

"Reimburse you? But I didn't—" I took a deep breath and counted to ten. "Let me go over to Celia's and get my dog back first. I'll discuss the financial ramifications of the retreat with her. Then I'll get back to you."

"You do that." She made a sweeping gesture at me with one hand. I took a step back, and she shut the door.

Julie, who was halfway down the block calling for Betty, looked at me as I reached the sidewalk. She cupped her hands around her mouth. "Does Lois know where she is?"

"Yes. Celia's got her," I called back.

"Thank goodness," Julie answered, smiling. She jogged back toward me and said, "I've got to get to the aerobics studio now. You don't need me to go speak to Celia first, do you?"

"No, I'm fine. Thanks."

Julie gave a friendly wave and jogged across the street and into her open garage. Just then, I spotted Joe's pickup rounding the corner. He saw me and waved. I waited as he pulled into Lois's driveway.

"Why, Molly Masters," he said happily, "if you ain't a sight for sore eyes."

I was sore, all right, though I wasn't sure about the part about the eyes.

Joe went on, "I can really use your help with a—"

I was already shaking my head. "Sorry. You're on your own with Lois."

As if on cue, Lois's door swung open and I could feel the heat from her glare on me as if it were a sunbeam focused through a magnifying glass.

Joe smiled and waved at Lois, but all the while said through his teeth, "Please? I'll pay you."

"Lois'd kill me. Besides, I have a puppy to collect and bring home to my children."

Joe shook his head. "Those damn brownies give me away, every time. The wife says she can always tell when I been over here, 'cause I smell like a Hershey bar. If only I could resist 'em, my wife would never even know I'd been at her house."

"Hi, Joe!" Lois cried. "Guess what I've got in the oven for you?"

He cast me a mournful gaze, and I said, "Good luck. Be strong."

Celia was carrying BC as she came to answer the doorbell. Beside her feet was a Boston terrier, yapping at Betty with unbridled jealousy.

"Hi, Molly. I just called and left a message on your machine that I have Betty."

I took Betty, who, fortunately for my ego's sake, seemed extremely happy to see me. Celia asked me to wait a moment and dragged away the still-barking terrier by the collar. She returned a minute later, and I thanked her for keeping BC safe for me.

"Oh, don't mention it. I don't mind in the least." She gave me a visual once-over. "You seem to have recuperated from your brush with Julie's beasts rather nicely."

"Save a few scratches and gray hairs, yes. Lois told me I still owed her money for the retreat. Do you have any suggestions as to how we can work this out?"

"I'm way ahead of you. This is what I do for a living, after all. I got in touch with the Red Fox Resort and demanded a full refund. The owners countered with half off. I'm still bartering with them. Just give me till the end of the week, and I'm sure I can get them down to just what the meals alone would have cost us."

While she spoke, I happened to spot her impressive set of keys on the end table. That reminded me. "Okay. Celia, something else has been bothering me for a long time. Somebody told me they saw you with your keys after you claimed they were missing."

Celia tsked and muttered, "Julie." She studied my face. "That's true. This is embarrassing." She took a deep breath, but otherwise showed no physical sign of embarrassment. "Whoever stole my keys actually did return them to my purse at some point. I pretended they were still missing, so that I could find out who took them. It backfired on me. They stole them a second time, then apparently stuck them in your purse. I thought it was you, at first. Otherwise, I would have admitted this to you sooner."

None of that made any sense to me, but I asked, "And why are you admitting it to me now?"

"I don't know who killed Allison. Up until I saw what you've been going through lately, I couldn't believe it really was murder. Allison had been so miserable, I was sure she'd taken her own life. But now, it's pretty clear somebody is after you." She opened the door for me. "Take care, Molly."

Jim was just circling the block as I stepped out. He waved and grinned as he saw me holding Betty. He reached across the seat and opened the passenger door for me. "All right! You found her!"

"She seems fine. I just hope she doesn't prefer her former owner to us."

"She's going to have a great life with us," Jim said, stroking BC's soft red-gold fur. "She's got Karen to dote on her. Nathan, too, once he gets used to keeping his door shut."

I stared at Allison's deserted house. There were only two reasons I could think of that could explain Maria Chavez's seemingly erratic and nocturnal visits to Allison's house. One of those explanations might just go a long way toward solving Allison's murder. If I could just get her to talk with me, maybe I'd get some answers. Betty was licking Jim's hand. "Can you watch her for a moment? I need to leave somebody a note." I grabbed one of my business cards from my purse that was still in the car and wrote:

Maria—Please call me as soon as you read this.
It's urgent.

        Molly Masters
        (the skinny lady who was chased up the tree)

I left the note in the doorjamb, and we headed home. We had an uneventful dinner and evening. At eleven thirty-four, the phone rang. I was still awake and answered on the fax phone.

"Is this Molly Masters?" asked a female with a trace Spanish accent.

"Yes. Maria?"

"Are you okay? Did the dogs bite you?"

"No. Julie got her dogs back under control in time. Thanks for calling her. Why did you take off like that?"

"I . . . can't talk to you. I don't want anything to do with the police."

"I won't mention this to them." I asked her the first of my theories that could explain her nighttime visits: "Are you living at Allison's house?"

"No."

"Then you must be looking for something."

Her pause, I thought, spoke volumes. "You said it was urgent that I call you."

"I need your help. I was in a cabin in the mountains with Allison and five of her friends the night she was killed. The police found my fingerprints on the murder weapon, and I never touched it. I'm trying to find out who killed Allison and why I was set up."

"I cannot help you. I'm sorry."

"Yes, you can. Tell me whatever you can about Allison's relationships with her female friends."

"I do not know anything. I know some of her friends, but not well. I used to work for someone who knows Allison. Nancy Thornton. She helped me get this job."

I was very surprised by this but asked calmly, "What can you tell me about Nancy?"

"She had many strange calls and messages," Maria said. "I think she was having trouble with one of her patients. One day, several months ago, I heard on her recorder a few strange calls from some man. Next day, I am out of a job. She told me she had changed her mind about needing a housecleaner."

"What do you mean by 'strange calls'?"

"He would say things like, 'So, Miss Nancy. You had better show up tonight. You know exactly what I'm going to do to you if you don't.' And like that. They were threats."

Chapter 15

When Dogs Dream

The next morning, I took a shower and came down the stairs, feeling the effects of my sore muscles more than ever. A snail with a brisk tailwind could move faster than this. DC raced over to greet me, giving me an excuse to catch my breath while petting her. It felt so good to get such an enthusiastic greeting that I knew Charles Schulz had it right when his Peanuts cartoon claimed that happiness is a warm puppy.

The phone rang, but in my slo-mo state, the automatic-answer function on the fax machine kicked in before I could get to the kitchen. Nathan was standing in front of the machine, watching as the fax emerged. "Hey, Mom. Somebody is faxing you a picture."

"A cartoon?" I asked, wondering if this was my lone new prospective customer, faxing me somebody else's cartoon to show me how superior my competition was.

"No," he said slowly, watching as the picture emerged. "It looks like a photograph."

That announcement alarmed me into some semblance of speed. I grabbed Nathan by the shoulders and gently but firmly shoved him aside. "Sorry, mister, but I'm not sure this is something that's okay for you to . . ." My voice drifted off as I caught sight of the faxed photograph. My worst suspicions had been verified. I snatched it off the tray and shoved it into a drawer, saying, "What do you want for breakfast?"

"I already got my own bowl of Lucky Charms. Why was that lady wearing a cat mask?" he asked, staring at the closed drawer where I'd stashed the pornographic photograph.

"It must have been Halloween," I answered, feeling my cheeks grow warm.

"What was that man doing to her?"

Shoot! He'd seen too much of the picture! I needed him out of the room so I could get the thing put away before he found a way to get a closer look. "Um, that's really a better question for your father. Where is he?"

"In the bathroom," Nathan answered, which I could have surmised for myself, had I stopped to think about it.

"Well, knock on the door and tell him Mom says it's time he had a talk with you about the facts of life."

While Nathan trotted down to the bathroom, I retrieved the fax. The top margin showed the current date and time, followed only by the user tag: COLO__ U_. Great. This could have been sent by any of the hundred or so fax machines on the C.U. campus—where Katherine Lindstrom happened to work.

I folded and stashed the picture in the pocket of my shorts. Until I could hand it over to the police, this needed to be some-place the kids wouldn't find it. The photograph was of the late Richard Kenyon, in bed with a woman naked except for a cat mask.

Nathan knocked on the bathroom door and shouted over the noisy fan, "Dad? Mom wants to talk about sex."

My jaw dropped. At only eight years old, Nathan had already made the leap from "the facts of life" to "sex." I suddenly felt like the world's worst mother for not handling—what? his TV viewing? external influences?—his upbringing better. The fan shut off. There were sounds of activity, then Jim, looking very startled, emerged, sports section in hand. He looked at Nathan, then at me. "What did Nathan just say?"

"Nathan, I need to talk to your dad alone for a minute. Why don't you go check the mailbox for me?"

Though Nathan knew as well as I did that mail didn't come this early, he slipped his sandals onto his bare feet and left through the garage.

"Nathan saw this on our fax machine and asked what they were doing," I explained, handing Jim the picture. "That's Allison Kenyon's late ex-husband in what, judging by the wallpaper, looks like the bedroom of Allison's house. I don't know who the masked woman is." One thing was certain, though. It wasn't Celia Wentworth. Catwoman didn't have Celia's blobby upper arms. I craned my neck around Jim's shoulder, tilting the picture to get a better look. "The woman's quite a contortionist. It looks like Julie."

"The aerobics instructor?" Jim let out a low whistle.

I snatched the picture away, now wishing I hadn't allowed my husband to see it, either. "It's time you had a talk with our son about the facts of life." Jim grimaced, and I added, "I already had my first talk with Karen."

"Isn't eight years old too young?"

"Maybe when *we* were eight. Not anymore." I gave him a friendly jab on the arm. "You can make it age-appropriate. I have complete confidence in you."

Jim grumbled, "Said General Custer to his troops."

Lauren emerged from the basement. Without makeup and wearing wrinkled tan cotton shorts and a camouflage T-shirt, she looked as though she'd just rolled out of bed. She said in a gravelly voice, "Morning. What sucks so far?"

Jim muttered that he was going to check on Nathan and exited through the garage. I told Lauren, "I just got an obscene fax regarding Allison's ex-husband, but otherwise, everything's great."

"Great? Hah!" Lauren shuffled into the bathroom.

She must be unbelievably upset not to even react to my mention of the fax. I wished I could offer some cheery comeback, along the lines of, *Okay, so you've split with your fiancé and are spending your hard-earned vacation dodging a homicidal maniac. The weather is lovely and I've got a great puppy.*

And yet, there truly was a bright side for Lauren. This fax was a reasonable excuse to get Tommy over here. Not a great excuse, since he obviously had no jurisdiction and therefore the fax actually should go to the Boulder police. However, I was willing to appear dense in order to help my two determined-to-act-even-denser friends get back together.

With Lauren still in the bathroom and out of earshot, I dialed Tommy's cellular phone. He answered immediately. I could tell by his eager tones whose voice he'd been hoping to hear. I said, "Tommy, can you come over? I've got a fax here I'd like you to see."

"Be right there," he said, and hung up.

Out the kitchen window, I saw him round the corner. He had to have been just up the street. Maybe he hadn't even bothered to keep his room at the Regency and simply planned to stay in his car. The doorbell rang as Lauren was coming up the stairs from the family room.

I quickly stuck my hands in the sink and called to her, "My hands are wet, Lauren. Could you answer the door, please?"

A moment later, I heard the sound of the door creak open, then silence. Tommy's first words were, " 'Scuse me. I'm here to speak to Molly."

I rolled my eyes, grabbed the fax, and marched into the room with it. "Tommy. This was just faxed to me anonymously." I handed him the picture. "There was no note or anything. The man's Richard Kenyon."

Tommy furrowed his brow as he studied the fax. "Boulder cops had better see this. Might not tell 'em much, but you never know."

"The woman might be Julie from aerobics, or Professor Katherine, or Nancy the therapist, but I can't say for certain. I'm relatively sure it isn't Celia or Lois. Their body types are completely different from the masked woman's."

"Uh-huh. Could also be none of the above."

"At least we know it was sent from the C.U. campus, where Katherine Lindstrom teaches. I can't imagine why she—or anybody else, for that matter—would send this to me."

"Uh-huh. I could take it down to the station for you, but they'll probably want to talk to you in person."

That plan would not allow for me to get Lauren and Tommy alone together. Lauren had already wandered out of the living room and was now in the kitchen. I was having trouble keeping the three of us in the same room, let alone the two of them. I took it back from him and returned it to my pocket. "I'll just take it there myself after breakfast. Since you're here, have a seat. I'll get you some coffee."

"But I—"

"Sit!" Betty Cocker promptly sat down, and so did Tommy, though the latter did so with a snarl. I muttered an apology to both of them for my tone of voice, then called, "Lauren, while you're in there, could you please bring me a cup of coffee?"

"Moll," Tommy grumbled, "do you ever even consider mindin' your own business?"

"Yes. I considered it and dismissed the idea." The moment Lauren entered, a cup in her hand, I rose and said, "You two stay and talk to each other. My favorite daytime TV show is on."

"What's that?" Tommy asked.

I never watched daytime TV, not counting football games. "Uh, *Ryan's Hope*. Excuse me while I go watch downstairs."

"Show was cancelled years ago," Tommy called after me.

"In that case, I have a lot of catching up to do."

To block out the sounds of their conversation, I flipped on the set, but made no pretense of watching it. BC followed me downstairs and was soon asleep by my feet. I smiled as she lapsed into REM, her feet flicking as if she were running. Chasing rabbits in her dreams, as my mom always used to say when our family's dog did this.

That gave me an idea for a cartoon. I grabbed my pad. I drew a man asleep on a couch, a sleeping dog by his feet. The thought bubble from the man shows him chasing after a rabbit in a field. The thought bubble from the dog shows the dog in a T-shirt and striped pants sitting at a desk, surrounded by human classmates staring at him in disgust as the teacher says, "Fido, all of your classmates knew about the fifty-page thesis due today! I'm calling your mother! And those'd better not be pajama bottoms you're wearing!"

"It's hopeless," Lauren announced to me half an hour later. Tommy had left, Nathan and Jim had returned, and all three kids were playing at a neighbor's house across the street. "Tommy is absolutely convinced that I'm never going to marry him. There's nothing I can do to change his mind."

"There is one thing you can do," I answered. "Marry him."

"What, you mean here in Colorado? But we wouldn't want to get married without his sons being present, and they're at camp."

I gave a quick look at Jim, who nodded. Though we'd never as much as discussed any of this, I knew exactly what he meant. "Lauren, if this is what you want to do, Jim and I will fly Jasper and Joey out here as our wedding present to you."

"I can't ask you to do that," Lauren said, shaking her head emphatically. "With no advanced purchase? That'd cost you a fortune."

"I can't think of a way we'd rather spend our money," Jim immediately said. That was the honest truth for Jim, who got more enjoyment out of generosity than from spending his money on himself. *A trip to Bermuda* popped into my head—I'm not as unselfish as my husband—but I quashed the thought.

That afternoon, Jim had to return to work at his former office headquarters. Both Karen and Nathan had been invited to friends' houses. Lauren and Rachel dropped me off at the Boulder Police station, where the police returned my rental car to me at long last. I gave them the obscene fax—neglecting to mention that I'd previously made a copy of it. If the police had drawn any conclusions regarding my—or anyone else's—guilt or innocence, they were certainly tight-lipped about it.

In case Professor Katherine Lindstrom had sent the fax, I wanted to check into the story behind her drug problems and relationship with her ex-husband, Julie's brother. Remembering all of those get-right-back-in-the-saddle pep talks from my horse-riding lessons, I decided to begin by confronting my saunaphobia with a return to Julie's aerobics studio.

Julie was seated behind the oak desk in her office, but judging from her glistening face—so far she's the only woman I could truthfully say "glowed" instead of sweated—she'd just completed a class.

Her first question upon seeing me was, "Is everything all right with Betty?"

"Yes, she's fine." I took a chair in front of her desk. There were two framed photographs on her desk—one of her golden retriever and one of BC's mother. None of her husband.

"You're not here to talk lawsuits, are you? My boss said she wanted to meet with you in person to tell you how sorry she is, but she wants to consult with her lawyer first."

I had no intention of suing Julie or anyone else, but the looming threat of my doing so might put me in the driver's seat now. "This is about something else. Katherine Lindstrom. Did you know she had a criminal record for drug abuse?"

Her eyes widened and she tensed, but then nodded. "She got me and my brother John into it, too, unfortunately. I was living with her for a while, back east, while they were married."

That was the exact reverse of what Katherine had said. Katherine's was perhaps the less believable story, since she, not Julie, was the one with the actual criminal record. "Where is your brother now?"

"He lives in California. He's remarried. He doesn't do drugs anymore, but he thought it best that we not contact each other."

"I'm sorry. That must be difficult."

She nodded, still poised for flight. "I had problems, a long time ago. I've been clean and sober for years now."

"How did you and Katherine both wind up in Boulder?" I asked, wanting to compare the women's stories. Somewhere within fact and fiction might lie a motive for murder.

"I'd lost touch with her completely. I was barely out of high school when all of that was going on. I moved out here to go to C.U. Then one day I ran into her. We had coffee together. She didn't recognize me at first, and she'd changed a lot, too. She used to have long blond hair, but she got it all sheared off and let it go its natural color."

"So you've gotten along with her pretty well? Despite what she did to your brother?"

"It's not like I blame her, Molly. I really don't. You can't turn somebody into a junkie by offering them drugs any more than you can get somebody off the stuff by offering them coffee. We make our own choices in this life." Her lip trembled as she took a halting breath. "I was simply glad and relieved to see she'd gotten her act together."

"Weren't you surprised to see she was teaching college again?"

She shrugged. "She told me C.U. was willing to give her a second chance. That she hoped I would, too."

"How would Allison have known about Katherine's past?"

"Allison?"

"Lois says that's how she found out about Katherine."

"I, uh, must have told her about it. But I told Allison never to tell another soul. You just can't trust people to keep secrets."

"Not in this neighborhood, anyway." I paused, but Julie didn't as much as crack a smile. She was sitting rigidly still in her seat, none of her usual constant motion apparent. I didn't know which version of the story to believe—hers or Katherine's—and had no way to know whether or not this had anything to do with Allison's murder. I decided to press a little harder. "I spoke to Katherine about this, by the way. She says that it was actually you who first provided her with the drugs."

Julie stiffened. "What else did she tell you?"

"That you were a . . . call girl in Boston. That your brother deserted her when she had breast cancer and got a mastectomy. She says that's why she turned to drugs. She was so depressed, she needed the drugs as a crutch."

"That bitch!" Julie slammed her fist onto the desktop. "She's a pathological liar! She never had cancer or a mastectomy. I've seen her in the shower, at my club. Katherine has both breasts. Ask anybody if you don't believe me!"

That would be an awkward question for me to pose: Have you ever seen Katherine Lindstrom's breasts? How many of them does she have?

Interesting, though, that Katherine had accused Julie of being a hooker, yet Julie ignored that and took issue with whether or not Katherine had had a mastectomy.

Julie rose, her hands clenched into fists. I expected her to do something drastic—scream at me to mind my own business, rail about her former sister-in-law. Instead, she swept up the photograph of Teak, her golden retriever, stared at it, then smiled. "You wouldn't be interested in a friend for Betty, would you? A cute golden retriever puppy, for instance?"

"No, thanks."

She set the picture down. "Dogs are so much better than people. They're so loyal. They ask so little from you."

I had run out of questions. I thanked Julie, assured her that I had no intention of suing anyone, and left.

To my unpleasant surprise, Celia was pacing next to my car.

"Molly, thank God you're here. I came over to talk to Julie, and I noticed your car. I have to talk to you."

"Go ahead."

"Not here. Julie might come out and overhear."

I let Celia into my car. As soon as we had the door shut behind us, Celia blurted out, "My lawyer just called. You have to help me, Molly. I think the police are going to arrest me."

"Arrest *you*? Why?"

"That night you were locked in the sauna, the police came to my door. I let one of the officers examine my key ring. Molly, there are copies of Julie's keys on my ring. I didn't put them there. Somebody is trying to set me up."

"How come you didn't notice this new set of keys yourself?"

"You've seen my key ring!" Celia held up her three-pound key ring. There were a dozen or more keys on it. "Look for yourself!" She jingled them in my face. "I've got a key to every door in the office building I own. Would you notice a new pair of keys on this key ring?"

"Well, no, but I'd never have that many keys on my ring in the first place. It's terrible for your ignition, for one thing."

"Molly, you're missing the point here! I'm about to be hauled off to jail, and you're worried about my ignition?"

Actually, I was enjoying this. "Who do you think might have put the keys on your ring?"

"Nancy Thornton."

"Nancy?" I had all but dismissed her from my personal list of suspects, as she had no discernible motive to hurt anyone, let alone kill Allison. Plus it just seemed too bizarre that this calm, quiet therapist could be a killer. "Why?"

"She had copies made of Julie's keys. I know she did. I saw them."

"How could you possibly tell that they were Julie's?"

"I went to Nancy's house a couple of weeks ago, and I spotted two pairs of brand-new keys on her counter. I didn't think anything of it at the time, but those had to be Julie's keys. Somebody made copies of them, and here's Nancy with a couple pairs of new keys, not even a month earlier. Don't you see?"

All I *saw* was that her spotting Nancy with a new pair of keys could be a coincidence. "Celia, I barely know you. Why are you asking me to help you?"

"Because anybody who *does* know me won't want to help. I'm not exactly Miss Popularity. You've got that friend who's a policeman. Get him to do something. Have him explain to the Boulder police that I didn't put the keys on my ring, and that I was at home, nursing a migraine, when the rest of you were here doing aerobics."

That seemed to be a reasonable enough request. Pointless, but reasonable. "Okay, Celia. I'll tell Sergeant Newton your story."

She grabbed my arm. "That's not all you're going to do, is it?"

"That's what you asked me to do!" I stared at her hand on my wrist till she released it.

"Aren't you going to at least talk to Nancy? She's at work now, and her office is right at the northwest corner of Folsom and Walnut."

"Talk to her about what? 'Oh, by the way, Nancy. Celia thinks she saw you with a key to the sauna. Did you put that on her key ring, by any chance?' She'll say no, and that'll be the end of it."

"So? That's no stupider than half the questions you've asked us ever since Allison was killed."

"Be that as it may," I said through clenched teeth, "I have my limits."

She harrumphed and attempted to toss her unmovable hair. She got out of my car, looked back at me, and said, "You know what you are, Molly? Selfish!" She slammed the door of my little rental so hard it rocked on its chassis.

While Celia marched to her own car, I drove away, silently phrasing a litany of comebacks to Celia's name-calling. While still in the process of doing so, I found myself heading in the direction of Nancy's office, rather than home.

I pulled into the parking lot and sat there with the engine idling, trying to decide upon my next step. Celia's "evidence" was so slight it was laughable, but if she happened to be right, then Nancy was both Allison's killer and the person who had attempted to kill me, too. I couldn't ignore that possibility, nor could I see myself marching into her office between sessions and demanding that she tell me whether or not she'd copied Julie's key to the sauna.

Nancy answered my dilemma for me by emerging from the building. She looked distraught. I did the natural—albeit despicable—thing and ducked down as she got into her car, then followed her. I kept silently kicking myself. She seemed like a nice person. Out of this group of five women, she was probably my favorite, though if I could get past my prejudices for stacked, perky women, Julie could have overtaken that role. But Nancy and I had more in common. Our age, if nothing else. Not to mention unstacked unperkiness.

We drove clear across town, with me just one or two cars back the whole way. Nancy pulled into Chautauqua, a lovely little park along the foothills. Now I was doomed. There was never anyplace to park here during the summer, and there was enough acreage that if I found a parking space, I'd never be able to locate her.

She pulled into one small parking lot and I continued past,

searching for a space. Ah, well. Seemed like a nice day for a hike, and at least now I'd not have to work quite so hard at explaining my presence if I eventually did manage to locate her.

In the last parking area before the dining hall—a high-porched, nineteenth-century building—a car was just pulling out, and I lucked into a spot. I parked and headed up the nearest dirt path, figuring that I'd endure a half-hour hike to loosen my bruised and battered muscles, then go home.

I'd abandoned any notion of trying to find Nancy in this large park, but I immediately spotted her long-sleeved white blouse and ankle-length denim skirt. She made such an impressive picture with those soft white tresses of hers that she was easy to notice. She was crossing a field below me, heading more toward Ninth Street than the mountains. I swallowed my conscience and made my way down the slight incline toward her.

I focused on my footing, periodically glancing up to trace our intersecting courses. Suddenly, she vanished.

Chapter 16

I'll Knead Your Dough

I forced my aching muscles into a trot and aimed at the spot in the rough terrain of the Chautauqua meadow where I'd last seen Nancy. The grass blades were almost up to my knees, but as soon as I rose on one last incline, I caught sight of her again, sprawled on her back. From this angle, it was impossible to tell if she'd fallen, fainted, or merely decided to lie down and bask in the warm sunlight.

"Nancy?" I called.

She sat up abruptly and looked my way, utterly startled. While I trotted the last few steps toward her, she slipped what looked like a photograph into the pocket of her denim skirt.

"Molly? I thought I spotted you in my rearview mirror, but I didn't quite believe it. Did you follow me here?"

"In a manner of speaking."

"And what manner would that be?"

"Well, the English language, I suppose. I'm sorry. This was totally stupid of me." Which was something of an understatement. How was I supposed to explain myself? I didn't want to say that Celia had pointed a finger at her; that could put me in jeopardy if Celia happened to be right. Nancy was still waiting patiently for me to explain. "Uh, this happens to me a lot. You see, I really didn't set out to follow you. You just happened to pull in front of me, and I . . . have some kind of compulsive need to see where people I know are going."

"You tail your acquaintances?"

"Sometimes, though not as a general rule. Maybe I have an obsessive-compulsive friend-following disorder. Do you think that's possible?"

In flat tones, she answered, "What you're talking about would normally be called stalking. Such behavior could indeed indicate an emotional disorder, which you might have. That is, if I believed you." She took a deep breath and turned her face up to the sunlight. "I come here to rejuvenate my soul. I like to consider this my private place." She smiled, and said in almost hypnotic tones, "Sit down, Molly. Tell me what you're really doing here."

While I slowly took a seat on the hard-packed ground, I considered my alternatives, determined not to let her know that I was here because Celia had named her as a prime suspect. "Actually, I followed you because I wanted to talk to you. I might know who locked me in the sauna." I waited for her reaction, but she gave none, her face still and her eyes focused on mine. "I think it might have been Celia Wentworth. Do you think that's possible?"

"Under the right circumstances, it's possible for any of us to have done that. Reasonable people can take absolutely bizarre, unreasonable courses of action when they feel desperate. Why do you suspect her?"

"She told me the police found the keys to the gym and the sauna on her key ring, though she also says she didn't put them there."

Nancy furrowed her brow. "She claims someone took her key ring and put the keys there to incriminate her, and she didn't notice until after the police found them in her possession?"

I nodded.

The corners of her lips turned up just slightly. "Sounds like Celia, all right. You don't believe her story?"

"No, and in fact, I'm beginning to suspect she killed Allison." Again, Nancy showed no reaction. "Yesterday, was I correct in gathering that you suspected Celia killed Allison?"

She shielded her eyes to look at me. "I said no such thing. I believe I told you I was not going to give my opinion about who killed *Allison*, because I could be mistaken."

She'd accented "Allison" as she spoke. "Do you know who killed *Richard* Kenyon?"

Her expression changed and she averted her eyes. Reluctantly she said, "The truth is, Allison had him killed."

I was very surprised, but did my best to hide my reaction. "You sound certain of that."

"I am. She hired somebody to do it. He was threatening to kill her, and she was certain he would succeed if she didn't kill him first. She considered it self-defense."

"But the police supposedly exonerated her."

She looked me straight in the eyes and said, "Maybe so, but she was guilty. She told me herself she'd hired the killer."

Now it was her turn to study my face. I was obviously not as skilled as she at keeping my reactions in check, for she said, "You don't seem convinced. That's natural. You don't want to believe ill of your deceased friend, and really, there's no reason for you to. Richard Kenyon's murder has nothing to do with you. I shouldn't have told you."

"Why did you?"

She stared off into space. "I'm tired of all the lies and obfuscations. I want this over with. I want the police to arrest Allison's killer and be done with it."

"Me, too." I rose, lost in thought. Having no other explanation for Allison's former housecleaner's behavior, I suspected that she had been hired to search Allison's house. Nancy, Maria's former boss, was the likeliest person to have hired Maria for that purpose. "By the way, there's another thing I

wanted to ask you about. I need to hire a housekeeper. Do you
know of any?"

"Quite a change in subjects. What brought that up?"

I shrugged. "Heck, I'd get dizzy if I tried to follow my
thought patterns."

Nancy gave me a long look. "Why do you want a housecleaner? I thought you were just here on vacation."

"I am, but I've got people moving into my Boulder house at
the end of the month, and I need to have the place professionally
cleaned first. Have you ever used any housecleaners here in
town?"

Nancy shook her head. "I used to have a semiweekly housecleaner, but I had to fire her. The experience was so bad, I've
given up on hiring out the job."

"Why? What happened?"

"She stole from me."

This was a conflicting story; Maria Chavez had said Nancy
recommended her to Allison, but had fired her for overhearing
the wrong things. "Did you report it to the police?"

"No. She stole some cash from a hiding spot in my house, but
she always took such small quantities—just ten dollars or so at
a time—that it took me a long time to know for certain what
was going on. Bringing charges against her seemed more
trouble than it was worth."

"What was her name, so I can be sure not to use her?"

She closed her eyes and basked in the sunlight. "I don't remember. Maria something."

"Thanks. Have a good afternoon." I left quickly. Once again,
somebody was lying. Maria Chavez might have lied to protect
her reputation. What reason might Nancy have to lie about her
relationship with her former housekeeper? None . . . unless
Maria had discovered something illicit or incriminating about
Nancy.

Mulling over the matter, I drove out of the lot and negotiated west Boulder's hilly streets. It was a little too convenient that Nancy Thornton was now willing to tell me that Allison had confessed to hiring Richard's killer. She'd had plenty of opportunity to tell me that earlier, yet she'd waited until now.

What if that was Richard in the photograph Nancy'd stashed in her skirt pocket just now, and she was in love with him, too? Could Nancy have killed Allison to avenge Richard's death? Then again, as a psychologist, surely Nancy had better control of her emotions than to fall for an avowed wife-beater.

Already in the general area, I decided to drop into the coffee shop on the Hill to see if I could speak to Katherine's assistant. It took me a moment to remember her name—Cindy Bates. I wanted to see if she or Katherine had easy access to a fax machine at the university. If Catwoman was Katherine, Cindy might have sent it to me to incriminate Katherine. Or perhaps Cindy was Catwoman, and Katherine had sent it for the same reason.

There was probably some potential cartoon there—catwomen having a fight over Batman, but my thoughts were too jumbled now to grab hold of it. I parked on the Hill and soon found Cindy at her "office" in the coffee shop. She was alone at her table, grading papers. She looked up at me and smiled. "Hello, Molly. Care to join me?"

I grabbed the chair across from her and asked immediately, "Did you know that Katherine had a major drug arrest in her past?"

"Oh, sure. It's sort of her bragging rights, her claim to fame, if you will. Several of the older professors have arrests and even convictions, of one sort or another. Usually just from having demonstrated in an antiwar protest back during the Vietnam War. But Katherine points out with all of this pride that she's the one with an actual felony."

"Doesn't having a criminal record prevent these people

from getting hired, when they have to put that down on their applications?"

"Applications? Professors don't fill out applications. They just send in their C.V.s. Then they interview with the department. Nobody ever asks about criminal convictions during the hiring process."

"So you don't feel Katherine's drug problems are something she'd want to hide?"

Cindy shook her head with confidence. "Not within her professional circles. I can't comment about her social circles, because I make a point of avoiding those."

The proverbial dead end. Katherine might be an obnoxious stuffed shirt, but she wouldn't kill somebody just for having divulged an ugly detail from her past. "On to other topics. I received an unusual fax from somebody at C.U." I snatched the fax out of my purse. My topic was moving from drugs straight to pornography. At least Cindy couldn't accuse me of being a dull conversationalist. "It's actually a photocopy of a faxed photograph, so it's not very clear. I'm wondering if you have any idea who the woman is, or who could have sent it to me."

Her eyes widened as she looked at my copied eight-by-ten. "That pervert," she snarled, yet there was obvious hurt mingled with the anger in her expression. "Richard suggested we do some sex games, and I told him I wasn't interested. He found some other woman who was."

"Do you have any idea whom she might be?"

She refolded the paper and handed it back to me. "No."

"Could it be Katherine Lindstrom?"

She shrugged, her cheeks flushed. "I've never seen Katherine nude, thank God."

"Did you know she had breast cancer?"

Cindy rolled her eyes. "Another of her personal claims to fame. She had reconstructive surgery, though, and I doubt you'd be able to see her scar on a faxed photograph."

"How hard would it be for somebody not on the C.U. staff to have gotten access to a fax machine on the campus at eight twenty-six this morning?"

"Fairly easy, really. I think all departments have one or two fax machines in their offices. There's also a copy shop in the U.M.C."

"So a student could have sent this to me?"

"Sure." She pursed her lips and turned her attention to her papers, her cheeks reddening. This was probably not her typical coffee shop conversation. "Listen, I've got to get back to work."

"Of course. Thank you so much for your time."

When I got home, Lauren, still in a funk, told me Jim had gone to speak to somebody at his office headquarters, which was located here in Boulder. I apologized profusely for leaving her with the children for so long, but she reminded me that that was our original agreement in return for my covering her airfare.

She obviously didn't feel like talking, so I decided to take full advantage of this chance to relax and headed upstairs to take a warm bath. The children were trying to brush Betty Cocker's teeth with some old toothbrush they'd found. I chased them out of the bathroom and poured myself a bubble bath, only to find Betty Cocker enthralled with what I was doing. She periodically whined outside the bathroom door as I luxuriated in the warm water and bubbles. In case of inspiration, I'd brought with me a pencil and a cheap pad of paper that I wouldn't mind getting wet.

My aching muscles slightly appeased, I drew an absurd— and wet—cartoon. A robber is looking perplexedly at a woman behind a counter of a bakery. She says to him, "I distinctly heard you say, 'I'll knead your dough, fast.' So take off that silly mask, put on an apron and a hairnet, and get back here. I can use the help." The caption reads: *One reason bakeries are seldom robbed.*

The doorbell rang while I was getting dressed. Lauren called upstairs, "That's Tommy, again, and this time I'm not getting it for you if you're stark naked."

"I'm *not* stark naked," I called back to her, "so that means you *will* answer the door, right?"

The doorbell rang again, but as I was brushing my wet hair into place, I heard the door open and the muffled rumblings of their quiet conversation. I waited an extra minute, then came out.

Tommy, hands in his jean pockets, was standing just a foot inside the door. Lauren was seated in the recliner a short distance away, with her back to him.

"Got some good news for you, Moll," Tommy said as I was still coming down the stairs. "They got a prime suspect for the murder of Allison Kenyon. They're close to bein' able to make an arrest."

"Celia Wentworth?" I asked.

Tommy's smile faded. "How did you know that?"

"She told me the police found copies of the key to the sauna on her key ring. She claims somebody planted them there. I didn't know they had any evidence linking her to the murder, though." While I spoke, Lauren leaned back on the arm of the stuffed chair, listening and yet removing herself physically from the conversation.

"Somebody anonymously turned in a series of written threats to your friend Allison a couple days ago. The Colorado Bureau of Investigation identified Celia's fingerprints on them, and handwriting analysis confirms that she wrote them. One's in verse and almost identical to the one you described getting during your group outing into the mountains."

"How did somebody turn them in 'anonymously'?"

Tommy raised an eyebrow as if proud of his knowledge of

the investigation. "Put 'em in a large envelope labeled 'Boulder Police' and dropped 'em in a mailbox."

"Do you know if Celia confessed?"

"To sending the threats, yes. She says she wanted to frighten Allison into confessing that *she'd* murdered her ex-husband."

"How do you know all this?" I asked Tommy, feeling a touch of injured pride at having been one-upped by his superior sleuthing.

"I got to be friends with one of the officers on your case."

"Which one?" Lauren asked, rising with arms akimbo.

Tommy eyed her for a moment, then answered, "I've been wining and dining one of the female officers, if you must know. *She* seems capable of sayin' the word yes."

"Oh, she is, is she? So what favors are you going to ask her for next?"

"'Scuse me, Molly. There seems to be a lack of fresh air in here."

Tommy left, letting the screen door bang behind him. He got into his car and drove off.

My cheeks were burning on my friend's behalf. I stayed put in the living room, while Lauren huffed and paced. "I sure walked into that one, didn't I? Now he's trying to shove some other woman in my face to get to me."

"But fortunately, you're not even slightly jealous."

My deliberate sarcasm coaxed her into a small smile. "So. They've almost got this thing solved. That's great news, isn't it?"

"Sure. If they're right. The thing is, though, Celia had no reason to try to kill me."

"Maybe she knew you'd figured out that she was in love with Richard and wanted to avenge his death."

"But Richard and Celia's relationship wasn't a secret. Every-body knew that. Lois said their entire neighborhood knew."

Lauren paused and considered my statement. "Maybe she

thought you were the only person who could have known she was the one sending those threats."

"Maybe so," I said with a shrug. It was hard to put myself in the killer's shoes—which was a bit ironic, since the killer had literally put herself in *my* shoes to frame me.

The phone rang. I barely had time to answer, before the voice on the other end blurted, "Mrs. Masters? I need to speak to you. Can you meet me someplace?" I immediately recognized Maria Chavez's accent.

"Yes. Where?"

"The Pearl Street Mall. I'll be by the stone rabbit."

She hung up before I could respond.

The stone rabbit was probably the carved rabbit at the east end of the mall. To be safe, though, I checked the business section of the phone book in case a new business called the Stone Rabbit had moved into town during my absence. None had, so I left Lauren in charge of the children once again and headed off.

I walked briskly along the redbrick walk of the open-air mall. I spotted Maria. She was clutching something against her chest and kept checking behind her as if very nervous. She smiled a little when she saw me.

"Mrs. Masters. I do not know if I'm doing the right thing, but I feel that I have no choice."

"Go on."

She handed me a manila envelope. "Those are photographs. I found the negatives for them and gave them to Nancy Thornton."

I was not overly anxious to rip the envelope open and study dirty pictures in front of a woman I barely knew. "Are these . . . pornographic pictures of Richard Kenyon?"

She nodded. "Nancy does not know I had these copies developed."

"Did she hire you to find them at Allison's house?"

"Yes. Though she gave me no money. She said I must help her, or she will have me deported."

"Did you fax me a photograph this morning?"

She gave a slight nod, lowering her gaze. "I did not know what else to do. I do not trust Nancy. She may still call the INS, now that she thinks I have no way to stop her."

"So, Richard hid the negatives in Allison's house before he moved out?"

"It might have been Allison who hid them. Nancy told me Richard took those pictures without her knowledge. And she said that Allison used the pictures to force Richard to give her a divorce."

"Thank you, Maria. I'll get them to the police right away. I hope she won't be able to get you in trouble with the INS."

"I hope so, too." She turned on a heel and walked away.

As soon as I was sure no passersby could see, I opened the envelope and flipped through the contents. Some of the pictures were with and some were without the cat mask.

Though the woman's hair was blond instead of white, the woman was Nancy Thornton.

Chapter 17

What Are the Odds?

Tommy had told me an anonymous source had given Celia's *threats* against Allison to the police. What about these photographs? I trotted after Maria Chavez and caught up with her just as she was about to get into her car. " You found these pictures in Allison's house?" I asked.

"Not the pictures. The negatives. I take a photography class at the university. I developed the pictures myself. I kept the pictures. I gave the negatives and the notes to Dr. Thornton."

"Notes?" I repeated, my heart pounding.

"Yes. They were rhymes . . . threats to kill Allison."

"Did you give any copies of the pictures or the notes to the police?"

Maria shook her head. "I told you. I do not want the police to know about me. I will be deported. I did not give anything to the police."

That meant *Nancy* must have given the notes to the police once she'd gotten them from Maria. Yet why, I wondered, would she do so anonymously? Unless . . . "The police found *Celia's* fingerprints on them, not yours."

"Yes. Dr. Thornton told me to always wear gloves when I touched them."

"Nancy specifically told you to find the notes for her?"

"Yes. My orders were to find the negatives and the 'nursery-rhyme notes,' she called them, and give them to her."

229

"How did Nancy know they existed?"

She pursed her lips and took a step away from me, growing annoyed with my constant questions. "I only know what she told me. She said Richard told her he gave the *negatives* to Allison. And then, I found Allison's hiding place—inside a curtain rod."

All of this confusing jumble was finally beginning to make sense. Nancy had killed Allison and had planned the murder for quite some time; I could come up with no other explanation for her actions. After Richard's death, Nancy had manipulated Celia into sending threats to Allison, then forced Maria to get those threats for evidence to frame Celia for the murder. But why? Why kill Allison? Perhaps Nancy had killed Richard, then had to kill Allison to cover everything up.

"I'll get these to the police. I can't thank you enough."

Maria put on her sunglasses. "The best way you can thank me is to keep my name out of this. I want to stay in this country."

"I'll do my best, but Maria, I'll have to tell the police something about where I got these. Otherwise, an innocent person is going to get charged with two murders she didn't commit."

Maria's lips quivered, but she nodded. She got into her car without another word.

Pondering the implications of what I'd just learned, I stood still and watched Maria drive away. Nancy had been having an affair with Richard Kenyon. She was intelligent, gorgeous, had a thriving practice as a psychologist. How could she have put herself in that position? I shuddered a bit at my unspoken pun, remembering the acrobatic move the camera had caught her in.

That brought up another question: Had Richard really taken these pictures without Nancy's consent, only to have Allison use them to strong-arm him into a divorce? That might have just been a story Nancy had concocted to convince Maria to search

Allison's house. Allison could have hired a private investigator to shoot the pictures. Either way, the only logical scenario I could concoct was that Nancy had killed Richard, then Allison. But these pictures proved nothing.

I had to call the police. Though there were closer phones, I decided to walk the couple of blocks and call from the Harvest. If Max Tucker happened to be working now, he might be able to give me some insight into Allison's relationship with Nancy.

I dashed into the restaurant, ignored the hostess, and spotted Max, waiting on a table with his back toward me. His face fell when he turned and saw me, but he approached anyway. I gestured for him to follow.

"Max, do you know how Allison felt about Nancy Thornton?"

He scoffed. "Once you know your friend and your spouse are cheating on you, things tend to get tense."

"Allison told you her husband had had an affair with Nancy?"

He shook his head. "She never talked to me about Richard. Said talking about him was too upsetting." Max let out a sad chuckle. "That Nancy was something else. Only therapist in town that can do splits like that."

"Excuse me?"

He held up a hand. "Never mind. Private joke."

"You've seen the pictures of her, haven't you?"

He stared at me in surprise, then averted his eyes and answered, "The guy that lives across the hall in my apartment building was a patient of hers. Someone sent him a photo of her with some dude. The photo was cut up, so the man's face wasn't shown, but I recognized the wallpaper in the background. It was Allison's bedroom. That's how I knew about her and Richard. Quite a Kodak moment, I gotta tell you."

"How did your neighbor get hold of it?"

"He said it came in the mail one day last winter. No return

address or note or anything. My neighbor seems to think it's funny. He hung onto it all this time and shows it to everyone."

Yuck! Somebody was sending pornographic pictures of Nancy to her patients. Who could do such a horrible thing? Allison? No, that was impossible. Last winter, Richard was still alive. Allison had been a battered wife; she couldn't risk the repercussions of such an act once Richard found out. Richard himself was the most likely person to have doctored the photograph so that Nancy was clearly shown, but he was not.

Max interrupted my thoughts. "Is that all you, like, wanted to ask me? 'Cause I really gotta get back to work."

I wished I'd never asked him about Nancy Thornton. He had already been through too much emotional trauma for someone so young. "Sorry. Thanks for speaking with me."

He strode toward the kitchen.

"Max?"

He stopped and looked back at me.

"Your mother is going through a really tough time right now, and she needs you."

"My mom? You sure you got the right lady? She never shed a tear in her life, not even when Dad died."

"Or maybe she just never let you see her cry. All I know is she's hurting now."

"Yeah?" he said, pointing a finger and struggling to keep his voice down. "Well, so am I! And she's never as much as tried to contact me since I moved out!"

I said gently, "Max, I think if Allison were here today, she'd tell you that life's too short to waste time waiting for someone else to take the first step."

He said nothing, merely marched to the kitchen. I returned to the phone in the lobby and called Tommy's cellular phone. I told him I thought Nancy Thornton was Allison's killer, as well as Richard's, and asked if he could meet me in the parking lot of the police station right away.

I left, but soon realized there was still at least one piece of the puzzle missing. I doubled back to the restaurant lobby and called Celia, grateful that she answered. She immediately cried, "Molly, have you talked to Nancy yet?"

"Yes, I saw her, but—"

"The police think I killed Allison! I can't convince anybody that I'm innocent! I have to talk to Nancy, but she's not home!"

"I've got to ask you a difficult question, Celia. Were you sending death threats to Allison?"

She sobbed, then said, "Yes, but only because Nancy made me."

"She *forced* you to send death threats?"

"She told me Allison killed Richard. She told me the only way I could ever feel closure was to make Allison pay for her crime. I know it sounds crazy now, and I can't believe I actually listened to her, but it sounded so right when it was coming from her. I can't believe I . . . Maybe she hypnotized me."

Hypnotic suggestion. That seemed far-fetched, but there truly was something almost intoxicating about Nancy's voice; she was so soothing and convincing. Celia was not one of the calmer people I've met, and she might have given Nancy more power over her than she let on. I thanked Celia and hung up. Just then, Max rounded the corner. He held up a quarter as he brushed past me and said gruffly, "'Scuse me. I gotta make a call." I raised my eyebrow, and he mumbled, "I'm gonna check on my mom."

I drove to the station, stunned that Nancy Thornton—a therapist and someone who's supposed to help people—was a murderer.

Though the photographs proved little, at least I was finally out of the loop. I would give my evidence to the police, and once they'd spoken with Maria and Celia, they would arrest Nancy. Plus, a little bit of good had come from my blasted greeting card retreat; I might have played a part in helping Lois Tucker to reunite with her son.

Tommy, sitting in his rental car in the parking lot, had beaten me to the police station. He lifted his chin to acknowledge seeing me, and I pulled into a parking space near his. He strolled over and opened my passenger door. "Moll, I gotta go soon. Lauren called, just after I left your place earlier this morning. We . . . kinda apologized to each other and promised to spend the afternoon together."

"Much as I hate to delay you and Lauren, this can't wait." I offered him the manila envelope. "It contains photographs." He made no move to take them from me, so I prompted, "Look at them. They're of Nancy Thornton and Richard Kenyon. Before Richard's death, somebody had been distributing them to Nancy's patients."

He still merely frowned and stared at the envelope in my hand. "What about fingerprints? Shouldn't you—"

"They're just copies that my source developed from the negatives."

"Did you just say your 'source,' Officer Masters?"

I rolled my eyes and got out of the car to stand beside him on the sidewalk. He opened the envelope. This was the fastest I'd ever seen Tommy look through evidence. He rifled through the photos as if he were shuffling cards, then returned them to the envelope. "You think Nancy killed both Allison and Richard?"

I nodded. "Everything I've learned tells me that Richard was using these photographs to control Nancy. She killed him and thought she got away with it, only she found out that Allison had the negatives. Maybe Allison was blackmailing her, or maybe Nancy couldn't take the chance that Allison might tell someone else what Nancy'd done."

Tommy raised an eyebrow. "But *Celia* was the one sending threats to Allison."

"Nancy could get an almost hypnotic hold on you just by talking to you. She has this incredibly soothing voice."

Tommy was looking skeptical, but I continued with confidence. "She probably even convinced Celia to set up the greeting card retreat. Then she killed Allison. Maybe she intended to get Celia's fingerprints on the syringe, but couldn't for some reason, so she got my fingerprints on it instead."

Tommy blew out a noisy breath. "This ain't much, Molly. BPD's gonna need way more evidence than this."

"Yeah, but it's a start. With any luck, they'll be able to get some more evidence, once they know Nancy's the one they should be looking at."

We went inside the building, and a total of four officers listened carefully to my story and accepted the photographs. I talked at length about how Maria Chavez desperately didn't want to get involved and was afraid of deportation. I'm not sure if they believed me. Eventually, though, they said we could leave. Tommy kept glancing at his watch, but he stayed beside me, then followed me home.

The house was strangely quiet, only our footfalls breaking the silence. I called hello as I dropped my keys on the counter, and Lauren called back, "Molly, is that you?" Her voice came from the basement.

"Yes. I'm with Tommy."

After a pause, she called back, "Tommy, can you come downstairs, please?"

He made a show of not being in a hurry, but he wasn't fooling me for a moment. Unless I misjudged Lauren, Tommy's mention that he'd gone out with a female officer had put a scare into her. With any luck at all, the wedding would be back on, and two weeks from now, Lauren and Tommy would be marching down the aisle.

The children were playing badminton outside, with BC

keeping the stakes high. When they missed and didn't retrieve the birdie quickly, she'd chomp on it. I called hello to them and sat on the deck, wanting to give Tommy and Lauren as much privacy as possible. Plus, I needed some time to think.

The police had told me they would handle this, and I had to have faith that they'd do just that. I ran the whole scenario through my head, over and over, to see if there was any way I could be wrong about Nancy. Yet, try as I might, no other explanation made sense.

Determined to distract myself, I thought up a silly cartoon that showed a recently robbed jewelry store. Lieutenant Columbo, wearing his trench coat over pajamas, is looking at a series of small circular markings. Columbo is saying, "What are the odds? The thief had not just one peg leg, but two. There's no other explanation for all these little circular marks leaving the crime scene." In the background, a street sign reads POGO STICKS: RENT OR BUY! and the markings lead directly to a pogo stick. The caption below the cartoon is: *Lieutenant Columbo experiencing a bad day.*

The phone rang and I hurried into the kitchen to answer. A high-pitched voice asked if I was "Mrs. Molly Masters," and then said, "This is Lucy Phillips, the owner of the Red Fox Resort. I've been talking to your associate, Celia Wentworth."

"Yes," I said, "we want a refund on the rental of two cabins last weekend."

"I have a check here, made out to you, refunding your deposit in full. I just need your signature on a form stating that you received a refund and that you will not hold the Red Fox Resort liable for any additional monies."

"Okay. That will be fine." Actually, it was almost an overpayment. The resort wasn't even getting reimbursed for our meals. If it weren't for the false advertising that got me and my group there in the first place, I'd feel guilty accepting the offer.

"How would you like to do this?" she asked. "I can put the form in today's mail for you, if you'd like, and can send you the check as soon as I receive the completed form."

"You'd send me the check afterward? That would mean I'd sign something that stated I'd received a couple hundred dollars yet to be mailed to me."

Lucy giggled. "Oh, dear. I hadn't thought of that."

"Can you come down to Boulder?"

"I'm afraid I can't. My car is in the shop. I have no transportation this entire week. Can you meet me in my office at the lodge?"

I felt uneasy at the concept of going back to "the scene of the crime," but this time I could ask Jim to accompany me ... which reminded me. Where was he?

I wanted to get this financial matter handled and would be up there for all of five minutes. "I can do that." The sooner the better, I thought. "Would an hour from now work for you?"

"Sure. I'm stranded till my husband gets back with the second car, so I'll be right here."

Jim arrived just as I was hanging up. To my complete surprise, Jasper and Joey Newton, Tommy's sons, were with him.

My heart started thumping. I greeted the boys as calmly as possible. It seemed as if they had grown in the couple of weeks since I'd last seen them, turning into exact images of their father. They said nothing other than "Hi"—from Jasper—and "Hey"—from Joey.

"What's going on, Jim?"

He didn't answer. The four of us stood staring at one another for a moment, my husband looking decidedly pleased with himself.

The only possible explanation was that Jim and Lauren had teamed up during one of my absences to get the boys here, and Lauren was planning to elope with Tommy. Unless Jim had taken it on himself to do this without Lauren's knowledge, which would be a fiasco. "Did Lauren help you arrange this?"

"Is Tom here? His car's out front," he said by way of evasion.

No sooner had I answered that he was downstairs, than the door to the stairwell opened and Tommy burst into the room. He had a goofy expression on his face. He looked at the four of us, blinked, then cried, "Jasper! Joey! You're here!"

Just then, Lauren stepped into the room behind him. She was wearing a white dress suit she'd obviously bought for the occasion. She looked absolutely stunning. My eyes misted at the sight, and I covered my mouth to keep myself from sobbing openly.

"Guess what, Molly?" Tommy said. "We're getting married today!"

Lauren slipped her hand into his. Tommy pulled her into a deep embrace. Caught up in the joy and romance of all of this, I would have watched them, except Jim kissed me. Afterward, I studied his eyes, astounded that he'd managed to keep Lauren's decision to suddenly get married a secret from me. Not to mention my surprise at *Lauren's* opting to keep me in the dark.

Reading my thoughts, Jim said, "Surprise. You're not the only devious planner in the family."

"But how—"

"Last night I arranged to fly the boys in and told Lauren to sleep on it, that I'd cancel at the last minute if she wanted me to. This morning, after you left, she told me she'd decided to go for it, if she could only find herself a dress. And, as you can see, she did."

While Jim talked and I struggled to mentally work out the logistics of how this had all come together so fast, the younger set—Karen, Rachel, and Nathan—heard some of the commotion and slipped in through the back door. Karen and Rachel were soon squealing with delight and hopping up and down at the prospect of a sudden wedding. Nathan was busy yelling "No!" at BC, who was also hopping, barking, and dashing through our legs. Meanwhile, we "adults" were engaged in a flurry of congratulatory hugs, explanations, and planning.

Lauren announced that they had all of two-and-a-half hours until they were scheduled to be in front of a judge at the justice center. First, they both had to be present to get their license.

Tommy insisted on going out and getting a suit. He, Lauren, and the boys took off, telling us to meet them in the lobby of the justice center at 2:20, ten minutes before the ceremony. My own wardrobe was so limited by my packing job that I rushed upstairs to put on my one nice dress, while Jim said he would make lunch for himself and the kids.

Fortunately, Lauren's sandals, which I still wore, looked reasonably nice with my blue dress and my pantyhose; I'd forgotten to pack dress shoes. Just as I was struggling with the dress zipper, it hit me that I had to reschedule my trip to the Red Fox Resort. I trotted downstairs to use the phone.

"Molly?" Jim said into my free ear after I'd dialed, "We don't have anything left in the fridge for lunch. I'm taking the kids out to McDonald's. Want to come?"

"No, thanks," I replied.

No answer, though I'd let the phone ring almost twenty times. Lucy must be out cleaning the cabins. I hung up and said to Jim, "Don't be late getting back. We all had better leave here at two, just to be on the safe side." For all of Jim's good points, tardiness was such a problem with him that if anyone could find a way to spend more than two hours at a fast-food restaurant, he could.

The house seemed incredibly quiet all of a sudden. My best friend was about to be married. Everyone else was swept up in all the details, and I was alone, supposed to simply get dressed and show up. I felt a little left out. I glanced at my watch. Ten after twelve. Two-plus hours with nothing to do. It would only take me an hour and a half to get to the Red Fox Resort and back, and I would love to have that matter behind me.

I jotted down a quick note to Jim about where I was going, and that if, for any reason, I wasn't home by two P.M., I'd drive straight to the justice center and meet everyone at 2:15.

I sped north, ambivalent about my decision to do this. There was no way I'd do anything to louse up this ceremony—such as being late. What if I got a flat tire? If that happened, I answered myself, it was downhill to Boulder. I'd roll as far as I could, then get a cab to the justice center.

There was also the little matter of the killer possibly not being under arrest yet. I'd feel infinitely more secure if I knew for sure that Nancy Thornton was indeed guilty and had been arrested. However, it was probably safer for me to be driving to Evansville—where only Lucy Phillips knew I'd be—than to stay alone in my house in Boulder. And, after all, it had been my idea to head up there today, no one else's.

Despite my rationale, part of my mind kept nagging at the other part that I'd just made an unfathomably stupid mistake. I drove with one eye on the dashboard clock, and felt relieved as I spotted the wooden sign and saw that I'd made the trip in just forty minutes.

A piece of paper slapped across the sign for the Red Fox Resort read: CLOSED. That was odd. Lucy hadn't mentioned anything about their being closed or out of business.

I pulled into the dirt lot by the front door of the lodge and got out. The place was quiet and deserted. I could hear nothing— not even the chirping of birds. I shut the car door behind me and looked around, hoping I hadn't just driven up here for nothing. Surely this hadn't been a prank—a fake phone call.

I headed up the stairs to the lodge. A deep, rumbling growl erupted from the direction of my car. My heart pounding, I whirled around to look.

There stood Nancy Thornton, one hand on the collar of her enormous Great Dane. She smiled. Sounding just like the high-pitched voice I'd heard over the phone, she said, "You made good time from Boulder, Mrs. Masters."

Chapter 18

They Do . . . Don't They?

Dear Lord! Nancy had pretended to be the owner of the resort over the phone and had lured me here, probably to kill me!

I decided to play dumb and hope that Nancy would let me near enough to my car to get safely inside. "I don't know what you mean," I said as casually as I could, though terrified out of my wits. "Great news. I got a call from the owner of the resort. She's going to give us our money back."

"That is great news. Unfortunately, there's nobody else here. Just you and I."

"Plus your dog." I saw a sparkle of light reflect off an object in her hand. A syringe. She was trying to keep it hidden so she could get close enough to me to use it. One very large dog. One murderous psychologist with a poison-filled needle. *Oh, shit!*

"Hi, Faldo."

"You're not still afraid of him, are you, Molly?" she said, still using those hypnotic tones of hers. "He won't hurt you, unless you should be so foolish as to try to hit me. Or to run away. He would simply chase you down and pin you, then perhaps bite clear through your neck."

She and Faldo moved between me and my car. Playing dumb hadn't worked. Maybe appealing to her sense of logic would. "It's too late, Nancy. I already gave copies of those photographs of you and Richard Kenyon to the police. So they already know everything. Killing me won't help you."

Nancy's eyes flashed with anger. "What exactly will they know? That I had an affair with someone who was tragically killed in a burglary. That's hardly a criminal offense."

"Except when it provides the motive for murder. You wanted to call it quits with Richard, so he started sending pornographic pictures he'd taken of the two of you to your patients."

"He was a deeply troubled man. That's how I got to know him, when he came to me for therapy. I thought I could help him. That is one of the common pitfalls of therapists, believing too greatly in one's own abilities to heal."

"You told everyone you'd decided to let your hair go to its natural premature gray. You're probably the only woman in America bleaching natural blond hair white. You knew Richard's neighbor had seen you when you were blond. You never wanted the police to make that connection between you and the blonde that Richard had struck the night he died."

Her features clouded with anger. "Richard deserved to die. He thought it was funny that he'd sent the negatives of dirty pictures of the two of us to Allison to protect himself from me. I didn't want to kill her, but I had no choice. Sooner or later, she'd have blabbed something to the wrong person . . . such as you."

Suddenly, thinking of Nancy as Catwoman in those damned photographs, it was all clear to me. "The cat killed curiosity," I said in a near whisper. "That's why you killed Allison. She'd said that at the retreat. She was referring to the photographs of you in that cat mask, in bed with Richard." Allison's words returned to me, now making perfect sense. I'd asked everyone to think of Christmas card ideas using cats, but Allison rattled off darker allusions—a cat burglar—another deadly role that Nancy had played. "She was getting too close to revealing that you'd killed Richard. So you wrote that threatening rhyme and tossed it in with the others to make it look like Celia was the killer. But why did you try to frame me?"

"It was supposed to be Celia," Nancy said with a hint of

regret in her voice. "I even switched batteries in her flashlight to mess with her head. She and Allison were the ones who typically drank to excess, but Celia chose that weekend to go on the wagon. Then Allison went and screwed things up further when she took the damned bottle over to your cabin. You were the only one who drank the wine and knew Allison. You made a lousy suspect, and you kept asking too many questions. So I had to make an attempt on your life and then frame Celia, to make it clear it was Celia all along."

"And the Dobermans?"

"I'd been keeping a watch on you. I spotted you leaving your house and walking toward Allison's neighborhood, so I released the dogs in Allison's yard. I just wanted to prevent you from talking to Maria." She patted Faldo's shoulder. "I have a way with dogs. They'll rip somebody's throat out on my command."

She shook her head and smiled. "You see, Molly, maybe it is too late for me to get away with it, but I'm in too deep now to stop. Your problem is, you have no proof. It's just my word against yours. And soon, it'll just be my word."

She held up the syringe. "I can drug you and you'll go peacefully and painlessly, or you can try to fight me, and I'll have Faldo eat you alive. Any preference?"

I eyed Faldo's massive jaws. "Given the lousy options, I guess I'd rather go with the shot." I held out my arm, but still stood on the top step of the porch.

"Wise choice." She took a step in my direction. "Don't do anything foolish, such as push me down the stairs, or I'll have to go with Option B."

Though I had no doubt she was correct, I couldn't go that easily. As soon as she was about to grab my arm, I push-kicked her. She went flying backward and landed with an *oof*.

I tried to run to the corner of the deck to leap off but only got a couple of strides before I heard Nancy shout, "Faldo. Attack."

I dove between the middle and top railings, just managing to break my face-first fall with my hands. I tried to get up and run but was knocked flat by Faldo as he leaped on top of me.

Then my leg was on fire. Faldo had sunk his teeth into my left calf.

I screamed in agony and somehow managed to turn over, wrenching my knee in the process. I tried to pry Faldo's jaws apart.

"You idiot," Nancy spat at me. "Didn't you believe me?"

The huge dog was actually in her way, but the pain was so all encompassing I struggled in vain to escape from him.

"Faldo, release!" she cried.

He promptly did as commanded, but my leg still felt as though it was on fire.

"This is your last chance to go peacefully," Nancy said.

As she tried to kneel to inject me, I grabbed a handful of sand and pine needles and threw it in her face. She let out a grunt and turned her face.

With physical strength born from my own intense pain, I bit her arm just above the wrist. She lost her grip on the syringe and I grabbed it just as Faldo barreled into both of us—pinning Nancy against me. He tried to claw Nancy out of the way to get to me.

All I had to protect myself was the syringe.

Nancy spotted the needle in my hand. She tried to grab it from me and yelled, "Faldo, no! Release! Release!"

In her attempts to grab the needle, Nancy managed to move so that my torso was exposed to Faldo.

His huge paws on my shoulders, he snapped his teeth at my face, barely missing. With Nancy still screaming, I jabbed the beast with the syringe and pushed down the plunger in blind desperation.

Faldo lifted his head. He got off me, took a couple of stumbling steps, and sat down, blinking at the two of us.

"What have you done to my dog?" Nancy cried. She wrapped her arms around his neck and wept.

I felt nearly crazed with the still unbearable pain in my leg. "If you want your dog to live," I said in groaning pants, all the voice that I could muster, "get him to a vet."

Blood was streaming down my ankle and soaking into the ground. Nancy looked at me, her eyes wild with fury. She took a step toward me, and I cried, "Leave me alone! It's too late for you to get out of this! Get your dog to a vet!"

Still sobbing, Nancy rose and tried to coax Faldo to his feet. Nancy started to come at me, hands set to strangle me. "I'll kill you for this!"

Automatically I held up an arm to fend her off. I was no physical match for her in this state. She stopped, then looked back at Faldo. "Damn you!" she yelled at me. "Look what you did to my dog!"

She returned to Faldo, now lying down, his breathing labored. She grabbed his collar and tried to pull him to his feet. "Come on, Faldo," she coaxed through her tears. "We've got to go."

While she struggled with her enormous beast, I got up on my one good leg and started limping toward my car.

"Stop!"

I kept going, bracing myself for an attack.

"You're right," she cried. "This is hopeless. The police already know I did it, and I can't lift Faldo by myself. Just . . . please send help for my dog."

I looked back at her, stunned. She dropped down and sat beside Faldo, then lifted his head onto her lap.

"I will." I dragged myself into the car to drive to the fire station nearby.

"I do," Tommy said.

"I hereby pronounce you husband and wife."

At the Boulder judge's words, a cheer went up from what was quite a large audience for such a small room. Their applause made me cry all the harder.

"You're going to have a hard time seeing what you're signing," Jim murmured in my ear, handing me another tissue. This time, I managed to use it without losing a grip on one of my crutches. We were the official witnesses and needed to sign the certificate.

Flanking us were all five children, though with Jasper and Joey's adult proportions they'd have balked at that description. Half a dozen uniformed officers were there as well, from both the Boulder police and the sheriff's department. Partially, I suspect, through their influence, we'd been able to delay the ceremony by twenty-four hours so that I could attend.

It was over. I was finally off the hook, and Allison's killer was behind bars.

Yesterday, after the police had responded immediately to my call from the Evansville Fire Station, Nancy Thornton had given them a full confession. Apparently her Achilles' heel had been her dog, something I was beginning to appreciate myself now that Betty Cocker was our newest family member.

Faldo, the police officers had assured me this morning, was recuperating. Furthermore, a dog psychologist in Boulder had been consulted to train Faldo out of his attack-mode behavior.

Lauren and Tommy were getting hugs or vigorous congratulatory handshakes. I watched but was determined to get my emotions in control before joining them. At length, Tommy broke off from the group and came over to me, shaking his head at the sight of my tears. "Now, I know I'm not good enough for her, but you don't have to cry quite this hard, do you?"

"It's not that. I'm delirious from all the painkillers." I laughed in frustration as a new host of tears burst forth and I lost hold of one of my crutches. Standing on my uninjured leg, I deliberately dropped the other crutch and held out my arms. "Congratulations, Tommy."

He held me in a tight hug for a long time, and as he pulled away, I saw tears in his own eyes. In an attempt to cover for his emotions, he asked gruffly, "You gonna have time to make your flight?"

Lauren was making her way toward us and I grinned at her. If possible, she looked even prettier today than she had when I'd first seen her in that dress.

I nodded. "We're leaving tomorrow morning," I told Tommy. We would be boarding a flight to Albany, New York, where we'd drive to a small suburb named Carlton. Otherwise known as home.

If you enjoyed *The Fax of Life*,
try another Molly Masters mystery . . .

THE COLD HARD FAX

by Leslie O'Kane